ALGORITHMIC TAXMAN

Christopher Cooke

Amazon

Copyright © 2024 Christopher Cooke

All rights reserved

The characters and events portrayed in this book are fictitious. Any similarity to real persons, living or dead, is coincidental and not intended by the author.

No part of this book may be reproduced, or stored in a retrieval system, or transmitted in any form or by any means, electronic, mechanical, photocopying, recording, or otherwise, without express written permission of the publisher.

ISBN 9798327462809

Cover design by: Art Painter
Library of Congress Control Number: 2018675309
Printed in the UK

Everyone hates paying taxes?
Here at the agency, we think not.

CHAPTER 1. AN EVENTFUL DAY OFF.

Mathew awoke with a familiar sense of dread, which he recognised only too well as the residual dregs of one of his most frequent anxiety dreams: he had been pursued again by a malevolent female armed with garden sheers. The grotesque female entity appeared alternately or as a composite of his mother, sister and first love, none of whom he'd ever fallen out with sufficiently to warrant so violent an encounter.

A cup of coffee and bowl of bran flakes later, he was sitting physically and mentally inert on his favourite section of the sofa in front of the TV which was disgorging the latest breakfast news trivia: the chancellor had made a firm commitment not to raise taxes above 20 percent which had for many years been a sacred threshold over which no political party dared overstep for fear of utter electoral demolition.

Mathew emerged from his mindless stupor seconds before the end of the report – just in time to be reminded that he needed to check his latest online payslip for that tax refund promised him by His Majesty's Revenue and Customs. It was his mid-week day off, so he could while away as much of the morning as he cared to. One of his favourite pastimes was an almost daily check on his personal wealth and using any and every excuse to fly into a deep inner rage at the slightest unforeseen expense or, heaven forbid, discrepancy on any of his financial statements.

To his great relief, Mathew's payslip showed the expected tax refund. However, his monetary urges being far from satisfied, and recalling the TV report featuring the chancellor, he decided to double check that there were no dreaded tax rises on the budgetary horizon. A quick superficial internet check confirmed, just as he had known all along, that there were to be no tax rises in the foreseeable future.

His semi-idle mind then drifted over to a couple of eye-catching key phrases turned up by his internet search. One particularly caught his attention: *Are you naturally good with money? Proud of your domestic accounting and budgeting? Do you feel you could use your talent to help others acquire financial acumen? Look no further – there could be a splendid career awaiting you just one click away on our web platform!*

Mathew was in his early thirties and, like most of his moderately intelligent peers, had found no particular fulfilment in the world of work. After gaining an average degree in business and IT studies, he had worked for a couple of firms including his current job analysing commercial data and having earned an equally average salary for the past ten years or so, felt it was time to move on to something a little more financially rewarding, if not overly stimulating.

With so much time on his hands and little incentive to budge from his laptop screen, he followed the line of least resistance which led him to the ad promising *a splendid career*. And, also as promised, with just one click, the HMRC government web page loaded up in a split second. It was the predictable online aptitude test. This one combined purely arithmetical with problem-style questions through which he raced well within the suggested 12 minutes and was awarded a 95% score. The one he got wrong was purely down to a misreading of the question in his rush to finish.

Seconds later, a table appeared inviting him to arrange his own interview. Giving himself no time to equivocate, he mechanically selected and submitted the first available slot at 15.30 that afternoon. It was half nine now, so he'd have time to get washed and dressed, come down for his mid-morning snack, log back onto his computer and do a quick bit of research on brushing up interview techniques. An hour or so later he was fully dressed and staring back at his laptop screen, returning to the HMRC website under *career opportunities*. This time he couldn't find the enticing ad which had lured him thus far, but there certainly were a number of jobs requiring similar qualities which he confidently believed he possessed.

After a snack lunch and having quickly absorbed the top five tips for interview success, Mathew set off early afternoon to the appointed venue in central Manchester. Like any self-disrespecting northerner, he was mildly surprised that a potential job working for the government didn't involve travelling down to London at his own expense, so doing the whole journey on his monthly saver train ticket on the final day of its validity felt like a real bonus. He had resolved thereafter to revert to the bus service and make only exceptional use of his car on environmental grounds.

As he stepped out onto the station platform in Piccadilly, Mathew felt a glow of pride at having made one of the most impulsive and yet confident decisions of his life so far. With a good half hour to spare, he quickly located the interview venue in a predictable office block on the city square and decided to collect himself by sitting for a few minutes on a wooden memorial bench. He calmly concentrated his mind on the persona he had resolved to project during the interview, inwardly rehearsed it, took a couple of deep body-calming and mind-focusing breaths and entered the building.

Within minutes of announcing himself at reception, a smart young lady had come down to greet him and asked him to accompany her to Mr Hudson, the recruitment chief's office. During their long walk down the corridor, he exchanged a few pleasantries with the lady who, though aesthetically appealing, wasn't too attractive to distract him from the focussed mindset and cool composure he was now striving to maintain in anticipation of the imminent interview. She ushered Mathew into a featureless office with a name plaque bearing the words: Mr P Hudson, Head of Recruitment. It struck Mathew that during his passage from reception through the long corridor and past dozens of office doors there had been no hint that he was in HMRC territory.

'Good afternoon Mr Bryant, and thank you so much for coming in at such short notice. Do take a seat and let me get you a drink. Tea? Coffee?' The niceties progressed smoothly with no social errors or awkwardness and within two or three minutes, Mathew's interview began.

Mr Hudson began by almost apologetically acknowledging the ease with which the initial selection process had been performed. The advertisement which had caught Mathew's attention was targeted precisely at internet surfers who frequently logged onto their bank accounts, browsed for savings and investment products and checked the financial markets – in a word, those who clearly had an above-average interest in all things money-related.

Observing Mathew's growing embarrassment, Mr Hudson at once put him at ease:

'There's nothing shameful about wanting to make the best of one's money in this uncertain day and age. Indeed, those of us who take our financial wellbeing seriously could be said to provide the backbone of the nation's fiscal health. We are the one and only agency contracted by HMRC to maximise the government's tax income. Over the past few months, we've been recruiting dozens of individuals such as yourself with an inherent interest in financial matters. I should say at this point that your interview today is not to establish whether you are suited to our kind of work, but rather *how* your particular qualities and aptitudes will best serve our purpose.'

It only now occurred to Mathew that he had not even been

asked to email his CV before coming to interview. However, he reflected that the all-pervasive and grossly intrusive vehicle which the internet had long since become no doubt made this redundant. He was a little taken aback once he'd digested the enormity of his current situation: from a lazy awakening and sleepy internet browsing session just a few hours earlier, he was now on the verge of being offered a mystery new job.

Mr Hudson then explained that he would now being handing Mathew over to another colleague who would begin the process of evaluating his capabilities, aptitudes and inclinations. For this purpose, he was ushered into another equally characterless office which differed from Mr Hudson's only in having no plaque on the door. The gentleman sitting at the other side of the desk this time appeared a little younger, closer to Mathew's age. He immediately stood up and shook hands with Mathew, making him feel welcome and relaxed just as Mr Hudson had done.

'I'm Roger by the way. Hope you don't mind being on first name terms, as we need a degree of informality to get the best out of this session. You could call me the psychologist in the works, but don't let the mention of psyche put you off. We're quite progressive here. We don't interrogate people like fabled shrinks in the days of yore; we'd much prefer the people we employ to reveal themselves to us on their own terms. Here's the smart way we do it. Instead of firing a list of questions at you about your personality, I'm going to show you half a dozen video clips of different people in interview situations and all I want you to do is rate them in terms of which interviewers' styles you preferred, which one is most like your own if you had to conduct a similar interview, and so on. You'll just need to answer a few simple questions requiring tick box answers about each scenario. Please be honest and try to go with your first reaction rather than agonise too much about any of your responses.'

Mathew settled in front of the computer screen as relaxed as well as he was able. True, at the back of his mind was the nagging suspicion that, simple though the exercise was, there could be a few trick questions. Or perhaps some of the interviews were 'staged' so as to tempt him to make obvious choices which he was actually meant to avoid. But then he recalled how he'd been assured a job was his whatever the outcome and quickly dismissed the notion of a ruse.

He must have viewed clips from about a dozen interviews in total. It struck him as just a little odd that they appeared to be with people applying for rather different jobs in the financial or tax field and he found himself giving most of the interviewers a good to very high score, but each time he hesitated over the question: 'If you were to conduct this interview, how similar do you think your own interview style would be?' In all but two cases, he ticked option 4 'quite similar' or 5 'very similar'.

When the test was over after what seemed to be about half an hour, Roger beamed a little smugly and told Mathew the results would print out in a matter of minutes and that they would end the session discussing them. Sure enough, just as Roger finished speaking, the printer served up the first of two double-sided sheets. He picked them up excitedly, scanned them quickly and surprised Mathew with the speed and depth of his analysis.

'I hope you don't mind, but we weren't completely on the level with you over these tests. We certainly were interested in how you'd score the various interview approaches and you were spot on. In our view, all but a couple of the interviewers had sound techniques. You picked that up and gave them top or nearly top scores. A less confident person would have given a wider range of scores, assuming they were meant to! We were also pleased to see you were troubled by the lack of range in performance, but stuck to your guns with the high scores anyway. You must have considered whether we were playing with a straight bat, decided we were and did the same yourself.

'The other questions were really ballast. We were actually measuring your body language above all else, as that's what tells us most about your personality and helps us point you to the right job in the right department. If you'd like to come in for the whole day sometime next week, we'll give you a full induction and by the early evening you'll know where you'll be working to begin with. Do you mind my asking how much notice you'll realistically need to give your current employer?'

Mathew answered after a slight pause: 'I think the standard notice term is four weeks, but I can't see leaving sooner would be a problem. I'll raise it with my line manager first thing tomorrow.'

Roger confirmed that the agency would be keen to have Mathew start at his earliest convenience, but that up to one month would be acceptable and the second induction session was agreed for the same day next week which again was his day off.

'Splendid,' continued Roger, 'And I'd like to pre-empt any concerns you may have about your prospective salary by stating that you will be sure to find our remuneration rates most generous.'

So, a mere two hours from the moment he entered the agency building, Mathew was sitting on the train homewards beset with a stream of impressions, thoughts and emotions arising from the day's events.

Over the first two or three days following the fateful day, Mathew's thoughts were dominated by a torrent of questions which had not occurred to him to ask his interviewers at the agency. He had allowed himself to be lulled into a false sense of security and submissiveness which, no doubt, was exactly what they had wanted and he began to reproach himself for his lack of initiative.

Why hadn't they even given him a contact number in case he needed further information, which was surely bound to be the case? Was he meant to ask for this before he left? Wasn't it normal etiquette to give the interviewee a chance to ask any questions before terminating the interview? He felt irritated at the idea that possibly he had been assessed as having a naturally super-compliant personality and this hurt his pride. Finally, however, his racing mind quietened and he regained his characteristic mental and emotional equilibrium.

His day off work had been a Wednesday so he faced two days in the office to readjust to the reality that his career in business analysis was coming to an end. He decided not to rush into an appointment with the HR chief to discuss his notice terms, but to reflect over the weekend. He needed to formulate a way of addressing the issue which would avoid burning his bridges in case his new post never materialised. If he broached the subject correctly, his present employers might reveal how much he was actually worth to them and offer him an enticing package to stay or at least return to the fold if found his new job unsatisfactory.

Mathew returned to work on Monday possessed of an absolute conviction that these would be the last couple of days of tedium he would be spending at least at this particular office. He handed a note marked URGENT to the Human Resources secretary on his way past reception and, as luck would have it, was summoned for a meeting later that morning. He found the HR chief perfectly unmoved at the prospect of his leaving the firm and only too eager to agree to release him with immediate effect upon his appointment at the agency being confirmed. To his relief, he would be paid to the end of the month.

When he returned to his office after a short coffee break, he was met by an IT technician who told him he would no longer have access to his computer and that if he had any questions, he should raise them with his line manager. Mathew intuitively knew that this was all about his employers' perceived need to closely guard their commercial secrets and so immediately dismissed from his mind any naïve or romantic notions he may have had about keeping the door open in case his new job didn't work out.

Mathew overcame his initial inclination to be super-compliant and insisted on remaining in his office while the IT man cleansed every last trace of him from the computer he'd worked on so conscientiously and loyally for over three years. He used the time to clear out his drawers and cupboards and collect any personal possessions. These amounted only to a chipped mug, a few of his personal stationery items and a packet of extra strong mints. His ex-company was welcome to all the rest.

Barely fifteen minutes later, he made off to what he was determined would be a fleeting visit to his line manager. He had got on passably well with Mr Houghton, but in his still numbed auto-pilot state, he really just wanted to get authorisation to leave the premises with the minimum of fuss and awkwardness. Mr Houghton had already been advised of the situation and made things easy for Mathew by briefly apologising for the rush to wind up his 'account' with the firm, as he put it and wished him all the best for the future. He would just need to call in (he nearly said 'pop in,' but that would have made too light of the occasion) and sign off with the HR's secretary to whom he'd handed his resignation note only three hours before. And he was free to go.

He walked hurriedly to his car. Among the confusing complex of emotions now welling up inside him was relief at it all being over, resentment at his former employers for such dismissive treatment and excitement at the prospect of beginning a new and exciting phase of his life.

CHAPTER 2.
EQUIVOCATION

Mathew's unexpected extra day off before induction into his new job had the effect of forcing him to reflect and assess the various aspects of his life. When he had returned home the week before, there was no obvious person in his life to be the first to share his news with. He had been single for almost a year now and though by no means estranged from his mother and sister Paula, neither was he particularly close.

There were just three people he could loosely call male friends, but none of them was a clear candidate for him to pick up the phone and announce his career change to. To make a special call to tell his oldest friend, Frank, would have been insensitive. Frank had been made redundant from his dream job as a zoo keeper three years ago. He had been unemployed and suffered from severe depression ever since.

Rory, the one person he'd kept in touch with from his university days, would be interested, but would interrogate him over every last detail. As details were something Mathew couldn't as yet provide, he would only feel foolish and wouldn't be able to bear Rory's competitive account of his own latest career achievements along with his recent romantic conquests.

That left just Andrew, his sister's ex-boyfriend. Mathew had got on quite well with him, for some reason especially after he and his sister split up. Despite not really regarding Andrew as a friend in his own right, talking with him about everyday matters seemed easier somehow. However, by due process of inertia, Mathew lost little time in deciding to tell no one anything for the time being.

Mathew's next thoughts turned to his general situation in life. His achievements so far had been limited to keeping down a couple of sufficiently well-paid jobs long enough to acquire a mortgage, hence a modest home in a fairly good area and decent second-hand car which he'd just finished paying for. Besides that, he had just enough disposable income to afford occasional holidays, a few other treats and put a little away for a rainy day.

Mathew, despite his preoccupation with money as an abstract concept, wasn't materialistic as such, but the prospect of a bigger salary excited him. He took pleasure in speculating about how much extra he would earn and whether new vistas would genuinely open up for him. Perhaps he would meet some interesting colleagues in his new post, even strike up a romantic relationship...

These musings took place between late afternoon and early Monday evening on Mathew's last day as a business analyst. After dinner, he succeeded in blocking the impulse to delve any deeper into his psyche by anaesthetising himself with two cans of moderately strong beer in front of the TV. The light intoxication also induced a mild sense of euphoria and enabled him to create the illusion of a mini celebration which he felt fully entitled to even if he had no-one but himself to celebrate with.

He got to the news. An uneventful day in most parts of the world, it seemed. Another interview with a junior government minister reiterating the usual mantra that practically the whole populace needed to hear: no tax rises for the foreseeable future. Income taxes would remain at 20 percent and be deducted at source at a blanket rate, but only on any earnings over £40 000 annual income. A simple and fair system which was easy to understand and straightforward to administer thereby preventing any more of working people's hard-earned cash than absolutely necessary from being sacrificed to the machinery of State. The incumbent government, which enjoyed growing public satisfaction ratings, could also boast of an unbroken year-on-year rise in the nation's wellbeing and happiness index.

There had been a national election only two weeks ago which had not excited much media attention either in the run up or immediate post-electoral period. Mathew took little interest in politics beyond voting in the annual online poll, either in the local or national elections. Since exit polls predicting results had become so consistently accurate around forty years ago, there was no buzz of excitement across the country on election nights. A good many citizens awoke the following morning blissfully unaware that an election had even taken place and of the rest few cared about the result.

Some political parties had retained their traditional words in their names such as Liberal, Democratic or slightly adapted them to the modern era such as the Conservationist Party, but since the Democratic Reconfiguration of 2035, old concepts of left and right-wing along with the historical bitter rivalry between the parties had more or less disappeared from public life and few traces of the political culture which had prevailed at the turn of the century remained. There was little indeed left of the generation that might have faintly recalled the ideological or philosophical debates which struggled on into the 1980s.

While daydreaming about what he would spend his extra disposable income on, Mathew suddenly experienced another nagging feeling about his prospective job. The question occurred to him: If all earners pay the same rate of tax at source on every pound earned after £40 000, why was an agency required to help the government collect this money? Surely this should be the simplest of tasks in the modern-day digital-technology-driven world. Perhaps there were nevertheless various anomalies to clear up, like in his case when someone changed jobs or moved house. Surely given today's smart tracking systems there couldn't be any tax dodgers?

Mathew then began to reproach himself for trying to second guess the inner workings of a realm of which he knew virtually nothing, except that, in the esteemed opinion of the agency recruitment team, he had the verified qualities required to master the tricks of the trade. All would no doubt be revealed during the induction beginning the day after tomorrow.

After the news, he indulged in another pseudo-celebratory moment by ordering a home delivery meal. Perhaps tomorrow he'd be clearer about who to co-opt into marking the occasion with him. He was edging towards a decision to invite his mother and sister, as they still lived quite nearby and he could give lifts if need be, as much as he'd prefer not to have to watch his alcohol units. Anyway, he'd sleep on it. No doubt his dreams would take an interesting turn tonight.

On awaking on Tuesday morning, Mathew in fact had zero recall of any nocturnal experiences. He decided to put this down to physical and mental exhaustion which no doubt had thrown him into a deep dreamless sleep. His subconscious must nevertheless have been at work, as he had firmly made up his mind to call his mother and sister to invite them round on Wednesday evening to celebrate his first day at the new job.

Before reaching for the phone, however, a sounder judgement caused him to reschedule to the weekend: What if he came home on Wednesday too tired and distracted to play the good host? And by the weekend he'd have a little more to tell, not to mention the fact that he could settle for lunch when everyone was likely to be on their best form. In fact, how silly of him to have considered the Wednesday evening in the first place.

He had a strange sense of this being his last day of freedom – a strange buffer zone in time between two vital phases of his life and was torn between two contrary impulses. The first impulse was to sit back and enjoy the moment, clear his mind of past woes and future concerns and put off any practical preparations for tomorrow until the latest possible moment. He defeated this temptation and instead listened to his wiser inner voice telling him not to put off till the evening what the morning might accomplish.

Making a meaningful call to his mother was a matter of fine timing. Between nine and ten in the morning, she'd be up and about, but largely inert and grouchy if engaged in conversation. Between ten thirty and midday was likely to be the most productive slot, as she'd be at her most alert, reasonable and responsive. By early afternoon, the loosening effect of the alcohol from her first couple of drinks risked turning any conversation into a minefield of potential slights, boasts and hollow promises. From the early evening her speech delivery slowed down and the volume lowered as the mood became increasingly maudlin. From eight or nine onwards, he could expect anything from a violently aggressive diatribe to unconsciousness.

After some minutes preparing exactly what he intended to say and how to express it, Mathew picked up his mobile at exactly 11am and speed dialled *mother*. She answered within seconds.

'How nice of you to call, Mathew, there are one or two things I'd been wanting to discuss with you,' she began in her lucid matter-of-fact, though self-obsessed tone. Mathew knew he'd have to cut in quickly: 'Yes, mother, I'm inviting you and Paula round to lunch on Saturday or Sunday, whichever suits you both best, so you can tell me all about it then. I'll have something to celebrate, I hope…,' he had added the insurance clause to the script just in case.

'Well, that will be nice,' continued his mother who proceeded regardless to outline the matters she had been wishing to discuss with little heed to Mathew's suggestion to defer this part of their conversation. Currently, her main preoccupation was with her imminent assessment to consider her eligibility for a top-up to her citizen's income allowance on grounds of deteriorating health.

Over half an hour later, with the conversation over, though mentally and emotionally fatigued, Mathew was relieved to have settled the invitation for Saturday midday. His mother had promised to talk to his sister too about a lift so the two of them could come together. Mathew, however, had learned from recent past experience not to entirely trust his mother to communicate anything reliably concerning arrangements. Although she hadn't yet hit sixty, he seriously worried what the next ten years or so held in store for every aspect of her health.

Mathew's call to his sister was much more straightforward. Although she was currently working for the council, he knew he'd be able to text her and arrange for a quick chat during her lunch break. Paula congratulated him on his prospect of a splendid new career and took no persuading to pick up their mother and ensure they both arrived at his by no later than half twelve on Saturday. She sounded quite cheerful and relaxed for a change, but Mathew a little guiltily checked himself from extending their chat longer than necessary given the ever-lengthening list of 'must-dos for the day' which had begun to crowd his mind.

Having overcome the hurdle, as he perceived it, of arranging a social get-together with his mother and sister, Mathew decided to treat himself to his favourite home-cooked lunch of boiled brown rice fried up with a mixture of steamed vegetables and mushrooms. For dessert he settled for ice cream. His default cup of tea was replaced by a mango, pear and banana smoothie of his own mixing.

With the washing up over, it was already half past two and roughly halfway through his waking hours. His thoughts drifted inexorably back to preparations for tomorrow. What should he wear? His smartest suit. Were the trousers properly creased? Should he prepare a packed lunch? How would he travel to work? He'd not enquired about a staff carpark. Momentary anger: why hadn't they mentioned that? Should he play safe and go by train like last week?

No, he'd drive, but give himself plenty of time in case he had to find a parking space a little distance away. But that would be too unpredictable and stressful. No, he'd use public transport after all and enquire about a staff carpark some time during the day. He would have time to research the routes and timetables for the bus – a mode of transport which he much preferred over the train for reasons which he'd never consciously analysed.

Other trivial concerns crossed his mind such as whether to bring along his own stationery for the induction and training sessions, what aftershave to wear, indeed whether to shave this evening or in the morning. With most of these issues resolved and a few practical steps taken where necessary, he could now think about his evening meal. That was easy – finish the rice and veg fry-up he'd made for lunch and wash down with a glass of wine. But as it turned out he didn't have any wine in, he had to settle for beer. Just one bottle, as he didn't want it oozing out of his pores on his first day at the job…

By mid-evening, he caught himself longing to talk to someone again, just for the sheer company and moral support, but he knew if he rang any of his friends without a specific reason, he'd feel awkward and it would be premature to talk about his new job tomorrow. Besides, any conversation along those lines would unnerve rather than reassure him. He gave in to the temptation to down another beer and allow the mild intoxication it brought him to assuage his mild sense of loneliness.

One last-minute panic before turning in: he needed to have all his bank details handy for the payroll admin tomorrow and decide which of his three bank accounts to have his salary paid into. This realisation cost him just a few minutes' anxiety and a brief online check: That was the downside to having so many bank accounts – not being able to memorise his account numbers and bank codes. By 10pm he was sinking into a relatively untroubled sleep after dismissing a final gentle self-reproach for allowing his last thought of the day to be money oriented.

CHAPTER 3.
INITIATION

Mathew arrived at his new building in good time with a sense of mild self-congratulation at having settled on the bus as a means of transport. In recent years, this had become the more relaxing and reliable, not to mention cheaper, option, as private motorists were increasingly coming to recognise. So many factors had come to militate against cars and in favour of public transport over the past few years. Steep road tax on all but the 'greenest' vehicles was part of the reason along with often prohibitive surcharges for driving in urban areas and heavily subsidised trams, streetcars, buses and trains. And at last, a political consensus had arisen over the need to green up transport in the face of unacceptable pollutions levels and the catastrophic technological and commercial failure of electric and driverless vehicles in the early part of the century.

Mathew was greeted at reception in much the same way as before, though this time he was led straight to Roger's room and invited to sit down after helping himself to a coffee and croissant. He was clearly the first to arrive and, on observing the single coffee pot next to a plate of just five croissants, he deduced the induction was to be a somewhat intimate affair. He was relieved to have a few moments alone to recollect himself before the next arrival: a tall ginger fellow, roughly his own age, awkwardly helped himself to a croissant and struggled a little with the coffee pot pouring mechanism before sitting down one desk away from Mathew. The two exchanged polite greetings, but Mathew didn't feel sufficiently at ease to begin a discussion of the day ahead or what had brought them there. A minute later, Roger himself entered with the remaining two induction candidates. The last of these was a moderately attractive lady, also of a similar age to Mathew.

'Lady and gentlemen,' began Roger, 'thank you so much all of you for getting here so punctually. We're sticklers for that sort of thing here at the agency, as I expect you may have guessed already!'

'My role today is to introduce you to the agency and explain the background of how we came into being, what our role is, our philosophy, our way of operating and our relation to the His Majesty's Customs and Revenue. You'll see we're a cosy little group today, which is how we like it, so don't hesitate to butt in and fire away questions at will. No need to put your hands up. This is an induction session, we're not at school!'

Mathew admired Roger's affable oratorial style and as at his previous encounter, at once felt at ease and confident he was going to enjoy his first day at his new job.

Roger continued, 'The first thing to note about our agency is that we have no name as such. We are the sole partner of HMRC in this field and hence have no need to distinguish ourselves from any other. You are probably all too young to remember, but we're not like those disreputable NHS and so-called teaching agencies of yesteryear which spent half their time pestering hospitals and schools for custom and the other poaching staff and intelligence from each other, not to mention the taxpayers' money.' Roger paused as if lost in thought for a moment. 'Anyway, I'm not here today just to sing our outfit's praises, but to explain, as I said earlier, how and why we came to be.

'Until 20 years or so ago, tax was a political hot potato. No one liked paying it whether income tax, value added tax or corporation tax and certainly no one wanted to pay any more than they already were. It was a huge source of resentment with so many press stories about how big stateless corporations virtually dodged paying it altogether and ordinary members of the public used every possible means to evade or avoid tax. This gave rise to a burgeoning industry employing various ruses to reduce their clients' tax bills. For a large commission, of course.

'Whichever political party was in power it wouldn't stay there long if it even so much as hinted at raising taxes by the slightest margin and any opposition party would be sure to stay that way unless it promised to reduce taxes. But politicians right across the political spectrum had to face the reality of growing demands on the State with overstretched budgets to provide more and better services, not to mention a Universal Citizen's income introduced in the late 20s.

'To cut a long story short, a coalition of the reformed political parties at last saw the wisdom of agreeing a consensus on the need to set and then freeze income tax at the rate it is now, 20 percent, and then look at various ingenious ways of filling the remaining hole in the State budget equivalent to a further 20 percent. Yes, a huge short fall in the public purse, so what was to be done about it?

'Giant steps have been made in recent years to change the public perception of money. In a sense the seed of that change had been sown over a hundred years ago with Premium Bonds which provided the government with a steady and quite hefty source of income on loan from the public while offering in return security for their money along with a bit of excitement every month with the prize draw. But how many bond holders really understood the true function of Premium Bonds and how long did it take successive government treasuries to appreciate their full potential?

'As you may recall, a few years ago, the government ran a campaign to raise their profile and urge all citizens with spare capital to invest in Premium Bonds. Why was the campaign so successful? Because it promised that the money on loan would be used to fund health, education and welfare services and subtly put across the message that this was a patriotic thing to do, as well as retaining the old excitement of the monthly draw. Who cared that the prize fund was a shade lower than inflation when banks were offering near zero interest rates and few citizens fully believed the legislation promising to keep their money safe.

'The banning of any non-state-sponsored gambling in 2025 gave a terrific boost to the National Lottery and was timed nicely to coincide with Local Authorities setting up their own lotteries and community bonds to fund many services previously starved of investment.

'There have been many other creative ventures to get people enthusiastically parting with a larger portion of their cash than in previous generations when higher taxes were perceived as the only way.

'Of course, today we have a much more powerful and diversified media to spread the word. By the end of the 20th century, celebrity culture had become embedded in society and was set to become ever more influential. This enabled voluntary organisations and charities to use famous people from actors to sports personalities to pull at the public's heart strings and guarantee a steady stream of regular and one-off donations. All the State needed to do was muster the courage to apply the same techniques in its own right and on a grander scale.'

Roger stopped at this point to take a sip of water. His delivery had become perceptibly more animated over the last minute or so, presumably to convince his small audience of his commitment to the cause.

'Now I'm about to get onto the agency's role in the latest government initiatives and where you come in. But before I do that, and in case you think I'm too fond of my own voice, I'd like each of you to briefly introduce yourselves to the whole group. Later on, we'll be doing some pair work and group work where you'll have a better chance to chat and learn more about each other.'

Mathew started the ball rolling, unconsciously prompted by a sense of entitlement at being the first to arrive. He confined his self-portrait to age, geographical origins and career in the money world to date. He rounded off by apologising for having jumped in first and made up for his social faux pas, in case there had been one, by looking across at the lady, as if to nominate her to go next. This evidently worked, as the lady immediately took the floor, introducing herself as Emily, thirty-four, originally from Derby and having had at least five jobs since university, starting out as a financial adviser with a high street bank. She too had done a stint as a mortgage adviser. In her last job she had specialised as a debt adviser for a charity and become thoroughly disillusioned with the role.

The two gents then briefly introduced themselves: Peter, a short dark stocky young man, 33, from Manchester, had worked in sales all his life. And finally, Jonathan, the tall ginger chap, 35, from Sheffield, who had started out as a bank cashier and progressed to the rank of mortgage adviser. Mathew hoped the other aspects of his fellow inductees' lives were a little less grey than their careers sounded. He'd no doubt learn this during social time out later on. But who was he to judge them on the basis of their past anyway? The others may have similar prejudices about him!

Despite what he'd said a few moments ago, Roger couldn't have minded the sound of his own voice too much, as he swiftly moved on, as promised, to outline at some length the agency's role, goals and policies.

He preluded this second speech with a joke or two about how the agency functioned as a latter-day 'tax enhancement extractor' or 'exactor' for people who still knew hard words, as he put it. The government needed to siphon off approximately 30% of its citizens' generated wealth to function and provide the services consensually expected of it. But the days of the taxman being seen as an enemy of the people were about to become a thing of the past, Roger assured his audience. All but the very oldest generation nowadays had been taught in civics classes at school what the State's role was and how various taxes played a big part in how it was financed. So that battle was almost won. Still, psychologists agree that owing to the dual nature of humankind – the selfish versus the altruistic –a good deal of work remained to be done.

Roger continued, 'Now for our first little role-playing activity. I want the person on your left to be a middle-income member of the public. The person on the right is, well, one of what you're going to be – let's call you a tax engagement officer. Your job is simply to persuade your partner to pay more tax *voluntarily*. I'll give you a few minutes to think through your respective roles and then off we go. Four minutes prep time starting now!' Roger set the timer on his phone.

Mathew was sitting on the left, so he had to play the part of the innocent victim of Jonathan, the 'tax extractor' man. It felt appropriate, to let Jonathan initiate the conversation which began clumsily as most role-playing attempts do. Jonathan was very polite. He introduced himself in his official role and then stalled in a frantic search for the right way to go about asking Mathew to pay more tax. Finally, he ventured, 'because the government needs it.... because ....it's foreign investments have yielded lower returns than anticipated over the last quarter.... or rather last two years.'

'Very good,' Mathew slipped out of character to congratulate his interlocuter on his commendable first effort before responding equally uncertainly: 'I suppose I *could* voluntarily pay a little extra tax.... at present, but before I agree to anything, may I just ask.... are you trying to get everyone to do the same?' He could have bombarded his unconfident partner with several more questions and challenges, but in the spirit of the exercise, graciously passed the baton back to Jonathan.

The inductees were told to change roles after a little while and after about ten minutes in total, Roger called time. After a brief feedback session from the participants, Roger summed up some common themes.

'The sticking points always seem to be: how do you broach the subject of paying more tax with anyone these days? Can we make it any easier through a change in lexis? Can we avoid the dirty word 'tax' altogether to make the conversation easier? Whichever way you broach the topic, how do you explain why people should or may want to pay more? What do people want to know? At least two of you, for example, asked whether they were being singled out or were others being asked to do the same. You've observed in just a few minutes that people are likely to be more amenable when they feel they are part of something bigger.'

Roger brought up a few other interesting points arising from the role-playing before breaking up for coffee and a *pain au chocolat*. These had been discreetly brought in as an apparent upgrade to the earlier croissants and felt like a symbolic reward for getting through stage one of the induction programme. All the new employees had enjoyed Roger's introductions and found the role-playing reasonably comfortable, though Mathew secretly resented not being teamed up with the only female in the group and still hoped there would be a chance to change partners or at least work as a group later in the day.

All four participants in the induction found themselves fervently discussing the training so far rather than using the opportunity to get to know each other better, but this just seemed the natural thing to do at this point. Mathew found himself confessing to Jonathan that he somehow sensed from the moment he set eyes on the internet ad that this new career opportunity was meant for him and that what he'd heard so far today confirmed that. Far from a tedious role as a tax inspector or admin clerk in another office, they would be working with people in a meaningful utilitarian way. Jonathan agreed, but said he slightly doubted his own ability to make people warm to him and get them on side. Mathew slightly pitied Jonathan as he heard these words and thought: *What is it about tall red heads that mysteriously lends them an inferiority complex?* Then he immediately felt a twinge of guilt for having had the thought.

The afternoon induction session provided an opportunity to get to know everyone a little better. Jonathan revealed he'd become disillusioned with his role as a mortgage adviser as he felt pressured to prioritise his bank's profit over his clients' best interests. Emily, who hadn't paid Mathew any particular attention, said she had enjoyed advising on ethical investments more than working with people in debt which she found depressing. Peter was the only one who had apparently enjoyed his working life to date. He had experienced no particular moral angst working in sales and only left the sector to take up a new challenge, as he put it. The glint in Peter's eye as he uttered the word *challenge* suggested to Mathew this was a likely euphemism for financial gain.

Roger finally broached the issue of pay which, as promised was generous. The good news was that they would all be earning up to 20% more than in their previous employment. He also explained that the agency had an equal pay policy for all employees. Increments were only paid for roles involving extra hours over and above the standard seven-hour working day. He would explain the anti-meritocratic equal pay policy on another occasion.

'But the bad news,' Roger paused for effect, 'is that all employees agree to set a good example by, you've guessed it, making voluntary extra 'tax' contributions! But don't worry too much; depending on your circumstances, you are free to set the rate anywhere between just one and three per cent of your gross salary.

'Now before sending you home a little earlier than the end of the official working day, I'm going to set you a homework task. I'd like each of you to come up with alternatives to the word 'tax' with all its negative historical connotations – Super tax in the 1930s game Monopoly, the 1990 Poll Tax, the 2013 Window Tax, the 2028 second home tax, and even everyday references to a taxing job, etc. I can guarantee you'll have your work cut out this evening!

'And finally, last week at your basic assessment I did promise to let you know at the end of your induction day what you'd be moving onto next. Tomorrow and Friday morning – yes, you'll have the afternoon off if you behave – is for training in our basic techniques. Then on Monday you'll be sent out on an assignment with one of our experienced agents to see how it all works in practice.'

On returning home, Mathew was somewhat surprised to find himself quite so drained. After all, he'd spent most of the induction day passively listening to Roger talk and the only activities – the role-plays and group discussions - had been relaxing rather than onerous. As he reviewed the day more thoroughly, however, he realised that his fatigue was more mental and emotional than physical. All the way on the bus journey home, his mind had been racing as different parts of his brain competed with each other to process the conceptual and interpersonal inputs it had just received.

Within five minutes of settling down on his sofa, cup of tea in hand, he was dozing in front of the TV. This was his usual habit on returning from work. That evening, he again toyed with the idea of ringing one of his friends, but on closer self-examination thought better of it. This would have been merely a self-indulgent excuse to think out loud rather than a sincere desire to engage in a two-way conversation. Or would it?

Perhaps he was just not prepared to make the effort to catch up with his friends who may well be wondering why he hadn't got in touch for so long in any case. Mathew, who was only too well aware of his propensity for self-doubt and overthinking, consciously called a halt to any further ruminations by immersing himself in his current favourite hobby – painting miniature military figures. This occupation safely absorbed him until bed time at about half ten. He'd be up bright and early tomorrow morning with a clear head and ready to roll for the training proper.

CHAPTER 4.
ALGORITHM

Mathew made a travel review the focus of his breakfast time reflections. He had agonised long enough yesterday about the virtues of public versus private transport and concluded he owed it to himself to drive to work today. This would enable him to make a fair comparison between the bus and car travel times and also assess how damned inconvenient driving to work had latterly become. He'd learnt on Wednesday that his new employers were subject to the usual workplace parking levy meaning that several hundred pounds a year had to be paid to the local authority for each and every staff parking space with the cash raised going to fund public transport and active travel. Half of the levy had to be paid by employees wishing to use their own cars, but this would only apply to new employees from the Monday of their first week in employment. If he were honest, Mathew would have to admit that his real reason for driving today was that he simply couldn't resist the offer of two days' free parking.

The car journey into work was just seven miles with an estimated duration of 20 minutes. With fewer private cars on the roads these days, traffic flow was appreciably quicker and tension between different types of road users had gradually begun to give way to mutual respect. Even cyclists, now more or less safely confined to their own dedicated travel space, had become a widely tolerated species.

Mathew had set off early and had no trouble following the signs to the workplace car park and finding a space. The trouble was, he mused, the car park was on the opposite side of the building from the main road and so it took him a further five minutes to orientate himself and walk round to reception.

As he stepped inside the building for the third time, he suddenly froze at the realisation that he'd completely forgotten about his homework. He at once launched into a frenzied mental search for a synonym for the word 'tax' until he recalled how early he was. The situation reminded him of his school days when he would hastily rush off most of his homework in the form classroom before lessons started, continuing through registration period and occasionally even skipping assembly to get the job done. Thank God this time it was a mental exercise requiring no written work and his subconscious must have been at work overnight, as an excellent solution occurred to him almost at once.

The training room felt familiar by now and he looked forward to meeting up with his class mates for the second time, but he noticed that the set-up on this occasion was different. First of all, there was no refreshments tray sporting cakes and drinks and secondly there was a lady's handbag on the desk by the white board and the eight desks were arranged more like in a traditional classroom. Again, Mathew was the first to arrive and this time he remained standing slightly uneasily until a moment later when Jonathan peeped gingerly round the doorway. Upon seeing Mathew, he beamed broadly in recognition and relief and the two of them sat down together towards the middle of the room. Before they could fall into any meaningful conversation, the other two trainees arrived together and sat down behind them.

At last, the handbag owner entered and introduced herself as Theresa Smale. She was young-middle aged and absolutely looked the part of a professional trainer.

'Good morning, everybody. I hope you enjoyed yesterday's jaunt through our little outfit's history and raison d'être with Roger. Today and tomorrow, my role will be to bring you up to speed with the nitty gritty business of getting to grips with our 'marks' as we jokingly refer to them.'

Mathew mused over the similarity in style and tone to that of Roger and his reference to tax extractors or exactors.

The morning consisted of a series of brief introductions by Theresa to a number video clips, some acted, some genuine, of practitioners interviewing members of the public at various stages of the 'conversion process,' as it was dubbed. Most of the action appeared to have been shot in the homes of the 'marks,' though one or two seemed to be in a more official setting. When asked about the reason for this, Theresa explained that the agency dealt with all types of people and saw it as essential to accommodate to the needs, circumstances and preferences of the individual. After all, people were unlikely to be amenable to parting with their hard-earned money unless in the most congenial environment possible. Some agency workers specialised in home visits, though the majority worked on the premises here.

Part way through the morning session, the remaining two places in the training room, which today felt more like a mini lecture hall, were taken up by trainee trainers who were clearly there to observe best practice in training techniques.

Lunch was brought in on a trolley by Roger at half twelve. He interspersed his presentation of the menu of sandwiches, salads and an assortment of canapés with a couple of witticisms and stayed for a few minutes as trainees, trainer and trainee trainers alike tucked into their lunch. Roger first of all explained that the agency's equal pay policy was reinforced by what he termed an 'no task too great or small for all' work ethic. 'We believe that equal status in an organisation is key to ensuring its success.' *No doubt another well-tried phrase out of the training manual,* thought Mathew.

The afternoon began with a discussion of the homework task. Theresa first asked if any of the trainees had noticed what linguistic devices the agents in the videos had used in discussing money matters with their potential clients.

Peter came in first, 'I think I can answer that pretty confidently, as I was listening out to hear whether anyone had come up with a better euphemism for 'tax' than the one I'd thought of. In fact, it's a trick question, because I don't reckon anyone used one.'

'Fair comment,' replied Theresa. 'But my question was actually: what *linguistic* or language devices did they use? So probably the best answer would be: 'avoidance.'

'Although *avoiding* saying something is strictly speaking a *non*-linguistic device,' Emily corrected her without a hint of smugness.

'Both valid points,' chipped in Mathew in a reflex attempt to impress both ladies simultaneously. Over a fifteen-year career of failing to learn adequate wooing techniques, he had barely assimilated two principles, namely – always let the woman speak the most and never appear to disagree with her. He had chanced upon even these arguably outdated principles during an internet search.

'But was it really a trick question?' hazarded Jonathan. 'I must admit Roger's warning was fair, as try as I might, I just couldn't come up with anything better than *civil dues*.'

'That's a really good effort,' Theresa encouraged him. I have a friend who pays 'dues' as a subscription to a club or society she's a member of. Subscription isn't a bad word either, by the way. The word 'dues' has the positive connotation of paying your dues to society or giving someone their due, which is hard to argue with.'

This prompted the others to make their offerings. Peter suggested *levy* which mustered little support given its association with the process of *raising* taxes and, even worse, it was from the French *lever*. Emily said she'd like to 'contribute *contributions*,' which Mathew was alone in finding rather witty. Emily argued effectively for the ease with which one could attach a range of persuasive adjectives to the word in order to drive the point home. She seemed particularly proud of the combination *national solidarity contributions*, which, were it not for his growing infatuation, would have struck Mathew as overly pretentious.

Finally, Mathew revealed his killer idea, which he had deliberately kept back until the others had all had their turn. This was to use a parallel with *pay as you earn* which might be *pay as you feel*. This idea struck him as more inspirational in concept form than when he actually articulated it aloud. Nevertheless, it elicited a positive or at least sympathetic response from the others.

In most of the full-day training courses Mathew had attended over the years, the key messages seemed to be presented in the first half, leaving the shorter afternoon session for more peripheral and forgettable elements. Today was no exception and the plenary which rounded things off at around four o'clock largely consisted of Theresa telling the training participants how well they had engaged and promising that if they continued in a similar vein tomorrow, they'd be sure to get home by early afternoon. The flattery too had a familiar ring to it. So apart from the better pay and conditions along with the jaunty philosophy, Mathew's new agency was beginning to appear far less forbidding than his paranoid imagination had presented to him as a worst-case scenario.

Friday was to be a workshop where the trainees would enact various case studies with a wide spectrum of potential marks such as they had seen and discussed in the videos. These would be recorded and played back to the whole team including a couple more experienced colleagues sitting in like today.

Mathew returned home brimming with pleasant impressions

from his day's labours. Indeed, he was so engrossed in his musings that he completely failed to note his travel time and even observe the route his phone took him. Well, at least that provided him with the excuse he'd been subconsciously looking for to use his car again tomorrow in order to make a fair comparison with his earlier bus journey. Just as he came to this conclusion it occurred to him that his new job would be likely to entail regular trips out to visit people in their home settings and this would surely only be feasible using his own car after all. He would clarify the matter tomorrow.

For the first evening since the fateful day just a week ago when he stumbled upon the taxman ad, Mathew was able to get through an evening with work mode almost entirely switched off. He at last resolved to call his old university friend Rory. It was about time he had something positive to report to his super-intelligent, overachieving, borderline-conceited friend who had just been promoted to senior marketing operative at his sickeningly virtuous green energy cooperative. Mathew now felt in a position to stand up to his friend's scrutiny, providing him with a convincing account of the worthiness of his new role while slipping in a subtle reference or two to its advantageous pay and conditions. A little counter virtue signalling wouldn't go amiss either.

His friend promptly picked up the phone.

'Hi Rory, what have you been up to these days? Swallowed up any more unviable mini-energy companies lately?' A reliable opening *pawn to King 4* move, he figured.

'Nice to hear from you mate, I was beginning to wonder if you hadn't been swallowed up by that big money tree in the sky yourself. How is it at…?' Even Rory with his near perfect recall couldn't bring to mind the name of Mathew's former employer, but then perhaps he'd never been sufficiently interested in his friend's career moves to commit it to memory in the first place.

'I left them only last week Rory, just felt I needed to move on as the cliché goes. Obviously, I'm growing itchy feet like you in my old age. Well, to be fair, I'd been through a fair number of jobs already even if I could never quite compete with you on that score.'

On uttering the word *score*, it seemed to Mathew that honours were about equal after the opening skirmish in their light-hearted conversational sparring match. It didn't last. The longer he continued to recount his latest adventure, the more his friend succeeded in undermining his confidence:

What about his work contract? What was his holiday entitlement? How far would he be expected to travel from home? Alright, so the agency was one of its kind, but did it have branches all over the country or would he have to travel all over the place and stay away from home for weeks at a time like so many civil servants? And that was just the beginning of Rory's negative fault-finding analysis. No, Mathew had definitely made a fool of himself yet again and should have followed his own advice of a few days ago and refrained from picking up the phone on impulse.

Rory didn't even give Mathew the satisfaction of hearing about any of his own recent woes such as how his confidence had taken a serious hit through a fall out with two senior work colleagues just days after rising to his new position. And, he'd had to undergo his first ever humiliation on the romantic front: that of being ditched by a girlfriend. In Rory's world, only he was meant to make or break relationships.

Not for the first time, when Mathew put down the phone he wondered why he had ever kept up with Rory after their university days and avowed he wouldn't contact him again. As on previous occasions, however, his resolve weakened as his sense of disappointment and embarrassment faded and he was already planning his next conversation once he had resolved all the questions and doubt Rory had caused to enter his thoughts. Rory hadn't meant to belittle him, at least not consciously, and, in a way, he was grateful to him for flagging up some considerations he ought to have arrived at by himself. Tomorrow, he would be armed with a suitable number of self-interested questions and would be better placed to defend his dignity in his next engagement with Rory.

So, having regained something of his earlier equilibrium, Mathew settled down to one of his favourite passive leisure pursuits - listening to lectures on MyTube about military history, particularly around the Napoleonic era. He was half way through a series on the defeat of the Austrians and Russians at the decisive battle of Austerlitz, and this fascinating conflict had inspired him to take up the more active hobby of painting miniature figures of soldiers representing the armies of the period. He was amazed at how easily he was able to obtain these figures, as manufacture of plastic children's toys or any items deemed non-essential had been outlawed at least 20 years ago. Clearly, some enterprising individuals with an eye for a speculative opportunity had bought up masses of these products for resale many years into the future. Mathew didn't mind paying the inflated prices, as a box of fifty soldiers would keep him occupied for over a month.

He slipped downstairs just before ten, mechanically turned on the TV and half-heartedly tuned into the late news. The same old monotonous and predictable political and economic non-events and sports reports. He forced himself to follow the regional weather forecast for tomorrow morning with a view to justifying his predetermined decision on his means of travel into work. It was set to be warm and dry so he'd have to dream up an alternative justification for choosing the car over the bus. And dream he did.

CHAPTER 5. FRIDAY: NITTY GRITTY

Mathew was no stranger to vivid dreams with apparent veiled significance often just beyond his grasp. He was sufficiently keen to crack his dream code, if indeed there was one, to enter details of his bizarre experiences in his diary immediately on rising before they faded away. He had read somewhere that dreams could be directed and controlled. If that were the case, he mused, this would mean using one's conscious mind to block messages which the subconscious mind was presumably trying to communicate.

Last night presented an especially prolific dreaming ground. It was no great surprise to find himself in the training room at his new job surrounded by many of the characters he'd recently been introduced to. It was as though all the others were engrossed in everyone else's animated conversations, but he was inexplicably out on a limb. He could neither quite make out what they were saying nor get clear in his own mind what it was he would like to get across to them if only he could break through the communication barrier.

Then, with no apparent transition, he was walking home, frantically attempting to push his miniaturised car along the pavement with his left hand. It kept slipping away, refusing to roll in the direction he was pushing it. He tried a number of times to climb into the vehicle, though at each attempt, apart from being ludicrously small, it seemed to exert a force field which repelled him.

On waking, he enjoyed for a moment the sense of satisfaction at having captured these dreams and set about analysing them. He was gratified all the more by his success at interpreting them so readily. The first could not have been a clearer representation of his social angst, his deep-rooted inferiority complex and fear of failure at his new work. The second was obviously his conscience pricking him for deceiving himself into taking the convenient option of driving into work rather than taking the bus. The dream's imagery was so strong that he resolved to follow its directive. He wondered how often people in general allowed similar dream-induced revelations to influence their behaviour. And if they did so, was this from a moral impulse or rather out of fear, superstition or too much Bible reading?

Once settled into his window seat on the bus, Mathew stared for a few moments at the traffic scenes outside before switching his attention to his fellow passengers. Under cover of stretching his neck, he managed to cast surreptitious glances around the cabin in search of any colourful individuals. Ten years ago, the introduction of the Universal Citizen's Income had amazed even its fervent supporters by eradicating the worst cases of deprivation within a very short period of time. The days when buses were largely regarded as the domain of Edward Bulwer-Lytton's 'the great unwashed' had almost passed into history.

In the early days following the Democratic Reconfiguration, campaigning groups and government ministers had worked in concert for once and had succeeded in re-popularising bus travel among all socio-economic groups barring the very wealthiest. Mathew could still recall some of the slogans from his earliest childhood: There were some terrible cases of alliteration and assonance with 'Bill says bus is best' and 'No fuss bus!' having indelibly imprinted itself on his memory.

Mathew's gaze flitted from one passenger to another, but he was unable to fix upon anyone in particular before the risk of uncomfortable eye contact became too great. In any case, the journey was short and he would soon have to look out for his stop. He spent the last couple of minutes trying to calculate his weekly saving by opting for the bus over private motoring. An almost impossible task, he found, at least if he tried to factor in all conceivable financial costs, let alone the incalculable environmental ones.

As he entered the familiar training room for what he imagined would be for the last time, Mathew was considering how and when he would field the questions suggested to him by Rory. He felt uncomfortable about putting them all at once out of the blue before the session began, as this would make him look unduly suspicious of his new employers and possibly provoke an adverse reaction from trainers and fellow trainees alike. Might it not be better to accost the agency staff discreetly during a break or after the session? But this could appear unduly secretive and self-centred given that most of the questions concerned everyone alike.

He opted for a hybrid approach. The newly introduced Theresa had arrived ahead of the trainees. Jonathan appeared a moment later so Mathew used the moment before the full company had assembled to ask about contracts: 'Theresa, I was wondering last night whether the agency has a particular take on issuing contracts...' The indirect question had the desired effect as Theresa needed no encouragement to explain that the agency was frankly a little casual about the process, preferring to email these as PDF documents, which was what many modern agencies tended to do nowadays. But he would certainly receive a contract by the middle of next week. She also alluded unsolicited to the holiday entitlement. Mathew sensed Theresa had assumed that this was likely to be what had partly motivated his question.

Mathew felt much relieved at getting two answers for the price of one half-question and inwardly smiled even more when Theresa repeated the information apologetically as the other two arrived. Reassured by her frank and ingenuous reaction, Mathew reckoned he could bear to wait till next week, if necessary, to learn about travel and away staying commitments. Perhaps it would be mentioned today in any case or one of the others would bring it up.

As promised, the final training session focussed on the need for agency workers to tailor their approach and messaging to the different types of individuals targeted. After recapping what had been covered to date, Theresa began with a short introduction in which she broadly classified 'targets' in terms of the appropriate level of voluntary contributions sought, how to present persuasive arguments to convince individuals with differing educational and socio-economic backgrounds, taking into account their belief systems and personalities.

Mathew was impressed if not a little alarmed by the psychology employed in convincing people to part with an extra portion of their often hard-earn cash. He was also surprised at the amount of detailed information which could apparently be teased out of clients: the trainees were told that algorithms enable the agency to assess their income and outgoings based on databases formed from their purchasing habits, travel patterns, holiday choices etc.

Theresa explained, 'The agency doesn't have access to their existing tax records, but of course the HMRC does have this knowledge and although it can't pass it on owing to the laws on data protection, it is allowed to send us what they call 'outline categorisations' of each client such as how stable their income is, roughly what proportion of their income was paid in tax over the previous few years, etcetera.'

'Surely,' interjected Emily, 'knowing what proportion of income was paid in tax would enable anyone with basic Maths skills to calculate pretty accurately what their actual income is!'

Mathew sensed the tension as Theresa paused to formulate her response to the most testing question anyone had ventured so far. But the hiatus was elegantly performed in the guise of a legitimate pause for thought and in no way suggested any discomfiture on her part.

'Appreciating that confidentiality rules around this area only allow HMRC to express this information in the broadest terms, a scale was created from one to seven. One means lowest while seven means highest. So, an individual ranked seven would be a particularly high earner.'

A related question occurred to Mathew along the lines of whether these numbers represented equal tranches of the earning population or not. In other words, an equal tranche would mean that about one seventh or 14 percent of the lowest earners would be ranked one, the same proportion would be ranked seven as very high earners. If the rankings were based on income brackets, say rising from the taxation threshold at £40, 000 in regular £20, 000 intervals up to £160,000, then the picture would be different. There would be a much higher percentage of earners in the lower bracket than the top bracket. However, he dismissed the temptation to ask the supplementary question for fear of sounding smug. Perhaps he would have the opportunity to impress Peter with his advanced mathematical thinking later. He was the one among them who seemed the most fixated on money matters.

Predictably, the rest of the morning was dedicated to representative persons from each of the seven categories being interviewed on film followed by a discussion and role playing. Mathew and the others had really fallen into the groove of the training methodology employed by the agency and acted out some quite convincing scenarios. After the work in pairs was peer assessed, each enactment had to be performed in front of the other trainees, Theresa and two agency staff observers.

But the most enjoyable aspect of the morning for Mathew was the opportunity at long last to change partners and work with Emily. During the break, he was able to monopolise her in conversation over hot chocolate and cupcakes – the menu had changed yet again – and by the end of the break he felt he had at the very least got onto her radar.

During the last hour and a half there was a quick assessment by Theresa of what they had achieved today and over the previous days' induction and training. This was followed by the long-awaited question and answer session.

Peter pre-empted Mathew's question regarding the issue of potentially having to work away from home and how this was arranged fairly between the staff. Theresa was fully prepared to answer this.

'Although we are one agency organisationally, we have several branches throughout the country. This one covers the city and outlying areas with a radius of no more than 20 miles so travel isn't usually a problem. Public transport is of course encouraged where direct links exist, but a generous mileage allowance covers reasonable motoring costs. In exceptional cases where, for example, a fellow agency branch is short staffed we might invite one of you to fill the breech a little further afield, but this is always subject to negotiation and never a matter of coercion.'

There were a couple more questions: how was payment of the extra 'voluntary' donation administered? Would they each be assigned a dedicated mentor during the first week? When would they be unleashed on the unsuspecting public unsupervised? Jonathan who out of the four new recruits still seemed the most tentative, asked whether they would be working with the full range of income types from the start or would they specialise with people of a particular profile.

Surprisingly, Theresa appeared uncharacteristically unprepared for this last question as if she had not come across it before, but quickly recovered her composure, saying they would be expected to become experts in dealing with people of all backgrounds and temperaments.

As if to break the slight tension induced by Theresa's brief moment of perplexity, the others, including Mathew rounded off with some fairly trivial queries about canteen facilities at the agency building, eating out arrangements and dress code.

Then suddenly Emily produced another of her gems and asked the obvious *But what if* question which had mysteriously not occurred to any of the others. 'I'm sorry if this sounds naïve and rather out of place, but do you mind my asking what happens if at the end of the day our client says an emphatic *No?*' Mathew had despised Peter for fielding his own question earlier about working away from home as his tone suggested he was primarily concerned about the financial aspect. But now he found himself inwardly cheering Emily on for taking teacher to task and was guiltily aware that this may be a case of one pretty woman trying to catch out another pretty woman with a smart question in order to impress the boys.

Theresa didn't lose her cool in the least this time and replied that *candidates* for persuasion (Mathew wondered just how many synonyms or euphemisms for *people* had been used to date) had been selected with extreme precision much as they themselves had been vetted before being taken on. Today's algorithms were so sophisticated as to almost preclude the possibility of failure.

Perhaps even twenty years ago the notion of a computer programme capable of analysing the human psyche to the nth degree would have sent a chill up the spine of most intelligent people. But the effect among the company today was negligible.

Class was dismissed early as anticipated at half twelve. Theresa was joined by Roger momentarily to congratulate the group for successfully completing their initiation into the ways of the agency. However, copious warm words were not backed up by lunch being offered on the house. Mathew knew it was now or never:

'Emily, would you fancy a bite to eat before darting off home? I thought we might explore the local eating places in case we find the canteen food isn't up to much.'

'I *am* in a bit of a hurry to be honest, as I'd been banking on using the surprise afternoon off to catch up with a couple of family matters, but I've just time for a quick sandwich if you want. There's this French bakery place just round the corner where you can sit in. I know the area quite well as I live only a mile or so away.'

In a sense, Mathew was relieved that the encounter would be brief, as he hadn't planned what he was going to talk about. Now he would have time to prepare a proper script to impress Emily for a future occasion.

On their way to the boulangerie-pâtisserie, Mathew opened the conversation proper:

'By the way, I appreciated your stunner of a question just then. To be honest, I've been dying to compare notes with someone from the group about one or two things which have been bothering me over the past few days. In some ways I've found the whole process a little spooky, haven't you?'

Emily smiled, 'Spooky isn't quite how I'd put it, but clearly the agency operates pretty much like most government-sponsored organisations these days. It's got a clearly defined purpose and a nucleus of core staff who are perfectly aligned with it and unquestioningly believe in it. Did you notice how passionate Roger was when he lectured us, especially on the first day. He's clearly bought into the whole ideology thing. We're the people on the ground chosen essentially for our above average intelligence, decent employment history in the financial field and valuable interpersonal skills to go with it.'

Arriving at the café, Mathew headed straight for the counter and asked Emily what sandwich she fancied. They both settled for an egg cress and mayonnaise baguette with a caffè latte. Mathew eagerly continued the conversation while waiting at the counter for the order. 'You speak about the agency more like an undercover journalist than a rank-and-file new recruit.' Do you think we may yet be in for some nasty surprises?'

Emily sat down with her refreshments and mused. 'My experience with any new job I've had is there are always one or two nasty surprises – difficult colleagues, excruciatingly boring tasks, ethical issues, and the first pay slip for some reason always disappoints. And, of course we've got the extra deduction to show to the world what exemplary model citizens we are. Do you resent that at all, by the way?'

'To be honest, no, not really. It's just I'd like to see my contract as promised early next week and whether there's a clause like that in it. I can't recall exactly how Roger put it, but I don't get the ethics or even the logic of *making* people do something *voluntarily*. I don't mind for myself and I suppose the ability to set your own rate of contributions makes sense ….and presumably you could adjust that if your circumstances changed.'

'A payment holiday,' Emily laughed. 'Takes me right back to when I first worked as a mortgage broker!' By now she appeared to Mathew to have become quite engrossed in the conversation. Perhaps she might delay her weekend start time by a few more minutes. And they'd only just started their refreshments.

'At least you wouldn't expect the government to commission a rogue agency these days. Labour legislation is so focussed on ethical perfection with a requirement for statements on everything under the sun… vision statements on equalities, climate emergency, staff and client safeguarding….' Emily ground to a halt. *She's frightened in case our chat becomes too impassioned and she risks sending out the wrong signals,* thought Mathew. As he took over the talking, Emily set about discreetly finishing off her sandwich, washing down each bite with a gulp of coffee and avoiding eye contact.

'That's an interesting point,' he resumed. 'I'd quite like to know how the commissioning process worked in this case. Did the government create the agency itself or rather set out the terms of reference and invite different organisations to come forward and apply for the contract?'

'The former.' Emily explained she had read enough about the terrible tangle the government had got itself into at the turn of the century over so-called *Public Private Partnerships* or *Private Finance Initiatives*. The private companies involved in bidding hired huge legal teams to hold government to ransom through intricate contracts and ultimately cost the taxpayer billions. The same mistake wasn't going to be made again in the face of today's public investment savvy public.

'Anyway,' she had by now finished her last mouthful of sandwich, 'It's time I was off. Thanks for the lunch and no doubt see you on Monday.'

Mathew had unconsciously mirrored Emily in her rush to consume her refreshments and so had also finished his lunchtime snack. As they got up to leave the café together, he wondered how likely he was to see Emily at work next week. Would the newly trained employees be working together as a kind of team? Yet another obvious question no one had thought to ask.

During the course of the conversation, Emily had appeared to warm a little more towards Mathew, but he had no sense of a romantic involvement being on the horizon. No doubt she was a young lady of her generation who saw the workplace as a forum for no more than professional relationships. If friendships were mainly forged at school or college then romance was strictly the domain of dedicated online forums or dating apps. Life partnerships were too serious a matter to leave to chance meetings or a limited pool of work colleagues.

Mathew, emotionally buoyed up by his chat with Emily, spent his journey home in an infatuated daze. Unlike during his trip to work, he had no appetite for fixing his attention either on life outside the bus or the people within it. Only after stepping off the platform onto the pavement, did he turn his thoughts little by little to his mini family reunion planned for Saturday.

As much as he found his mother and sister irritating each in their own way, he was still looking forward to seeing them tomorrow and remembered to stock up with the essential groceries for the occasion just in time to avoid mechanically walking too far past the local supermarket. Of course, he hadn't planned ahead and so had no shopping bag, but this didn't matter. The store would be sure to have a supply of cardboard boxes on hand for absent-minded customers such as he. It would just mean he wouldn't earn the tempting two percent bonus for bringing his own canvas *bags for life*. Given their disastrous impact on the planet's ecology over many decades, it was hard to credit that plastic bags had still been in use until eleven or twelve years ago.

CHAPTER 6. MUM AND SISS

Mathew sprang out of bed at seven o'clock. He probably would have lain in till about eight had it not been for the momentous occasion of a family visit. Theoretically, all the food preparation and attendant tasks could be accomplished in an hour or so, but he wanted to take his time to avoid leaving himself open to any explicit, or more likely, implied criticism. Mathew was quite capable of having sharp words with his mother and particularly his sister on a one-to-one basis, but on the rare occasions the three of them met together, they had tacitly agreed a non-aggression pact.

Mathew tried to pace himself with today's preparations by punctuating the series of tasks involved with activities from his normal weekend routine – checking on the financial news, ordering a couple of paints online for his miniature figures and listening to his favourite music on MyTube. By half ten he'd made two reasonably appetising salads, steamed the rice and veg for the main course and taken out of the freezer a range of deserts to please all palates. To supplement the wine, he'd provided fruit juices, smoothies and mineral water and his coffee maker was loaded with ready ground beans and a jug of filtered and dechlorinated water standing by.

He inwardly praised himself for being so well organised and having practically everything ready including a mental outline of the conversation topics he intended to introduce and those he would try to steer clear of. Then there were the topics he'd sooner avoid, but knew he would have to deal with starting with his mother's hope or expectation of a top-up to her Universal Citizen's Income which, out of a habit acquired during an earlier generation, she called Universal Credit. Universal Credit had clearly been a stepping stone or halfway house towards the government's next move – to bring in a Universal Citizen's Income. It hadn't removed the stigma of receiving a benefit, but it had at least got people used to the terminology.

His mother was not in a healthy financial position. She could have managed on her basic citizen's allowance were it not for her expensive alcohol dependency. Living alone in a three-bedroom house, she could have taken a lodger to boost her income, but the embarrassment and shame she felt on account of her drinking made this unrealistic. This left her no option but to re-mortgage her modest dwelling.

Mathew's father had walked out on them when his mother was approaching forty and he was fourteen. Left in the lurch, and sensing how hard up they were, Mathew had always been protective towards her. However, he resented his mother for leaning on him for solace rather than supporting him as an unconfident teenager. When much older, he realised his sister, Paula, had had an even tougher deal. Consciously or unconsciously, she must have felt the urgency to find a job, move out and get into a relationship to ease the pressure on the family finances. He recognised that his own growing obsession with acquiring financial and other forms of wealth could be traced back to his family situation.

Mathew started at the sound of his phone alarm. Then he relaxed again, instantly recalling that this was the reminder he'd set himself the night before to go off at half eleven. He'd calculated this would give him just the time he needed to get ready to pick up his sister and mother from where they both lived just over a mile away. Within ten minutes his sister was sitting beside him in the car and they were on their way to their mother's. 'Perfect timing', he thought out loud.

'You always were a stickler for punctuality and wanting to hold everyone to the same standard,' Paula commented. 'Remember, you did say to mum "no later than half twelve" and it's going to be barely midday when we get to hers. How likely is it she'll be ready, assuming she hasn't forgotten the arrangement in any case?'

Mathew didn't terribly mind whether or not his mother was ready when they arrived. He just liked to feel in control of his own timings. Paula had made a fair point that he was a stickler for being punctual. This no doubt went back to his own insecurities as a child, but the barbed end to her observation wasn't fair. He couldn't remember recently nagging anyone not to be late, least of all his sister. But it was as if she had read his mind:

'Oh, I know you don't go round mithering everyone about hurrying up, but it's just your impatient body language that speaks volumes. They reckon about eighty per cent of communication is non-verbal, you know.'

Yes, he did. Or at least if Paula was to be believed, as she had said the same thing or something similar many times before. Surely not eighty per cent! She must have been watching some of that discredited Neuro-linguistic Programming clap-trap on MyTube from the end of last century. This harked back to an era when the internet was taking off and all sorts of plausible smooth-talking fraudsters were peddling their snake oil on the various platforms it provided. He inwardly applauded himself again for not being provoked by his sister into an unseemly and gratuitous exchange. Was Paula unconsciously warming up in readiness for dealing with their mother?

They arrived at the neglected-looking 90-year-old semi a few seconds before a minute past twelve. It wasn't just being on time he was obsessed with, but time itself, he reproached himself. He was always toying with micro calculations as he went about his daily business. Exactly how long had he slept the night before in hours and minutes? What was his weekly average arising time? How many minutes would a normal wet shave take him? Could he wash his hair in the sink and rinse twice within five minutes? How much time (and water) would he save if he washed his hair first and then used the water from his second rinse to shave in? No doubt a psychiatrist would want to attach a compulsive obsessive disorder label to him or, better still, invent a subtly different syndrome precisely tailored to his unique condition.

Paula got to their mother's door first as Mathew manoeuvred the car into an acceptable parking space between two residents' drives. When he joined her at the front door, Paula was still patiently waiting and turned towards him with a slightly smug *told you so* expression. Mathew reached for his phone as he had seen many young people do as their first reflex to call friends at home even when standing right outside their front door. Malfunctioning door bells nowadays usually stayed unrepaired and the few remaining door knockers were viewed by most people over 50 as a quaint salute to a clunky bygone era.

Mathew's call did the trick. His mother answered almost at once and declared she was on her way downstairs. Moments later she appeared at the front door in her dressing gown.

'Come in for a few minutes. It'll only take me a moment to get dressed.' With which she hurried off back upstairs.

This was a better start than either of them had expected, as their mother was quite capable of not getting up to open the door to them at all and later claiming she – or most likely someone else - had got the time or day mixed up.

Being invited in was also a rare treat. In fact, Mathew couldn't recall when he and his sister had both sat in their mother's front room together; certainly not within the last two years. It also augured quite well for the afternoon, as he couldn't imagine his mother being so hospitable had she already been well into her boozing cycle.

During their few minutes' wait, Mathew asked Paula how she was faring at her council job. She had recently gained a modest promotion for exhibiting a degree of initiative in her role working for the waste collection and recycling department. Among other things, she had suggested to one of the staff in communications what she had thought was a fairly obvious way of seducing residents into signing up for the garden waste service.

This simply consisted in a 50% reduction for the first year's subscription provided they opted to pay the modest fee up front and ticked the automated renewal box which could easily be unticked at any time. Research had shown that in practice, over 85% of subscribers would automatically renew and only a handful of those would go to the trouble to seek reimbursement after accidentally failing to cancel.

Mathew applauded the shrewd psychology and sound ethics of his sister's intervention.

'Of course, so-called 'inertia sales' techniques before they were outlawed in the private sector were utterly immoral. But nudging people to do the right thing environmentally for a very modest fee is more than justifiable, it's essential.' No sooner had he declaimed this, than he immediately doubted himself: *Would any price hike on renewal be made clear to customers?*

Their mother's prompt reappearance prevented Mathew from exploiting this natural lead into a conversation about his own new job. Never mind, that could wait till later this afternoon, although on reflection probably he should have used this brief interlude to ask Paula if she'd had any contact with her ex-lover, Andrew. Another topic to try to introduce at an opportune moment later on.

The short car trip back to Mathew's confirmed his reasons for optimism: had his mother already embarked on her daily drinking session, this would have been evident at the first intake of breath in confined quarters. Over the years, he had acquired the skill of accurately assessing what kind of alcohol his mother had consumed, how much and when she had consumed it, all according to how she looked, behaved and the nature of the fumes she exuded. Today she was 'clean' and had probably not imbibed for at least 24 hours or so.

Paula had generously opted to sit in the back with their mother and the two engaged in small talk for a short while, leaving Mathew to enjoy the company of his own thoughts. Naturally, he was wrenched from his daydream on overhearing a first reference to his mother's ongoing claim for increased Universal Citizen's Income, but before a meaningful discussion could develop, they arrived at his place.

Just gone half past twelve. Mathew left his mother and sister in the lounge talking for a further ten minutes or so while he saw to the lunch for which he'd already laid the table in the dining room. The only further preparation required was to turn on the oven to heat up the main course and to uncover the salads and bread which he'd felt wise to slice just before leaving the house under an hour ago. He ushered in the guests and the three of them sat down to lunch together.

Even when Paula was with Andrew, family occasions always seemed short on people. Mathew was playing his mental numbers game again and imagining: *What if he had a partner and Paula had not only stayed with Andrew but they had brought two or three children into the world between them. That could have made for a family reunion of six or seven without even considering that his mother too might by now have found a partner despite her alcohol dependency and personality defects. Or was the fact that they were so thin on the ground just as much to do with his own and his sister's acquired or inherited character flaws?*

Mathew had travelled down this thought path before and knew it risked leading to rumination and ultimately depression. He brought himself round by recalling his own rosier recent past and at last introduced his much-anticipated conversation topic.

'Well since both of you are too shy to ask me about it, let me tell you about my amazing new job with the tax office!'

He kept the account short and to the point, concentrating on how he came to apply and get interviewed, the training focus and how he was ready and raring to go on Monday. He didn't think to mention where he was working or describe the actual job he would be doing. That would have been boring, anyway.

'Well, you or your colleagues will be wasting your time if you come knocking on my door for any tax payments...' his mother chipped in, thereby effecting a natural transition to the theme dominating his mother's life at present – enhanced Citizen's Income payments.

Paula had been expecting a plea to help her mother tackle the more recondite questions in the application form, but both brother and sister were relieved to learn that she had been helped in this area by a social advocate who had sat down with her for a good two hours and advised her that the outlook was good.

'So, on what grounds exactly have you applied for the top-up payments?', Mathew asked, relaxed, now that he was only required to play a supporting role in his mother's narrative rather than engage in it as a principal player.

'Well, as you both know, ever since your father walked out all those years ago, my health took a turn for the worse. It was with the stress of it all – financial insecurity, the responsibility of looking after you two and then there was the car accident that left me with a back injury. I'm sure that was linked to everything else and they do say woes come in threes. I'm sure I was distracted by everything that was going on, as I'd never had so much as a bump before or since for that matter.'

She hasn't driven since the accident, mused Mathew. '*It never rains but it pours*, my English teacher never tired of saying.' he encouraged her, willing himself not to betray any outward signs of impatience.

'Exactly,' she continued. 'And I know it was hard for you both too, being children and …'

'Mum,' his sister profited from her mother's hesitation to interject, 'you were going to tell us what medical reasons you gave for applying for an increased benefit.' Paula for once was evidently less patient than her brother.

'Yes, well I've been meaning to tell you both that I had some worrying blood test results a couple of months ago showing I had poor kidney and liver function. And before you say it, let me just say that the bad news comes with some good news. I know I've indulged in the Devil's brew rather too freely these past few years, but this health scare has given me pause for thought and I've decided to kick the habit. At first, I thought I couldn't, that I was probably an alcoholic and …unredeemable. But I really seem to have found the will to make it work. I haven't had a drink for over two weeks now.'

Mathew and Paula listened reverently to the rest of their mother's account as though any interruption risked weakening her vow of abstinence.

She had been told by her doctor that she had suffered organ damage which may not be completely reversible, but that drastically cutting down on or ideally cutting out alcohol altogether could yet give her a good chance of living a long and reasonably healthy life. Paradoxically, she had only mustered the courage to apply for the extra benefit after a week of sobriety when she was already beginning to feel much better. Hence, she felt a little fraudulent. But she explained that while she was still drinking, though financially in greater need, she felt she had no moral right and was too ashamed to apply.

Had Mathew wanted to punish his mother, he could have interjected with a comment along the lines of: *What a pity it took getting really ill to make you decide to give up the booze.*

There's little merit in that! Despite all his mother had put him and especially his sister through over the years, he wasn't vindictive by nature and applied himself instead to planning a discreet way of removing the bottle of light wine standing squarely in the middle of the table. A shiver shot up his spine as he realised the bottle wasn't there. Then he relaxed again as he recalled he had left it in the fridge by an oversight. How miraculously well his day was turning out!

With the most dreaded conversation of the afternoon over and everyone still emotionally intact, the next item moved up the agenda. It was time for Mathew to tease out of his sister where she was up to with her ex-lover and his unlikely friend. The opportunity to bring this up arose when his mother went up to the loo.

He began tentatively, 'I don't suppose you've heard any more from Andrew lately?'

'To be honest, I've not really had the time with my new job or even felt inclined to get in touch. He seems to have come to terms with our relationship having come to a natural end, and I'd rather leave it like that. I know you two got on well together, or should I say *get* on well together?'

The ball was resoundingly back in his court with a clear sense that Paula knew what really lay behind his question. In fact, it wasn't entirely straightforward. It was true that he had got one well with Andrew, particularly after his sister had split up with him. Mathew found the more he got to know him, the more strongly he felt he would be a suitable, if not flawless, partner for Paula. But would that then risk undermining his own relationship with Andrew? Did he value his own friendship over his sister's potential happiness? Or should he just stop trying to influence the situation and let events take their natural course?

For now, at least, he spontaneously opted for the latter and continued, 'I won't deny we've been getting on well. It's not like we have deep philosophical discussions or anything, I just find it easy to talk about mundane everyday things with him. He's great on DIY suggestions and nearly anything practical. We certainly don't discuss his feelings for you, past or present, by the way. That's tacitly off limits. But, the more I know him, the more I like him and I have a gut feeling that you could do …., you two would be really good together.'

He inwardly kicked himself, knowing he'd gone too far into the phrase not to give way that he was about to say 'a lot worse.' He knew the psychology of persuasive talk: that you should always avoid the negative 'half empty' in favour of the positive 'half full.' So why couldn't apply it in practice?

Suddenly, both brother and sister were seized with the same fear and exchanged anxious glances. Their mother had been gone a little longer than a normal trip to the loo warranted. But their moderately pleasant afternoon together continued unspoiled as she came down the stairs chatting animatedly on her phone to what, judging by her tone, sounded like a close friend.

Twenty years ago, it was quite a common occurrence for their mother to make an excuse to go upstairs only to come down an hour so later, clearly the worse for drink. A quick assessment by both of them ruled out any such ruse on this occasion as she rejoined them for a further hour or so of convivial conversation. Just before Mathew was about to resume his role as family chauffeur, Paula hazarded the question they had both been wanting to ask since the phone chat on the stairs:

'So, do you mind my asking who you were having such a lively natter with earlier on? It sounded very friendly.'

They could tell from their mother's expression she was only too pleased to oblige.

'Not at all, it was my doctor. A handy relationship to cultivate when you're in my precarious state of health, don't you think?'

Indeed, thought Mathew, though he couldn't for the life of him imagine why a doctor would be attracted to a middle-aged lady patient with battered internal organs. But then doctors aren't generally too squeamish about bodily decay. After all, his mother looked quite good for her age on the outside and wasn't totally lacking in charm. She probably reserved her unappealing self-pitying air specially for her son and daughter.

He checked himself from indulging his involuntary disparaging thought pattern any further. Was his residual resentment preventing him from being pleased for his mother as if, so soon after mending her ways, she was undeserving of happiness?

The trip back was one of the most cheerful times Mathew could remember having spent with his mother and sister for quite some years. The afternoon had been as near perfect as he could realistically have wished for: His timings had gone well, the meal had been well received, no sharp words had been exchanged. There had been good news about her benefit application and blossoming relationship with her doctor. Even the unwelcome news of his mother's poor health seemed to have been outweighed by her response to it. He would also feel much more at ease next time he reached for the phone to talk to Paula. The secret was not to leave it too long before arranging to meet her again.

On getting back home, Mathew took a little time out to recover his equilibrium. He'd learnt that high stakes social occasions could be as tiring as a demanding day at work, or even more so. This had been no exception, despite its positive outcome. Buoyed up by his good mood, he wisely resisted a strong urge to make those calls he'd been putting off lately in order to catch up with Andrew and Frank. First of all, he needed to absorb today's events and think over what he actually wanted to say to his friends. The worst thing he could do would be to launch straight away into a chat with Andrew before he'd assimilated what his sister had told him. It would be better to postpone that conversation until tomorrow and ring Frank with the clear aim of finding out how his least fortunate friend was faring.

Mathew spent nearly an hour restoring his vision of normal domestic order. He put on a dinner jazz album with five long tracks, roughly timing each to coincide with completing a task. The first track served as the background to clearing the table and putting everything on it into its rightful place – the fridge, freezer or wash basin. He had never liked dish washers and found washing up therapeutic. He completed this task with a minute to spare during the second track which was a little longer than the first and this allowed him ample time to thoroughly rinse the last saucepan, dry it meticulously and replace it on the hob.

Track three was for wiping the surfaces on the dining room table and the kitchen, and rearranging various items back in their usual places.

Track four accompanied his vacuuming of the lounge and dining room carpets and cleaning up in the bathroom.

Track five was held in reserve for anything he may have overlooked, but as he had apparently remembered everything, he was free to sit down and enjoy the music in its own right.

He still didn't feel quite prepared for calling Frank and so took a further ninety minutes or so 'down time' which he chose to devote to painting his current set of miniature soldiers. He had ordered this set of French Cuirassiers some months ago and and was totally enamoured of the figures per se – their historical accuracy, realistic and varied poses, beautiful sculpting and clean moulding.

However, he had equivocated far too long over one important detail. The Eastern European manufacturer had clearly aimed to surpass all others in producing as much accurate detail on the figures as possible. This had been achieved, however, by slightly enlarging the scale of the figures so that at one seventy-second scale, the cavalry figures would have stood to a man almost six feet tall. Two hundred years ago, this was unlikely when average heights were at around five foot six. The figures were also more heavily built than those of most of his other sets and so the difference in stature would be visible when these fellows were placed alongside certain others and risked appearing incongruous even at this tiny scale.

Finally, a little research helped Mathew out of his dilemma. It came to light that these elite 'heavy' cavalrymen would have mostly been selected for their above average stature and build, enabling them to handle a large horse and wield a particularly weighty sword. The miniatures' greater torso size was also justified by the body armour worn – a breast plate and back shield. They would have certainly cut formidable figures on the battlefield next to most enemy foot soldiers who, being generally from a lower social order, were mostly less well fed and attired in a far flimsier uniform.

Mathew had refined his painting routine to the point where he could set out the equipment and figures to be painted within two minutes. He had a special drawer in his office desk where he kept his accoutrements in a sturdy old biscuit tin: his paint thinners, selection of brushes, cleaning rags and the dozen or so paints required for this particular set. There were a few other items which took up very little space such as cocktail sticks for stirring the tiny tins of paint, tweezers for opening the tins, lids from plastic bottles for mixing paints and spare corks for mounting the figures to be painted. He usually kept the figures currently being painted on a shelf positioned at eye level above his desk so he could admire their progress each time he looked up from his laptop.

The tidying up routine took slightly longer, as there were brushes to clean and thinners to pour back in the bottle or absorb into a rag if too discoloured through use. Mathew enjoyed the planning, precision and degree of creativity involved in painting his figures. Also, it was one of the few pursuits, whether at work or play, which provided him with something tangible to show for his efforts at the end of the day. In case further justification were required, Mathew had once read a self-improvement book which stressed the importance for a balanced personality of maintaining a link with one's childhood, even if it meant continuing with a childish hobby.

Mathew returned from his Napoleonic painting distraction physically relaxed and with a quieter mind. Now he was feeling in a much better mood to ring Frank – energetically and morally fortified. The need he had felt earlier for a specific agenda with pre-prepared questions had melted away and been replaced by a simple desire to find out how his friend was and lend a sympathetic ear if this was what was required.

Frank sounded reasonably upbeat as he answered the phone. A quick catch-up revealed that a few weeks ago he'd found a rewarding outlet for his love of animals. His new job was working for very modest pay for a nearby veterinary practice which offered a pet sitting service for clients away on short holidays. Frank's role was to care for a variety of creatures in a range of settings. Some animals were accommodated at the vet's premises while others had to be visited at their owners' homes where his duties depended on the nature of the animal. These could be anything from feeding, entertaining and walking dogs to cleaning out rabbit hutches or aquariums.

On learning this, Mathew wished he'd contacted his friend earlier, as he could have saved himself a degree of heartache. One of the reasons he'd put off making the call was his awkwardness around Frank's depression and failure to find work. Although unemployment as such had largely lost its social stigma over the past twenty years since the introduction of the Citizen's Universal Income, it was widely recognised that most people had a deep-seated need to be valued for contributing to society in some way. While it was generally possible to live comfortably on the Citizen's Income alone and acquire a certain social status by working for a voluntary organisation, few people felt truly worthy citizens unless they were engaged in some form of paid employment.

Attachment to the need for 'gainful employment' was so ingrained in the popular psyche, that no public policy or educational programme seemed capable of eliminating it. Mathew came to realise too from his conversations with Frank that a much under-estimated negative impact on people's mental health occurred when people were deprived of responsibilities which supported their self-esteem. In Frank's case, loss of his responsible role at the zoo when it was forced to close down at short notice, had multiple effects all of which contributed in some measure to his near emotional breakdown in the space of just two or three weeks. Along with a sense of personal failure at being unable to save the zoo and concern for the fate of the animals he had looked after for quite a few years, he had to contend with a blow to his confidence and loss of routine. The impact on his personal finances was the least of his concerns.

In the course of their conversation, Mathew made the briefest possible reference to the latest episode in his own employment story. This was partly out of a desire to avoid stealing his friend's thunder, but also because he was genuinely interested in listening. Frank was quite a witty raconteur when the mood took him, and the disparate bunch of creatures he had encountered so far had already supplied him with abundant anecdotal material. By the second amusing account, Mathew had satisfied himself that Frank was well on the way to restoring his mental health and inwardly prayed that his friend's good fortune would continue.

Towards the end of their lengthy conversation, the two friends agreed to meet up for a meal next weekend at the latest and Mathew promised to provide an update on his own exciting new job over pizza and ice cream.

It was after ten o'clock and whereas Mathew would normally still have sufficient energy to write up his daily journal, on this occasion he felt it had better wait until Sunday morning. By now, he was fairly exhausted and feared any further stimulation ran the risk of overtiredness. With nothing yet planned, tomorrow would provide ample opportunity for reflection, journal writing and looking after his own needs after having expended so much energy lately on attending to others.'

CHAPTER 7. LET THE BATTLE BEGIN!

Mathew had another of those baffling anxiety dreams which seemed to plague him whenever he was at a major or minor crossroads in his life. As the dream unfolded, he was beset by a number of perplexing, interrelated, but ill-defined crises which intensified. As usual, each time he drifted towards wakefulness, he coaxed himself back to sleep against his half-conscious will as if an unknown force in his psyche could only be satisfied once the dream had run its course.

When he was finally allowed to rouse himself from his dream-state, he lay still for a few minutes attempting his habitual interpretation exercise. No one from the real world featured in the dream this time, though one female entity may have been a composite of his mother, sister and Emily. Before it melted away, Mathew fixed on a residual scene involving himself and a distraught individual which he sensed to be one of his 'tax marks.' This was easy to interpret as resulting from unease over the prospect of his first casework in the coming week.

Once discussing dream life with his friend, Frank had commented that his own dreams had often presented as an antithesis of his wakeful state. Of late, this had meant a stark contrast between his deep daytime depression and a much lighter mood when dreaming.

Despite the extra time spent on his post-dream analysis, Mathew nevertheless rose earlier than usual for a Sunday. As he stood up, he at once felt a heaviness in his eyelids and the blurred vision associated with a poor night's sleep. He would be better shelving his plan to ring Andrew today and instead focus on getting himself fully awake. To this end, he took a cool invigorating shower followed by a brisk morning walk around the garden. On coming back inside, he recalled with irritation that he'd also put off writing up yesterday's journal until this morning. This would now have to wait until he had rewarded himself with a fragrant cup of coffee made with freshly ground beans.

Back in his office in front of the computer, his cosiest of comfort zones, Mathew typed up yesterday's events, knowing only too well that twelve or more hours on, he would never quite capture the vividness he would have achieved had he written the journal before retiring last night. On the other hand, he could begin today's journal with the fragments of the dreams which still remained in his memory.

Just as Mathew's self-indulgent day began to take shape in his imagination, Andrew called. As sometimes happened when he was trying to be decisive and assertive, Mathew had completely overlooked the fact that while he was largely master of his own actions, he couldn't determine those of other people. But by automatically accepting the call, he overlooked another fact – that he could have chosen not to respond. This realisation occurred to him a split second after he had pressed the *reply* button on his phone.

In the first few moments of talking to Andrew, Mathew had to suppress his annoyance, not at his friend, but at himself. The suppression wasn't difficult, however, as Andrew made matters easy by kicking off with questions about how the home maintenance jobs had held up that he'd helped with in recent months – the dripping tap in the bathroom, the ignition problem with his cooker and the ballcock in his toilet cistern. Andrew had not just fixed the problems, but explained what he was doing as he went along to enable Mathew to manage by himself next time they arose. Online tutorials would have been a poor substitute for Andrew alongside him in person as a discreet and skilful teacher.

The conversation took an unwelcome turn for Mathew when Andrew suddenly mentioned that he missed Paula. This was by no means an unexpected topic, and had Paula revealed an interest in keeping in touch with Andrew yesterday, Mathew would have been only too pleased to pursue it. The situation was rather different now, however, given his sister's express desire not to maintain contact. Or had he been wrong to take what she said at face value? May she have been defending her own self-esteem? Mathew took a gamble in the heat of the moment:

'I was talking to Paula yesterday when she and my mother came to mine for lunch. I asked if she'd spoken to you lately. She said not and that she thought you'd come to terms with your relationship being over. But I wasn't convinced by her tone. She's got a new job and claimed she's been preoccupied with that, but I wouldn't be at all surprised if she were secretly hoping you'd get back in touch.'

Mathew paused for a quick self-appraisal of what he'd actually said before concluding:

'Of course, I'm biased; you and she both have probably realised, I'm keen for you to get back together. I know it's for you two to work things out between yourselves and I shouldn't really get involved, but since you kind of asked, I just felt I had to say what I think. At the same time, I feel a bit disloyal to my sister talking behind her back and passing on what she told me tacitly in confidence. so I think I should leave you to sort things out between you from now on.'

Mathew was quite proud of himself for his spontaneous outburst on this occasion: he'd found the courage to grasp the nettle, say what he really wanted to and be as faithful to the truth as appropriate without committing an indiscretion. Or at least that was the outcome of his first self-assessment. He knew himself well enough to expect that some of what he had said could well come back to haunt him – or even just doubts about what he had said or the precise words he'd used to say it. He'd not done such a great job yesterday when he almost blurted out *could do worse than Andrew* to his sister!

He appeared to have produced the desired effect, however, as Andrew wasted no time in seizing the lifeline, 'Well thanks for the news about Paula's new job, anyway. At least I'll have a pretext for getting in touch if only to congratulate her. It should be clear from how she reacts whether she really wants to have anything to do with me again... I don't imagine she'll take it amiss that we've talked and you happened to mention her new job to me?' His doubt appeared to have returned.

Mathew again came to the rescue: 'She might if you rang her this evening, barely twenty-four hours after I've spoken to her! Better give it a couple of days at least.'

So that was settled, then. The two of them continued their chat for another ten minutes or so ranging across their usual favourite topics until Mathew realised he'd been so distracted by the unexpected nature of the call and how it had turned out, that he'd not even mentioned his own new job. He decided to downplay the significance of this, pretending he was undergoing a trial period, which was in a sense objectively true, and he promised to report back in more detail to his friend in a couple of weeks' time.

Mathew often wondered how universal human psychology was and how much his own feelings and thought processes were mirrored by the people around him. Having completed quite a complex exchange with Andrew, he found his mind racing and going over each detail of what he had just said and his friend's reactions – a process he'd begun while in the midst of the conversation.

His main qualm was that he had probably stretched the truth or even lied about his own gut feeling about his sister's feelings for Andrew. So, what had impelled him to misrepresent them?

His own wishful thinking? Or was it more to spare his friend's feelings? If the latter were true, was he genuinely concerned for Andrew or was it more a case of people pleasing to avoid an unpleasant conversation?

Was switching to 'auto-pilot', an honest way to conduct a conversation or should he have been more reflective, analytical and measured in his interactions? Perhaps then he would have a better chance of remembering exactly what he had said. He had no clear answer to this or to the other questions which sped through his mind.

Had he betrayed his sister's trust by disregarding her express wish not to communicate further with Andrew, irrespective of what his motives were for doing so? Had she actually been so explicit about this? He couldn't remember the precise words she'd used and be sure of her real intent.

Was he overthinking the situation again? *Definitely*! The answer came back at once. If the conversation had gone badly, leaving his friend upset and perhaps angry at both him and his sister, Mathew's self-knowledge told him that he would now be operating in reverse and reconstructing the conversation in order to put himself in a more favourable light.

And did Mathew believe that all the people he had spoken to recently – his mother, sister, friends, Emily and other future work colleagues – conducted the same sort of post-performance analysis of each conversation as he did? Almost certainly, yes, but to what degree and how successfully? He then embarked on another line of enquiry as to how far this process was conditioned by one's education, upbringing, temperament and intelligence. Or genetic makeup?

Enough. It was time to return to his own inner fantasy world and source of profound enjoyment and fulfilment: his Napoleonic era wargaming.

As a fifteen-year-old, Mathew had painted a hundred or so

Napoleonic Era British infantry figures to a reasonable standard, albeit with scant regard for historical accuracy and he had planned to add a similar number to his collection year on year. However, even before he got round to painting enemy counterparts to pitch against this first mini army, competition from the demands of school work led him to direct his energy towards less creative pursuits.

When Mathew rediscovered his passion for military history about four years ago, he faced a dilemma. The era in question spanned a whole generation from the revolutionary wars of the 1790s right up to Napoleon's defeat in 1815. Over that period, the uniforms of the various warring parties changed – even the warring parties themselves. In addition, manufacturers had marketed literally hundreds of sets to choose from over the last two decades of the 20th century before the ban on plastic toys was imposed. Spoilt for choice, Mark finally solved the dilemma by restricting himself to the last ten years of the wars and hence to just fifty or so sets of figures from this period which were still available. Over the past four years, he had already acquired and painted about half of these sets.

He had an equal passion for skirmish wargaming and had evolved a cycle of alternating these with his painting sessions. Typically, on completing the painting of a set of figures over say a month to six weeks, he would then enjoy a 'rest' phase during which he staged one of his wargames. Over the years, he had elaborated a complex set of rules which he never tired of refining as new scenarios arose in the course of his games. He had bought several books featuring different authors' attempts at codifying wargaming rules and had researched the relevant facts on various dedicated websites. He reached a point about a year ago where he had synthesised his own set of near-as-dammit complete rules sufficiently well to post on the internet. To his delight, several dozen fellow enthusiasts from around the world had 'liked' his self-published manual with many sending him complimentary feedback as well as suggestions for enhancements which he gladly incorporated into future 'editions' of his manual.

The beauty of living alone in a three-bedroom house was that it allowed Mathew the luxury of a hobby room. Needless to say, a large wargaming table was its centrepiece. This was about the size of a ping pong table only closer to a square in dimensions. He had sprayed the surface various shades of green to add a greater degree of realism to its medium density hardboard surface. For additional realistic effects, he had purchased a range of miniature trees and scale model farm buildings and walls as well as defensive structures such as redoubts and chevaux de frise, the latter being grotesque anti-cavalry devices. These had been invented in the Middle Ages and consisted of central shafts of wood with metal spikes protruding at regular intervals along their length.

Mathew's battles were always protracted affairs. Their sophistication didn't lend themselves to being played out over just one evening. Each 30-second *phase*, in which every unit on the field had to *move*, typically took up to half an hour with each skirmish wargame lasting between ten and twenty minutes in real time. Then the attackers would follow in the same sequence. The defenders' turn was first, always starting with artillery, followed by infantry, then cavalry. A *move* might be a literal move – advancing or retreating across the *field*, or alternatively units may be firing, reloading or be engaged in hand-to-hand combat.

The first session of a new wargame consisted in Mathew inventing a scenario, deciding which soldiers to pitch against each other, followed by the painstaking, though infinitely enjoyable procedure of setting out all the units in their starting positions. Some were initially 'off the table' and yet to advance to the field of conflict. Their position would nevertheless be minutely recorded on a large spreadsheet containing columns for each group of units with rows to pinpoint and record details for each 30-second phase of action.

The setting up process normally required at least one and a half hours and consumed as much reserve mental energy as Mathew could muster in one day. Furthermore, at least half the second session was needed to evaluate all the forces in terms of their quality, speed of movement and initial morale. Today was no exception to the general rule, and Mathew contentedly left his hobby room to go back downstairs, conscious that last night's poor sleep was already catching up with him.

It was after one o'clock and so time for lunch. Despite his tiredness, Mathew felt it wiser to put off his doze until he'd eaten. A stomach full of food to digest might help him to sleep more deeply and get his napping over with in one stretch, allowing him to enjoy a normal fully refreshing sleep tonight. He quickly knocked up a quick meal consisting of a bowl of vegetable soup with toast followed by a cup of tea and biscuits. Annoyingly, while eating this, his desire for a doze passed and he found himself wishing he'd given in to it as soon as it arose.

Mathew had almost the whole afternoon ahead of him as well as the evening with nothing as such planned except a nebulous notion that he ought to spend some time preparing for tomorrow and his first real week at his new job. But what could he do that he'd not already considered such as dress code, mode of transport and less important matters like whether to take a packed lunch or try out the works canteen?

For want of any practical business to attend to, his mind was soon astir with all manner of concerns about the nature of the work ahead itself. A question came to him which he hadn't considered before perhaps because, until it was just hours away, the new job had been merely a theoretical proposition. Mathew found himself wondering who he would really be working for. Technically and contractually, it was the government, of course, through an agency. However, who would he come to feel he was actually serving – the agency managers, his immediate colleagues, or even possibly the clients? But in what sense could he be said to be working for ordinary members of the public when he would be aiming to persuade them to part with a slice of their excess wealth?

Until this point, Mathew had given scarcely a thought to what tomorrow would hold for him. This wasn't through any special effort of the will or deliberate tactic of self-distraction. He had simply found it easier and more natural to focus on other matters arising from the recent past such as yesterday's family get together and his talk with Andrew or engrossing himself in whatever he happened to be doing in the present moment.

On reflection, he realised his snap decision to stage his next war game was an unconscious bid to put off any untoward thinking that would be liable to interfere with his night's sleep. He was reminded of how as a child he and his sister would be so excited on Christmas Eve that they feared being unable to get to sleep and risk preventing Father Christmas's from delivering their presents during the night. One year, his sister being a little older and wiser, suggested they run round the block in the neighbourhood several times before bedtime in order to tire themselves out. It had been in vain: they both still lay awake excited and worried until the small hours.

So now, Mathew was almost resigned to one of two possibilities. Either he would struggle to get to sleep until about three in the morning or else get to sleep easily enough, but then wake up at about four in the morning and be too alert to have any hope of getting back to sleep.

He decided his best tack was to relax in the near certainty that whatever happened tonight, he would catch up on any lost sleep tomorrow after what promised to be a day filled with intense learning experiences and impressions. This decision taken, he set off upstairs once more for his hobby room where he broke with tradition by indulging in a second 90-minute wargaming session on the same day.

This would be a larger-than-average-scale skirmish involving over four hundred soldiers in total in thirty phases or fifteen minutes of real time. He spent the first twenty minutes or so rolling dice to determine the values for each of the eight different types of fighting men. For example, combat quality was on a scale of one to five: -20%, -10% zero +10% and +20%. So elite infantry coming up against the weakest possible opposition would have an advantage expressed as a ratio of 120:80 simplified to 3:2.

Troop morale was another important factor along with rate of movement which could be crucial, for example, in determining the number of casualties suffered before a unit reached enemy lines.

Mathew was now ready to launch the first phase of the actual battle and looked forward with glee to the opening sallies. The Russians were defending a farm house and so, according to the rules, were due to fire first. At the outset or *point de départ*, the advancing French were out of range of all but the single Russian cannon which fired shot at a range of 400 yards and inflicted two casualties. The rest of the phase was over to the French whose infantry used it to advance 33 yards towards their enemy.

The worst offence to realism so far was the fact that the 150 French infantrymen were set up at the opposite end of the wargaming table just five feet away from the British. To faithfully represent 400 yards would have required a table at least 17 feet long! As a child, Mathew had overcome this problem by transforming his bedroom carpet into the battlefield, but this had the drawback of being vulnerable to intruders such as his mother wandering in and inadvertently ploughing through the ranks on an innocent mission to make his bed or empty his waste paper basket.

Before the allotted time was up, Mathew succeeded in completing two more phases of the game leaving the French infantry just exactly 301 yards from the Russian defensive position with just five men falling to a second cannon shot. At a range of about 200 yards, the fourth phase would open with the Russian cannon switching from standard round shot to case shot. This would spray up to one hundred musket balls over a stretch of several yards across the front rank of the enemy and was certainly something for Mathew to look forward to on returning from work tomorrow!

Mathew was delighted to discover on regaining the kitchen that he had transmuted his sleep-plaguing nervousness into sleep-inducing tiredness born of three hours of intense concentration and pleasant excitement. A cup of warm drinking chocolate was all he now needed to send himself to a deep restorative and amazingly dreamless slumber.

CHAPTER 8.
FIRST MARKS

Mathew awoke, as often happened, just a few minutes before his alarm rang at seven. He was grateful to have benefited from such a rare treat: a dream-free night of refreshing sleep ahead of such a momentous occasion. He resisted the temptation to rush breakfast, ensuring he chewed his jam-topped toast adequately before swallowing and sipped his cup of tea down more slowly and mindfully than was his usual habit.

There was none of the anticipated dithering over his clothes choice as he opened the wardrobe doors. His hands automatically fished out his best-fit suit and a well-coordinated shirt. He was ready to leave the house at a quarter to eight and with a start time at work as late as nine, he could well afford the luxury of choice between private and public transport.

Oddly, this was his most agonising dilemma of the day so far. The angel on his right shoulder had almost successfully nudged him towards the bus for all the right reasons when the demon on his left shoulder intervened with a suite of arguments against: *The bus won't turn up and you'll be late on your first important day, you'll get wet, hot and mithered, you'll arrive at work in the wrong mindset to meet clients and be kicking yourself all the way home! Anyway, you'll be tired at the end of the day and driving home will be therapeutic and a well-earned treat. You can take the bus tomorrow.*

Mathew briskly quelled the demonic voice and bravely resolved to take the bus. His sound reasoning reassured him that however erratic the bus schedule might be he'd arrive in good time and no adverse weather was forecast, certainly not any rain. In reality, he had been subliminally conditioned by the *Tempter* who had simply re-emerged in another guise: his deeper reason for reverting to bus travel was his uncertainty of getting a space in the works carpark on a Monday morning when traffic always seemed heavier and, an even greater deterrent: he had omitted to investigate the financial implications of the workplace parking levy which would be in force from this week.

It wasn't until Mathew had boarded the bus and made himself comfortable in a window seat that the strongest subjective argument in favour of public transport re-entered his mind. Now for the next twenty minutes or so, he could quietly observe the world around, reflect on a problem or simply to bathe in his own passing undirected thoughts. This prospect was far more appealing than looking out for potential traffic dangers and other road users, negotiating junctions and traffic lights, timing gear changes and braking, getting into the right lane at the right time or out of the wrong one.

With his attention directed inwards, Mathew instinctively knew that this tactic of avoiding external distractions would better prepare him for the day ahead. He used much of this gifted travel time to review his work experiences to date. He began by recalling the key messages of the first couple of induction days before returning to the more recent training days and considering what they had taught him about the role he was to fulfil.

He then moved on to a review of his new colleagues, both the trainers and his fellow trainees. He still had very little idea as to how much of these people he would be likely to see in future and whether this would just be crossing in the corridor or through collaborative working. This wasn't of particular concern to Mathew except in the case of Emily who had occupied his mind at various times over the weekend.

As he entered the reception area, he caught sight of Jonathan who had obviously signed in just before him and was already being whisked away into a room a little way down a corridor to the right. If his insights of last week were anything to go by, Jonathan was just the sort of nervous character one would expect to be the first to arrive!

Mathew would have preferred to use the fifteen minutes or so before the nine o'clock start to daydream a little more in the lobby, but his priority was to ask the receptionist about the workplace car parking levy. As if to allay his guilt, he preluded his enquiry by informing her that today was the third time he'd travelled to work by bus.

Julie, the receptionist, as indicated on her name badge, concisely and clearly explained the system: the council levy for each parking space was six hundred pounds annually. This was shared equally between the agency and its workers and would cost Mathew three hundred pounds, roughly six pounds a week. On request, employees were allocated a parking space and would be liable for the whole levy irrespective of how often they used it. Lot shares were permissible with two colleagues sharing the fee, but only where a car sharing arrangement had been made. This was to avoid two colleagues driving into work on the same day in error and fighting over a single parking space.

The agency owned two cars for use by colleagues who were occasionally required to work some distance away from the building. Otherwise, they were expected to use their own vehicles or public transport for local trips out to clients. It was theoretically possible to book a space in the car park on spec, but the 'extortionate' daily rate of £12 for the privilege was a clear and effective nudge either to subscribe to the levy or use public transport.

Julie pronounced *extortionate* with a matter-of-fact intonation suggesting she didn't understand all the word's connotations. Mathew mentally attempted to correct her, but while he knew this was the wrong word, he couldn't immediately bring a more appropriate alternative to mind.

In the course of attempting to absorb all of the intricacies of the parking rules, Mathew realised how wise he had been to catch the earlier bus today. Presumably, if he had driven to work, he would have been faced with committing to the annual levy or the one-off surcharge. It was this thought which caused his true motivation for opting for the bus to emerge from his subconscious, namely his fear and loathing of unpredictable expenditure. And this awareness in turn led him to feel fraudulent for misrepresenting his motives for catching the bus today.

Mathew snapped out of his self-deprecatory mode and collected himself with just moments to spare before a smart middle-aged lady appeared out of an office door and headed towards him. He took her outstretched right hand into his own, instinctively realising he was destined to be this lady's shadow for the foreseeable future.

'Good morning Mr Bryant. I am Margaret Bentley, the colleague who you will be working with today. I hear you and the other new staff had a most successful induction and training last week. I couldn't get to sit in on any of the sessions, but have watched several of the recorded excerpts. I'm sure you'll fit in very well.'

As she led Mathew down a long corridor in the opposite direction to where Jonathan had just disappeared, she went on to explain their schedule for the day. This would begin with an interview with a gentleman who had come in to follow up on an earlier discussion about voluntary contributions. They would then discuss this together during a mid-morning coffee break and hopefully have time before lunch to prepare for a second interview in the afternoon. This would be more interesting, as it involved a middle-aged couple who had been contacted by the agency recently and had agreed to come for their first interview, knowing very little yet about the agency's programme.

'Just to let you in on the background to this case, we researched into this gentleman initially on the basis that he had been living alone for upwards of five years in quite a well-to-do road in the upmarket district of Didsbury. Do you know it? This, along with his tax returns, suggested he may have considerable wealth surplus to requirements. Oh, and I should have pre-empted a question which will no doubt have occurred to you: how did we ascertain he had been living alone for so long? Well, the quickest method is usually the Electoral Register. Everyone has access to this via the local library and we are happy to use this traditional public route for much of our routine research. I think you've already been briefed at induction or training about the discreet and proper use we make of data supplied by His Majesty's Customs and Revenue.'

At this point, Margaret paused, as if sensing that Mathew may be about to reach information overload, then continued, 'We'll talk more about the research process later in the morning, but as we're due to meet Mr Johnston in just a couple of minutes, I suggest we get settled into the interview room just down here. If you can just sit by me looking reasonably official and try to take as much in as possible.'

With that she led Mathew into one of the rooms towards the end of the long corridor. Margaret motioned him to sit down by her at a table positioned so that they were both facing the door. In due course an elderly gentleman was ushered in to be greeted by them.

'Good morning Mr Johnston. Do take a seat. I hope you don't mind, but I've brought along Mr Bryant today. He is new to the job and is sitting in on our discussion to learn the ropes, as it were. Thank you so much for agreeing to come back to us for more punishment. I hope they treated you well at reception, but don't hesitate to say if you need anything else.'

In much the same way as new recruits, potential clients to the agency were welcomed with a choice of hot and cold drinks and croissants served by a agency worker with consummate communication and interpersonal skills.

'I trust you have been able to think over the various options we suggested at our first meeting?' Margaret asked and continued, reading from his body language that the answer was affirmative.

'So may I start by asking what form would you like your contributions to take?'

Mr Johnston needed no further encouragement to reveal his preference: 'As we discussed the other week, I think you more or less persuaded me to go for the option B I think you called it. I've slept on it more than once and frankly can't see a better one. In view of my age, I think it makes most sense to have you become my executor and guarantee that 90% of my liquid assets and the same percentage from the sale of my property to go to my nephew in Durham.'

It appeared that this was going to be the shortest interview ever to settle a man's estate, but Margaret projected the image of one conscious of her mentoring role and pressed the old man for a little more information:

'I must confess that I was expecting you to come to that conclusion, but just to reassure me that you are acting in your own best interests and for Mr Bryant's benefit, could you outline for us why exactly you came to this decision?'

Mr Johnston momentarily appeared just a little discomfited by the request to justify himself, but obliged following a short pause to gather his thoughts: 'Well, as I've already mentioned, it's my age more than anything else. I can understand why it would make sense for a younger person to make modest regular contributions, but I don't expect to cling on to life much longer at eighty-eight and my main concern is to be absolutely confident that my nephew and his family will benefit from my estate. And given my mixed experience with lawyers and solicitors, I'd much sooner trust you, as in the government, to handle my estate when I go.'

'Nevertheless, even allowing for one or two shenanigans, you will still almost certainly be handing over a much larger slice of your wealth to the State than if you did the conventional thing and appointed a solicitor as executor....' Margaret added tentatively.

'Yes, but the difference is, as I've just said, I trust the State and it doesn't feel like a fee or a sacrifice when I know the money is going into the nation's coffers and will serve the public good. And it's hard to explain, but just knowing how much my nephew and his family will get feels reassuring, never mind the fact that it's probably less than through a solicitor who might be more concerned with lining his own pocket or be just plain incompetent.

'You hear so many stories... When one of my old school mates died suddenly a couple of years ago, his children were left in the lurch. Their family solicitor, who was their executor, had retired without telling them. Eventually, it turned out he had passed on all my friend's legal documents including the deeds to his house and will to another solicitor. Until they eventually found out what had happened, they spent months imagining everything had been lost or worse – stolen!'

This was enough by way of rationale to satisfy Mathew despite his having only just been introduced to the case.

Margaret spent a further fifty minutes or so discussing the finer details of the arrangement between Mr Johnston and HMRC and presided over the signing of various papers. The only other fact of any special interest to emerge was that the agency undertook to liaise with health and care services and any other agencies Mr Johnston may have occasion to use over the remaining years of his life. Indeed, this was another source of reassurance to him, as the agency would from now on be his first point of contact in his declining years.

Mathew was quite touched by the scene of this old man confidently and trustingly placing himself in the hands of Margaret – an agent of the State. How uncomfortable it would have been if he had had to rely instead on a member of the legal profession who like so many were motivated primarily by personal gain. He was nevertheless troubled by something about the situation which he just couldn't quite put his finger on. No doubt it would come to mind later...

Margaret bade the old man farewell after assuring him that the agency would keep in regular touch and that he was always welcome to call them with any queries. She then took Mathew, as promised, to the works canteen for a debriefing session. Their arrival was nicely timed to coincide with the half hour at mid-morning when the usual agency refreshments were served for free. Mathew guiltily went for the fresh coffee and a couple of chocolate biscuits rather than the healthier options: a one-off special first-day treat, he told himself.

As he settled down to his mid-morning snack, the elusive concern at last came into Mathew's conscious mind.

'I don't suppose it's necessarily of any great relevance, but I was wondering, Margaret, if you had the chance at all to meet Mr Johnston's nephew. Did the agency feel the need to contact him to explain his uncle's plans?'

Margaret answered as if she'd been anticipating his question or at least regarded it as perfectly natural.

'Yes, it's all part of our service making sure the beneficiary of the will is informed.' She paused, sensing that Mathew was not yet entirely satisfied with her answer. But she continued, suggesting her basic grasp of human psychology enabled her to guess correctly what was troubling him. 'We also needed to do a background identity check given that he was living so far away. Elderly people often get confused and out of touch with relatives whom they may not have seen for a lot longer than they imagine or who may have left the country, forgotten all about them or even died! And then, of course, there may be concerns about the probity of certain individuals who stand to benefit from an inheritance...'

Mathew used Margaret's pause this time to continue her thought. 'Yes, no doubt there are sad cases where an elderly person has been manipulated by a young relative for selfish personal gain.'

'Exactly, and so we always take utmost care to ensure that anyone engaging with us is doing so completely of their own volition and insist where possible on interviewing future beneficiaries or, if they live too far away, getting a colleague from a more local agency to do that for us.'

Now confident he was on Margaret's wave length, Mathew asked; 'I think rather naively I'd imagined you'd spend most of your time just interviewing one potential client after another, but it seems the background searches and follow-up work must take up a good part of the working day.'

'Well, to be honest, although we all aspire to be competent at every aspect of the job, over time we do tend to find that some of us gravitate more to the interpersonal side of things and others to the clerical and research side. Anyway, we're now going to spend the rest of the morning - an hour or so - examining together the background to our next *mark*.' Margaret smiled. 'I've yet to meet them in person. It's a very different case, a young middle-aged couple with no hint of wills or beneficiaries of questionable integrity!'

She led Mathew to a small office near the canteen for the prospective preparation session on the next potential clients. On a substantial desk there several paper folders, ring binders and box files lying alongside the expected computer. Clearly, a considerable amount of paperwork had been prepared ahead of this introductory meeting. Mathew enquired:

'If I'm honest, I'm rather surprised to see so much evidence of physical paperwork. I thought most people worked almost entirely on computers these days given the strong incentives for businesses to go entirely paperless. In fact, aren't there laws prohibiting paper-working unless an absolute need can be proven?'

By her expression, Margaret appeared to relish the opportunity to answer this question.

'There are two points to bear in mind here. Firstly, you've hit the nail on the head as regards the law. I'd sound cynical if I brushed off your question with the pat answer along the lines: 'As we're working for a government department, *we* make the laws around here!' There's an element of truth in that, however, and no doubt if we had to, we'd find a justification for using so much paper even if there really wasn't one. But in fact, - and this is the second point - there is a good reason which will become clear as the interview unfolds and it will make it more interesting if I leave you to work it out for yourself!'

'Well, it'll certainly make sure I stay alert, at any rate!' Mathew played along.

Margaret asked him to take a seat beside her and explained where the agency was up to in preparing this case, making it sound somewhat like a court proceeding. The couple had been selected via the usual algorithms on the basis that they were moderately high-earning professionals, approaching the end of their career, had no apparent debts, no dependents and supported a number of social enterprises.

'And how much will they already know about what your, or I suppose I should now say, *our* agency, is about and what they might be signing up to?' Mathew probed further.

'We approached it from the viewpoint of their interest in supporting social enterprises and explained we are here to assist them in achieving that goal.

'Now let me show you the main areas we're looking at. We have estimated that the couple earn an excess disposable income of around eight to twelve hundred pounds a month. And by that, I mean excess. We're already allowing for what the average couple in their position would want to spend on leisure, holidays, save for a rainy day and the rest of it.'

Mathew was intrigued: 'I can see how you can work out roughly what their income is, but how on earth you can estimate what they typically spend on recreation is beyond me!'

Margaret was clearly ready for this: 'I think you're underestimating the power of algorithms. Knowing key facts about a person – their age, educational background, work, their house, car and other main possessions is a fantastic start. Then we look at half a dozen other bits of information about them that is readily harvestable from easily accessible sources – this is all that's needed to get our assessments right nine times out of ten.

'You may have read about algorithms being used up to twenty odd years ago with scandalous effect to influence voting in elections. We've fine-tuned the same essential practices to ensure that both the means and the ends are ethical. Once we've identified likely individuals, the aim is to approach them in a sensitive way which allows us to harvest a mass of additional useful data such as causes they support, as I've already mentioned. Another way of looking at the process is to conduct a thought experiment. So far we've been considering the positive factors that help us go looking for suitable individuals…'

Mathew had anticipated what Margaret was about to say on hearing the word 'positive' and couldn't contain his eagerness to impress her:

'Yes, forgive me for interrupting: might that be ruling out people on the basis of a couple of negative facts about them such as…' He hesitated, unable immediately bring anything to mind, but Margaret graciously accorded him thinking time, '…some outward sign that they are self-obsessed, selfish and unlikely to sacrifice money for some altruistic purpose.'

Margaret conceded, 'Exactly, but you've bought yourself time there. I was hoping you would come up with a concrete example or two!' she laughed.

Mathew continued to play for time, waiting for inspiration.

'Well, an outward sign obvious to a neighbour, for example, even one who had never actually really met or spoken to the person concerned, might be that they owned a huge caravan and parked it on their drive so that only a gymnast or contortionist postman could squeeze past to reach their front door. And then when they do reach the door, they have to stoop down to the ground to reach the letterbox fitted with an armour-plated draft excluder designed to scrape every last bit of flesh of the postman's fingers if there isn't actually a vicious pet dog to do the job.

'But your agency surely wouldn't be investing in reconnaissance missions along residential roads to pick up data like that.' Then a splendidly simple idea came to him. 'I've got it – that visit to the library to check the electoral register and look for people living in a posh part of town, but who never vote, especially in local elections!'

'Bravo!' Margaret warmly congratulated Mathew. 'It was worth the wait: you've hit upon the very simplest yet most effective method we use to weed out the least likely responders. I can only award you seven out of a maximum ten points, however, as I'd mentioned the ER earlier, but still very clever of you to see how it can be used negatively to rule people out.'

Now let's have a quick look together about the information we already had about Mr and Mrs Travis and then consider what extra data they supplied us with and the use we can make of it.'

There followed a rigorous examination of much of the data stored in the files and folders on the table by the computer. During this process, Margaret showed Mathew the initial basic data gathered on the couple, the predictions furnished by the various algorithms and – the most interesting part of all – the additional information they had provided about themselves just prior to today's meeting. The match between the algorithm's projections and the factual information produced by the couple was startling.

'This is the bit I like best of all,' Mathew offered, 'where it predicts they are just left of centre in political outlook, socially liberal, spiritual theists, but not members of a particular church, have shown an interest in world religions other than Christianity, donate between £40 and £50 monthly between them to voluntary organisations, though they aren't active in any as such, and have a circle of about eight close friends they regularly socialise with. Such bold precision! And their answers are spot on in every detail, except that she used to be quite radically left-wing politically and he was an active member of the campaign for nuclear disarmament up to ten years ago.'

Margaret betrayed her appreciation of Mathew's keen eye for what was relevant.

'Yes, well done! This is a typical near ninety percent match. You could argue that it's made easy by the fact that most responses are prompted by a numerical scale, for example, the political outlook question has just five options: far right, right of centre, centre, left of centre and far left. Hardly anyone will admit to being remotely on the right of the political spectrum, few like to be seen as boringly in the middle. That just leaves left of centre and far left. Far left is too frighteningly radical for even traditional socialists given its connotation of extremism. So, all we have left – apologies for the pun – is left of centre. Would you care to have a guess at how many opt for this?'

Mathew caught the twinkle in her eye and went for seventy per cent.

'In fact, it's over ninety per cent,' Margaret proudly announced. 'But think about it for a moment: Why isn't that surprising?'

'I've got it.' Mathew had no need to temporise this time, 'It probably would have been just over half if you'd asked a complete cross section of the population at large, but the point must be that you've already weeded out most of those with the least social conscience from the very outset.'

'I couldn't have put it better myself.' Margaret acknowledged. 'So that particular question can be seen as one of the most effective in its confirmatory role. Essentially, that's what all the questions are for to a greater or lesser extent. Remember, we are only interested in the information people provide us with insofar as it convinces us they are the folk most likely to be persuaded to volunteer extra contributions to a good cause.'

Mathew suddenly had qualms. 'I heard once that when charities used to be the main vehicle for people donating to good causes, usually one charity's gain was another's loss. In other words, people's generosity had limits, so if they were persuaded to donate to a new charity, they would usually switch from another one rather than actually increase the overall amount donated. Isn't there a danger of that happening with your- sorry - *our* clients?'

Margaret had no pat answer ready this time, but following a moment's slightly pained reflection, she replied, 'We can't absolutely guarantee, of course, that getting people to sign up for extra tax contributions won't tempt them to reduce donations elsewhere. However, we're not really comparing like with like here and I'm sure that most of our clients will view extra tax payments as serving a completely different purpose from more modest payments they're already making to specific causes. It is something we probably ought to look into seriously, however.'

Mathew appreciated the honesty of her response, but it didn't entirely dispel his own sense that the agency should already have looked into this displacement problem.

The two of them spent the next half hour or so before lunch

examining the rest of the data collected so far on Mr and Mrs Travis. As the material to assimilate was more than Margaret had anticipated, they continued for a further half hour over a working lunch served to them in the office. Mathew apologised for adding to the time pressure by asking so many questions, but Margaret replied that it had been a pleasure to answer them.

The couple were finally ushered into the office. Just as they sat down, the agency's usual hospitality appeared: a trolley bearing an assortment of cookies, coffee pot and bottled water. Mathew was a little disappointed, not by the refreshments on offer, but because on this occasion he was unable to recognise the agency worker serving them.

Margaret followed what was clearly the tried and tested house etiquette. She warmly welcomed the couple, introduced Mathew, getting him to serve the refreshments, and provided a preview of what she hoped to achieve by the end of today's discussion. She then went on to outline the function of the agency in a short presentation, stopping once or twice in case the couple had any questions. As if complicitly, Mr and Mrs Travis did not avail themselves of this opportunity.

When the couple's turn came, Mrs Travis was the first to speak. It was immediately apparent that she was the dominant member of the partnership. She had worked as a secondary school teacher for a quarter of a century and was now considering leaving the regular workforce at the end of the current academic year aged fifty-eight.

Twenty years ago, this would have been called 'early' retirement, the normal age being sixty. Society, however, had moved on and the concept of retirement with its negative connotations of withdrawal from work, hence from life and society, had been largely eroded. The idea of becoming a pensioner too, with its old-age associations, had become outmoded largely thanks to the citizen's guaranteed income for life. In theory, the only issue remaining for most people was what income they felt they needed in order to maintain their chosen lifestyle.

Mrs Travis had enjoyed her work as an English teacher at her local comprehensive school, but didn't relish the prospect of having to adapt to yet another major curriculum overhaul in her subject area. These had already occurred four or five times in her twenty-five-year career and she was beginning to feel the appeal of a more varied and relaxing mode of life. This would entail spending more time with her husband with whom she shared many pastimes, developing her interest in reading and taking up one or two new hobbies on the creative side such as painting and learning to play a musical instrument.

At this point, Mr Travis took over. Five years older than his wife, he was an accountant by trade and, as he worked for himself, was in a position to power down gradually over the next couple of years so that by the time his wife left the workforce, he would have very few private clients left and they would be able to spend more time together.

After this small contribution to the discussion, he looked nervously across to Mrs Travis tacitly inviting her to conclude their unassuming self-portrait. She obligingly continued:

'In our younger years, like most couples we dreamt of having a family of two point three children, or whatever it was in those days. But sadly, they never materialised. Without the financial burden of raising little ones, we found our savings grew steadily. We were able to pay off our mortgage well ahead of schedule and nowadays it seems almost obscene to have accumulated so much money to no obvious purpose.

'We've done all the sensible things like put plenty away for a rainy day and take out insurance for all reasonable risks. We've spent a decent amount on improving our home over the years, but any more modernising would just be a source of stress rather than pleasure. In our forties we travelled about as much as we really wanted to before the law came in to restrict people to just one flight abroad per year. Since then, we've been happy to stick to occasional coach and train trips to places nearer to home.

'Our motoring costs are very modest. We have just the one low tax car. I've never driven and Harry, only drives when he has to, which is usually just to visit clients who mostly live nearby. In fact, many are happy to come to us. So, our lifestyle is pretty low cost. We even struggle to spend money on our hobbies – not like some folk with their golf and second home.'

At this point, Mrs Travis paused as if having run out of steam and tacitly inviting Margaret to introduce the topic of how the couple's surplus financial reserves might be put to good use by the State. She explained that most people preferred to donate their extra contributions to some specific cause rather than into a global government fund which would involve apportioning a certain amount to unpopular though arguably necessary expenditures such as defence. The Travises immediately opted for the children's education and social welfare fund.

Mathew had once seen a TV documentary which appeared to conclude that the State had seriously mismanaged public education around the turn of the century. A chaotically diverse and divisive system had evolved in the course of the twentieth century, leading to a crisis in the early twenty first. Against a complex social, political, cultural and religious background, almost every conceivable type of secondary school had emerged in the state sector – selective versus non-selective, coeducational versus single sex, faith schools versus non-denominational or humanist, Local Authority run versus so-called academies. Even the latter were divided into single and multi-academy trusts and were funded by a variety of organisations.

By the mid-2020s, it was widely recognised that even without considering the private sector which educated around six per cent of children, public education was at best stagnating, at worst deteriorating. A lack of any coherent philosophical basis for determining the school curriculum had led to frequent and often ill-considered tinkering and sometimes major controversial reforms. Successive governments had unwisely favoured a business model for reorganising any schools deemed by inspectors to be failing until, at last, it was recognised that the school inspections regime itself had been a major contributor to their failure.

Overpaid top-heavy self-interested senior management teams who cared more about performance targets than the wellbeing of their staff, as in other public services, often generated a toxic atmosphere. As a result, the teaching profession was being abandoned on mass by newly qualified and experienced practitioners alike.

In recent years, a degree of stability had been achieved by granting teachers professional status and trusting the teaching collective to largely determine its own curricula and run their own classrooms. An act obliged all single-sex, academically selective and faith schools to become secular, coeducational and comprehensive. Charitable status was removed from private schools and a surtax on fees soon led to their virtual disappearance. Given that schools are a microcosm of society at large, the educational deficit of children from less affluent backgrounds had been significantly reduced in years since the reforms had been introduced and worked through the system.

Nevertheless, many schools were still struggling to cater for all their students' special educational needs and so a dedicated fund was created by the government to support this effort. This is the fund the Travises chose to allocate their extra voluntary tax contributions to as well as to a children's social wellbeing fund.

Margaret then took the couple through the various methods of payment open to them. She explained that in the past, people would often leave substantial donations to good works in their will, but until their death, the money had been languishing for years in savings accounts with banks who often held this in a cash reserve fund rather than investing it. The appeal of voluntary extra contributions is that the money is invested straight away in a worthy project whose results can be seen by the donors in their own lifetime.

The couple also had control over their contributions. They could have them deducted at source from their pension or regular pay, or set up a mandate to pay a fixed or variable amount from their own account. HMRC would keep a reliable record of payments made just as in the case of standard tax and send them an annual statement. They would also receive a periodic report of achievements made possible by the fund or funds.

Mr Travis pointed out that he felt much happier about contributing in this way compared with twenty years ago when he, like many folk, used to give to the big charities until it came to light that they wasted a lot of the money donated, did little to account for how it was used and paid their top people fat cat salaries. Margaret explained that this was why the government as a trusted operator had largely taken the place of the big national charities and was keen, along with local government, to nudge people to donate more to local charities and voluntary organisations whose work they knew about or were even directly involved in.

Hearing Margaret say this further quelled Mathew's earlier concerns about charities losing out when the agency's clients signed up for voluntary contributions. However, he wanted to be doubly sure and took advantage of a quiet moment when papers were being signed to ask the couple innocently whether they thought they would still be able to support their favourite local charities and voluntary groups. Mr and Mrs Travis exchanged glances and confirmed this as one, nodding and looking Mathew in the eye as convincingly as he could have wished.

Immediately after the interview, Margaret smiled meaningfully at Mathew and congratulated him on his intervention:

'I could sense something was eating you and realised as soon as you opened your mouth, I should have known what it was given your comments earlier! I think you put the question very well and elicited an honest response. I trust you got the reassurance you needed?'

'I certainly did,' Mathew replied and continued, 'I think I have the answer to that other question too about why there was so much paperwork on the desk rather than having everything done on the computer which, for that matter, I don't think you even switched on!'

'Go on, surprise me,' Margaret grinned.

'Well both Mr and Mrs Travis must be competent at using computers for their work – she's a teacher and he's an accountant after all. But I tried to visualise how different the discussion would have been if while talking you'd been staring at the computer screen all the time with awkward pauses while waiting for spreadsheets to load up and print out. Less eye contact with the couple, hence less bonding….'

'Spot on as always,' Margaret jumped in, 'and you no doubt noticed too how the papers they signed at the end were already there in the folder rather than printed off while they waited. It's been proven that people give greater weight to signing contracts produced from folders than the same contracts printed off in their presence by a computer. As a species, we must harbour a residual mistrust of anything not produced by the human hand.'

'Yes, and given what magic computers can perform nowadays with artificial intelligence, it's hardly surprising.'

Margaret finally asked if Mathew had any more questions or thoughts. He asked what the success rate was once the agency had got to this stage with clients. In other words, how many changed their mind during the cooling off period. She replied that the Travis case was atypical in that it had progressed from an initial contact to outright agreement to sign up in the space of just one face-to-face meeting. With the standard two meetings, the success rate was initially in the region of 85% reducing over one or two years to about 75%. The reasons for people dropping out were usually down to changes in personal circumstances rather than a change of heart.

Before clocking off at the end of the afternoon, it occurred to Mathew to ask Margaret one last question about the work rhythm of the agency. He had envisaged a typical working day as being divided into perhaps as many as half a dozen interviews with clients and potential clients, whereas today they had dealt only with one individual and a couple. Was this typical or was it just because he was shadowing today and so much time had been given over to discussion between himself and Margaret?

Margaret, precise as ever, gave a nuanced answer: 'It's normally something in between. On a typical day, I will probably interview one or two more people, but it's not like visiting a bank where a financial adviser will see about six or seven customers in a day. You have to bear in mind that the returns for every extra minute spent on meticulous data collection, analysis and careful interviewing produces fantastic returns for the government. Just imagine if Mr and Mrs Travis are worth an extra three thousand pounds to us annually over a period of twenty years. That's sixty thousand plus a potential huge bonus we may stand to inherit when they pass away.'

Before letting Mathew go, Margaret briefed him on tomorrow's agenda which involved a similar shadowing session with another agency worker, but where he would be encouraged by degrees to take a more active part in the interviewing process.

As Mathew made his way to the reception area to sign out, he momentarily switched off from today's work-related events and allowed himself to daydream a little. Despite finding his discussions with Margaret intriguing and the interviews eye-opening - in many respects even heart-warming - he nevertheless felt slightly cheated at being unable to catch up and compare notes with any of the people he had met last week, especially Emily. Even his encounter with Jonathan first thing had been fleeting. He sat in the reception area for ten minutes feeling rather conspicuous on the off chance he might catch one of the others as they signed out, but to no avail. Tomorrow, he would make sure he got to have morning break and lunch in the canteen.

As he returned home, Mathew had that familiar buzzing sensation which he'd experienced before when confidently settling into a new job. Along with a sense of euphoria, he actually felt as though all the cells in his body were vibrating with an invigorating life force which was raring to carry him physically and emotionally to great new heights.

He found himself unable to focus properly when performing routine tasks such as making himself a cup of tea and changing out of his work clothes. Even when sitting in front of the TV to catch the latest news, he was too restless and distracted to follow the presenter's meaning despite hearing all the words. It was at least two hours into the evening before Mathew's racing mind had powered down sufficiently to enable him to concentrate on anything other than the impressions from his day at work.

Mathew was by now sufficiently familiar with this syndrome to recognise its various stages and prepared himself for the sequence which almost always followed the powering down phase. This would entail being assailed by self-doubt, anxiety and even depression. Before this change in mood took hold, he had already armed himself with its antidote: His antique record player was gently filling the room in stereo with the pleasantly discordant tones of dinner jazz and on the coffee table before him were a plate of his favourite nibbles and a pint glass of cold and exuberantly fizzing lager.

Two years ago, he had wisely replaced his habitual bottle of strong ale with an alcohol-free variety. He had learned that the short-lived fuzzy and euphoric sensation produced by the alcohol usually gave way to a headache and almost always to a lower mood which lasted considerably longer than the pleasurable feeling it had ousted.

CHAPTER 9.
MORE MARKS

The precautions taken by Mathew the evening before enabled him to escape the worst effects of his earlier euphoria. He transitioned gently from this heightened state into one of mild excitement in which he spent an hour or so engrossed in his current wargame until physical tiredness and mental fatigue finally overcame him. A relatively untroubled night's sleep ensued and Mathew awoke refreshed and pleasantly unburdened by any perplexing dreams demanding urgent interpretation.

Another source of relief was his automatic decision to continue his virtuous and by now almost habitual practice of taking the bus to work. The brisk walk to the bus stop around the corner from his house filled his lungs with the invigorating early autumn air. He was the only one to board the bus at this particular point, which caused him to feel strangely privileged. Most of his fellow passengers were unavailable for social contact, at least half of those sitting within his field of vision were staring down at their phones, others, judging by their distant facial expressions, were presumably wearing the modern invisible earphones and engrossed in music or at least some form of audio entertainment.

Mathew cast his mind back. Once on holiday in a strange town, he and his parents had become separated during a sightseeing trip. He must have been about eight at the time and though the experience was quite frightening, he kept his presence of mind.

As he remembered the name of his hotel, he decided all he needed to do was to ask a passer-by where it was. At least then he could get back there safely and wait for his parents to return should he fail to find them.

The difficulty was catching anyone's eye, as nearly everyone who passed was either absorbed by their phone screen or listening intently to music with their gaze fixed at a distant point ahead, presumably in the direction they were heading. How could he capture their attention? Calling out to those with the earphones would go unnoticed and, in any case, he feared importuning anyone.

At last, Mathew saw an elderly gentleman who, presumably having noticed his forlorn appearance, slowly began to approach. However, before the man had come close enough to speak, Mathew's parents called out and all was well. Only many years later did Mathew ever pause to consider whether the old man's intentions had been benign.

Mathew returned to the present and mused: modern-day earphones were as good as implants and the only clue their host was wearing them was generally a vacant gaze into space which turned to confusion or even resentment if they were addressed. How alienating! These reflections reminded Mathew how he valued or ought to value social contact and was partly why he had caught the earlier bus today in the hope of also 'intercepting' a new colleague or two on their way into work. This was the North after all where people were still meant to be warmer and more open than in the South... .

On nearing the entrance to reception, Mathew couldn't help producing a hierarchy of who he would most and least like to meet. The list naturally ran from Emily at the top, followed by Jonathan, then various trainer colleagues. At the very bottom of the pile was Peter with whom he had felt the least affinity from the beginning. This was no doubt down to his over assertive manner and the fact he'd unashamedly spent all his professional life in sales. Mathew realised he was succumbing to his own prejudices again and smiled at his self-rebuke that the agency's algorithm could not possibly have committed a selection error.

Mathew's prayer was answered. As he entered reception, Jonathan, his second most favoured work colleague, was just checking in. This time he wouldn't allow him to be whisked away before they had had a chance to chat. Receiving a firm tap on the shoulder, Jonathan agreed to wait a moment while Mathew himself checked in.

The two of them faced each other again for the first time in what seemed quite a while, although it had been only four days since their training ordeal together. Jonathan spoke first in his characteristically nervous manner. He appeared eager to talk as if to get one or two concerns off his chest, and spoke in a confidential tone, indicating with his body language that they should move as far away from the reception desk as possible. This was Mathew's instinct too, as he disliked the idea of an eavesdropping receptionist whether or not the role had been officially assigned to her.

Jonathan had undergone a similar experience to himself in most respects. In the morning, he had been placed in the capable hands of an experienced and socially adept agency worker, Denise, with an individual lady client who had already more or less pledged voluntary contributions. The interview discussion had covered how she proposed to make the payments and her preferred beneficiary of the funds. In the afternoon, they had tackled a younger higher professional couple with an acute social conscience on their first interview. Jonathan had found their virtue signalling rather overbearing. He stressed, though, how much more gratifying it should be to work with people who were keen to give extra money away. As a mortgage broker his clients were usually intent on parting with as little money as possible and would often even challenge his fee at the slightest excuse.

CHAPTER 9. MORE MARKS

Given the promise of his colleague's agitated posture, Mathew felt a little let down by the banality of Jonathan's account, but at least it was reassuring to note that the least confident member of the team had so far come through the process ethically unchallenged and without undue trauma.

In his own account, Mathew spared Jonathan excessive detail and simply stressed the essential similarities of their experiences. He preferred instead to sound him out on lunch arrangements which was one area where their fortunes had differed: Jonathan had at least made it to the works canteen for half an hour yesterday.

'Yes, lunch was fine – not a huge choice, but at least something for everyone - carnivores to rabbit food eaters. Nice desserts too, though everyone seems either too rushed or health conscious to enjoy them. I eat quite well of an evening and so a piece of fruit and a cake would do me any day. Nice to sit down and have a chat, though.'

'Were any of the others we met last week there?', Mathew enquired as casually as he could, not wishing to reveal his aspirational romance with Emily.

'I saw Peter and one or two of the trainers, what's her name, Theresa, and the chap who ran the first session... can't remember his name now. I wasn't particularly looking out for anyone, as I felt I had to spend most of the time talking to Denise, my mentor.'

Not as much intel as Mathew had hoped for, but they agreed to try and meet up for lunch today, work schedules permitting. Here too, they both appeared to have a similar practical induction programme and they promised to exchange a few notes at the next opportunity.

It was five minutes to starting time and Jonathan headed in the same direction as yesterday having been told which office he'd be starting off in. Mathew's own agent had told him to meet in the lobby, so he continued to wait, clinging to the hope of a brief but more interesting encounter.

Just as he caught sight of Emily about to push on the reception door from outside the building, Mathew was hailed by his date for the day. He turned round rather too sharply for decorum to find Theresa smiling and with an outreached hand. A three-pronged flash of resentment instantly shot through his psyche: he'd been cheated of at least two minutes of his own time, he'd momentarily lost his composure in a manner which must have shown, hence causing him embarrassment, and, worst of all, he'd been robbed of an opportunity to brighten the start of his day chatting with Emily. There was yet a fourth reason for his resentment which refused to break through into his conscious mind.

Theresa led Mathew down the same right-hand corridor as Margaret had done yesterday. In his temporary ire, he told himself this was no doubt part of the plan to keep the newbies apart, all the better to indoctrinate them. But the emotion leading to this reflection faded as they approached the office intended for today's deliberations. When Mathew sat down on the opposite side of the desk to face Theresa, the fourth reason for his earlier momentary ill feeling revealed itself to him: whereas Emily had instantly appealed to his masculine nature, Theresa was achieving a similar result on a slower fuse. Strangely, he had not been aware of this process towards the end of the session spent with Theresa and could only attribute it to the wondrous incubational capacity of his subconscious mind.

But why the resentment? A split-second self-analysis provided a complex answer: on the one hand, Emily might have sensed his discomfiture as she entered reception and saw him being greeted by Theresa. Her woman's instinct would have enabled her to detect his attraction for another woman even before he himself was aware of it. Thus, his future chances with Emily were at best damaged, at worst ruined.

Theresa brought Mathew sharply round from his ruminations with a lively preview of the morning's casework. They would be examining the file of a professional couple whose algorithm profile suggested a high likelihood of suitability for recruitment to the voluntary extra tax scheme, but before meeting them they needed to weigh up the most appropriate interview technique. Mathew observed in the ensuing discussion that Theresa repeatedly used the abbreviation VETS in place of the long-winded Voluntary Extra Tax Scheme and wondered how many more acronyms he would be privileged to learn during their time together. He couldn't decide whether her use of the acronym use enhanced or diminished her allure.

The data analysis session for this younger couple differed from yesterday's in a few important respects. To begin with, there was no pile of paper and plastic folders on the desk this time, as Theresa had everything stored on her computer. Mathew couldn't help resuming his role as teacher's pet by announcing that he had worked out the reason for this. Namely, the couple's formative years would have been when practically all information resources were served up via computer screen, whether teaching materials at school or games and social media in the home. They were perfectly happy to sit facing their interrogators holding wireless screens which allowed all four members of the company to switch from one display to another at a slightest whim.

There was nothing superficially striking about the data itself which Theresa extracted from the couple's algorithm profile. It contained a multitude of banal facts about their comings and goings, tastes in entertainment, shopping habits and the like. But Mathew had come to accept by now that this sufficed to predetermine their donor suitability to within 90% accuracy. He anticipated that it would be fun one day to encounter a rogue mismatch, which sooner or later he surely must.

Theresa explained which intel they were looking for in order to establish the best possible interview techniques to be employed with this couple. Mathew found these indicators rather too esoteric to grasp at once, but quite looked forward to acquiring the necessary mindset.

There was far less warmth at this meeting compared to both interviews yesterday, but Mathew was not at all fazed by this and felt perfectly comfortable when Theresa called on him to take part in the questioning alongside her. The gent was in his mid-forties and worked in education as a curricula organiser and his partner, just a little younger, was a senior home health care professional. In common with yesterday's clients, they were childless and supported social enterprises, both local and national, as well as two international former charities dealing in humanitarian aid. One of these had been salvaged from the wreckage of the Red Cross which ran aground in the 2030s following a fat cat nest-feathering scandal involving the CEO and many of her entourage.

Similar arguments were put forward to those which Mathew had heard already as to the advantages of supporting good causes via a government agency as opposed to private or independent ones. This was all well and good, he thought, provided the government continued to behave properly in the public interest and was effectively monitored by a trusted scrutiny body. He was a little concerned also by what he felt was a subtle suggestion that this couple might transfer their generous contributions to VETS rather than add them to their current portfolio. He was reassured, however, when they made it clear that their commitments to existing causes would not be affected.

At the end of the interview, Theresa praised Mathew for asking his questions skilfully and helping them to 'get a result', as she put it. He marginally preferred Margaret's manner to Theresa's questioning technique and general demeanour, but that didn't detract from Theresa's attractiveness.

Finally, Mathew was able to enjoy his first proper lunch in the staff canteen as a regular employee of the agency. He and Theresa had arrived a little early and so he was able to keep an eye out for familiar faces as other folk began to trickle in. At last, Emily entered the canteen and sat down next to Peter, which wasn't such good news. He monitored her movements for a few moments until she got up again and headed for the self-service drinks table. He used this opportunity to join her and strike up a conversation while simultaneously trying to get his coffee pot to pour, fumbling with a stack of paper cups and frantically looking out for the milk.

Seeing that Mathew was on the verge of a multi-tasking disaster, Emily took pity and stepped in, holding his cup steady and assuming responsibility for the idle chit-chat, while he was just left to pour the coffee and scan the table for the milk jug. With barely a drop of liquid spilt, the two of them sat down together to continue their conversation in a more favourable context.

Mathew recalled the first golden rule for winning a lady's heart from his trusted webpage and so, following its advice, sat back and prepared to let Emily do the talking. She clearly did need to get a thing or two off her chest, as by the time she first paused for breath, he had already drunk half his coffee. As she sipped her own, Mathew hurriedly searched for an appropriate response, after realising he'd overlooked another important heart-winning rule, namely: *listen* to what the lady has to say!

'Yes, I can see where you're coming from. Talking to Jonathan earlier, it's clear we've all been having a similar experience.' He realised he'd produced a grammatically flawed second sentence containing a misplaced gerund, but at least it fulfilled the third and possibly most important golden rule – that of *agreeing* with the lady.

Fortunately, when Emily resumed, she recapped much of what she'd already said, thus confirming Mathew's educated guessing had been broadly on target. She'd been subjected to a similar diet of practical induction as himself, probably the most notable difference being that one of her trainers' clients had been rather less inclined to fulfil their algorithm's promise. It emerged, however, that since the lady concerned had expressed an interest in becoming a public benefactor, her financial position had been compromised through unexpected redundancy from her senior management post. Emily's mentor, a young gentleman, reassured her that she could always come back to the agency once she obtained a new post, as he was sure she would do in due course.

Mathew, now fully attentive to what Emily was actually saying, learned something new – that donors were potentially signing up to a goodwill contract with the government. In the event of their personal circumstances deteriorating to the point where they were in financial difficulty, they could apply to draw down on their voluntary tax contributions! This element of insurance in the scheme struck Mathew as eminently sensible and an excellent enticement or inducement for people to join VETS. He would ask Theresa or Margaret why they hadn't mentioned this, though he imagined it was just a case of their not wanting to burden him with too much information.

They had been talking 'shop' for quite a while now and Mathew knew he needed to direct the conversation to more personal matters before the forty-minute lunch break came to an end.

'What do your family and friends think of your working for the agency, Emily?' he ventured as an opening gambit.

'I can't really answer that, as I've not had a chance to talk to anyone much about it yet. Or perhaps I should say I've been putting off telling people because I'm still working out what I think about it myself. I did tell my mum I'm now working for the government and I think she sees that as preferable to the private sector. I only have a couple of girlfriends that I talk to about anything work related. They know I've got a new job, but I've not really had much to report as yet.'

Mathew found some comfort in Emily's reply which though banal in content came across as thoughtful and suggested she was at ease talking to him and more or less on his wave length.

'Yes, I know what you mean. I've only told my mother and sister in passing and perhaps a bit more to a couple of friends. Unlike your mum, mine has a low regard for public sector jobs and will take some convincing I've not foolishly taken a step down in the world. I do have this bright university friend who's instinctively suspicious at any mention of the word 'agency'. He insisted on briefing me on all the pitfalls to look out for....' Mathew felt a slight pang of conscience at his slight misrepresentation of Rory, but this was overridden by an unmistakable sense that Emily had warmed towards him, as she had maintained eye contact almost throughout their conversation.

Over the few minutes that remained, Mathew learned from Emily that she shared his opinion about Peter's presumed mercenary nature and she plainly stated that the clumsy drinks episode just now had provided her with an opportunity to escape his company. What better cause could Mathew have for daring to hope that, albeit cautiously, she was signalling her availability?

By the time the lunch break ended and people began to make for the canteen exit, Mathew knew that his own unfaithful wavering and veering towards Theresa was over.

As he stood up to join the parting crowd, he noticed that Peter, presumably following abandonment by Emily, had found another conversation partner in one of the lady staff who had sat in on their training sessions last week. Despite his largely irrational antipathy towards Peter, Mathew still intended to catch up with his induction buddy one day soon, if only to confirm or challenge his initial feelings about him and allay any residual fears regarding Emily.

The afternoon held no particular surprises for Mathew, though it provided a couple more insights into how the whole VETS business operated in practice and brought home the sheer variety and complexity of the situations with which agency staff were faced more or less every hour of every day.

Theresa had a caseload of two interviews. The first was a professional woman in her early thirties who had shown an interest in making modest VETS contributions now with a view to stepping them up in the future should she progress in her career. She came across as a very earnest and pragmatic lady whose social conscience was embedded in a strong religious faith which made Mathew a little uneasy. His first reaction was to wonder why she didn't just donate to her church or, for example, a children's charity. It emerged, however, that her particular sect expected its followers to support public projects where feasible and this reminded Mathew once more of how in recent years the government had rehabilitated itself in the eyes of most citizens, whereas traditional charities had come to be viewed with suspicion.

The second case, was another couple with the difference that one partner, the male, was manifestly more enthusiastic than his long-standing female partner. Again, Mathew presumed to read the situation almost from the moment the pair were introduced. *Here*, he thought, *we have an elderly gentleman with considerable personal wealth partnered with a younger woman dependent who is naturally concerned about her future security and that of her children from a previous marriage. He too has a child, admittedly grown up and independent now, but all these facts from her perspective as a dependent will make his wish to 'donate to the State', as she put it, something of a luxury, not to mention a threat to her own position.*

Mathew was impressed with how Theresa handled the situation from start to finish. She explained at once that the agency did not normally deal with couples whose feelings about VETS substantially differed.

'We are not in the business of sowing disharmony or driving

a wedge between the people who come to see us. I suggest that you discuss your concerns with each other and return to us in a while if and when you are able to reach an agreement on contributing to VETS. Let me hand you this booklet which explains the key principles as well as the ins and outs of how people choose to make contributions. There are some benefits listed which few people are aware of, such as the insurance aspect.'

Mathew inwardly applauded Theresa for subtly sowing that particular seed having only just mentioned her wish not to sow discord in her previous sentence. The lady would be sure to read the booklet now and hence be much more susceptible to persuasion.

'I'm really sorry we've been wasting your time. I'm sure there must be far less difficult people than us you could be spending your time with.' the lady answered, feigning an apology. *If she'd really felt guilty, she'd have used the first person singular rather than the plural we,* mused Mathew, *but then again, I suppose it was both their fault: if this fellow had talked the whole business through with her earlier, this situation could have been avoided.*

Theresa naturally denied any time had been wasted for either party, as the whole discussion process was intended to bring clarity to all concerned and undoubtedly this had been achieved today. The last thing the agency wanted was to pressure people into making a decision which they might later regret.

When the couple had at last left the office, Theresa turned towards Mathew with a confident smile which he took as a signal to provide feedback in the form of the lavish praise he felt she deserved.

As Theresa modestly received his accolade, Mathew recalled he had wanted to ask her why she or Margaret hadn't referred to the insurance element in the VETS, but decided there was no need as it had come up naturally in the discussion just now. Besides, it would have been socially awkward for him to follow his warm praise of Theresa with a question which might challenge her professionalism.

So ended another day at the agency, leaving Mathew with the cosy glow of a job well done. He had further initiated himself into the secrets of VETS and largely, though not as yet entirely, found the reassurance he had been looking for from his new employers. Of no little consequence either was the fact that his determination to get to talk to his new colleagues had paid off, particularly in the case of Emily who had shown promising signs of wanting to become more closely acquainted.

As before, he took his time signing out at reception and lingered a while outside in the hope of meeting her again. When she failed to materialise, however, he wasn't at all despondent, confident that tomorrow would bring more opportunities.

On his return home at about five o'clock after another early finish at the agency, Mathew experienced none of the extreme physical and mental fatigue of yesterday, nor the racing mind. True, he still needed a while to assimilate the day's events, but much of this was completed during his bus journey. A further half hour spent in front of the TV over a cup of tea and two biscuits sufficed for the rest of the recuperative process.

The regular news bulletin suggested that very little had happened in the world. There were the usual reports of more flooding and severe winds wreaking havoc in remote countries whose economies were still too weak to provide adequate climate mitigation defences. It was hard to see what more humanity could achieve collectively to protect the environment now that population growth was largely under control and renewable energy had virtually supplanted fossil fuels. Air quality around the planet had markedly improved compared with a generation ago and safe drinking water and essential healthcare reached eight of the earth's nine billion souls. Climate change, or global warming, as it used to be called, was simply a fact of modern life – the inescapable legacy of earlier generations' mad rush towards economic growth based on a consumerist lifestyle which had gone unchallenged for too long.

The only barrier to social and economic equality seemed to be human nature itself. No definitive solution had been found to most people's inherent greed and their desire to accumulate wealth at the expense of others. In the absence of traditional forms of overt exploitation of the bulk of humanity by a privileged elite, the vast majority of societies stubbornly held on to a strictly meritocratic and hierarchical rewards structure. This meant that in a given organisation, the most senior employee could still expect to earn up to twenty times more than the lowest paid. True, in recent years some of the most outrageous cases of excessive executive pay had been addressed. However, this only served to raise awareness and further fuel vociferous public indignation at the persisting gross income gap between rich and poor.

The worst effects of social inequality were indeed mitigated by the universal income which had as good as eliminated absolute poverty. However, study after study suggested that it was the perceived inequality itself which remained the prime underlying cause of any residual social discord.

While Mathew prepared himself a light tea, he reflected on the fact that the past couple of weeks had imbued him with a renewed zest for life and taste for engaging with people. Previously, after work he would tend to take refuge in solitary activities to wind down such as his music and wargaming, whereas now he felt motivated to continue the social exchanges he had enjoyed at work.

Only days ago, he had agonised for hours over who among his friends or family to phone about his new job, or indeed whether to call them at all. This evening, had time and energy allowed, he would gladly have called them all – his mother, sister, Frank, Rory and Andrew – just for the sake of hearing their voices and learning their news and with no particular pre-prepared script of his own. As it was, he settled for 'family first' and began with his mother. Three days had passed since their weekend get together and she must surely have more to tell of her romantic adventures.

Optimistic that her health warning and newfound love interest had continued to hold her fondness for the bottle at bay, he called his mother much later in the evening than he would normally have dared. She answered at once sounding unmistakably cheerful. She had heard no more yet about her social security top-up claim. Without prompting from Mathew, she confirmed her resolve to remain alcohol-abstinent and had managed to fit in another dinner with her doctor friend. Her ebullient and talkative mood did not, however, extend to showing an interest in her son's affairs and so when Mathew put down the phone, he had imparted very little news of his own except that he was enjoying his new job. After all, he thought, that was all parents really wanted and needed to know.

Mathew allowed himself a few minutes to reflect on his mother's words before continuing with his calling schedule for the evening. It was only as he dialled his sister's number that he recalled the tension that had arisen between them over Andrew and realised he would have to deal impromptu with this if it came up in the ensuing conversation.

Paula took a while to come to the phone, but sounded reasonably pleased to hear from her brother whose reflex was to open with questions about their mother. This was an instinctive ruse to avoid plunging straight in with more sensitive topics. He knew that Paula would have seen their mother at least once since the weekend and that she may be able to fill in a few facts which had not emerged in his earlier conversation just moments ago.

Paula in fact had very little to reveal which his mother hadn't already told him or which he had been able to surmise for himself. She confirmed all the essential facts, adding only that further blood test results were expected which might provide

CHAPTER 9. MORE MARKS

more information about their mother's general state of health. Paula confessed to her ambivalence about what to hope for.

As she put it, 'obviously, we both naturally hope the results won't be really bad and show up anything too dire, but on the other hand, if they're too reassuring, it might undermine mum's resolve to stay off the booze!'

'Which is why it's so good she's got a couple of other things going for her at the moment,' commented Mathew. 'Do you think this doctor friend is a real prospect for her? I should have asked if you've ever met him, as you share the same medical practice don't you?'

'I've seen Doctor Clarkson walk through the health centre once or twice, but never had an appointment with him. He seemed quite nice, as I recall. I hate to say it, but to be honest, I don't really get what he sees in mum. For a start, he's probably a few years younger than she is.'

Mathew's next move was to ask Paula how she was getting on with her new job. She paused before answering and sounded uncertain as to what to report. Her scheme for inducing more residents to opt into the fee-paying garden waste service offered by the council was due to be implemented within a couple of months and she had been given a role in organising this. She was pleased that her new responsibilities hadn't adversely affected her working relationship with any of her colleagues and so all in all her experience had so far been positive.

Paula was modest and self-effacing by nature and so it was no surprise to Mathew that she quickly changed the subject to ask him about his own new job. Just like his sister, he wasn't entirely sure where to begin, but he spoke at some length on this topic sensing this would enable him to muster the courage to broach the other matter which he still hoped was closer to his sister's heart, that of her relationship with Andrew.

As expected, Paula's curiosity about her brother's new

employment was strictly limited to the rather banal details he shared with her. The only question she asked was predictably about his pay. He couldn't honestly remember quite what the salary was, and was content to dismiss the subject by stressing that although the salary was a little more generous than his previous job, with the compulsory VETS it probably worked out about the same. Oddly, he had never been able to read his sister's capacity for sibling rivalry and envy, but judged that playing down the pay element was the safest bet on this occasion.

At this point, both sensed that the relatively neutral phase of their conversation had been exhausted and each waited for the other to field the next topic. Finally, Mathew was relieved when Paula obliged by introducing the sequel he had been hoping to hear – her saga with Andrew. Andrew had shown at least a little patience by waiting over forty-eight hours after talking to Mathew before ringing Paula to congratulate her on her promotion. A little hasty though he may have been, it had gone well in any case.

Paula had been pleased to hear from Andrew after all and allowed herself to be persuaded to meet him again next weekend at a local café. Mathew felt that this vindicated his own bold if clumsy attempt to fix things between them. He was delighted to see how the renewed promise of romance had added to her self-confidence which had already been boosted by her recent promotion.

Once this potentially tricky threshold had been crossed in their chat, both Mathew and his sister relaxed and tacitly switched to discussing more mundane and even trivial matters. As he put down the phone again, Mathew was left with a profound sense of satisfaction and achievement. He had fulfilled the aim of his alter ego by being instrumental in fixing the rift between two people and making both happier as a result. Sensing her implicit gratitude, he noticed his feelings towards his sister were becoming distinctly warmer, just as they had towards his mother now that she appeared to be making a fresh start and entering on a more fulfilling phase of her life.

This pleasant reflection partially gave way to a more wistful observation on how cruel life can be in the realm of personal relations. Unfortunate souls with afflictions such as illness, addictions, depression or just plain unhappiness tend to push others away precisely when they most need human contact and support. Whereas happy, healthy, well-balanced and confident individuals who least need the support of other people, often attract them in droves.

Mathew sometimes felt that pity was the keynote which defined his relationship with members of his circle of family and friends. It was feeling sorry for others that motivated so much of his behaviour. He recalled now that it was in order to spare his friend Frank's feelings that he had postponed calling him about his own new job. At the agency, it had again been unconscious pity which had drawn him to Jonathan, because he was seemingly the most vulnerable and unconfident of his new colleagues.

He had engineered to mend things between his sister and Andrew because the thought of their unhappiness caused him anguish too. At bottom, without really knowing why, he even pitied his friend Rory despite his perceived superior intelligence and outwardly successful life. Perhaps it was because he saw Rory as essentially shallow and as having inferior values to his own, a character flaw which must ultimately lead to a lack of fulfilment in life.

Had these reflections not caught up with Mathew, he may well have gone on to call his friends too, but he realised all his will power and remaining mental energy would now be required to restrain himself from proceeding even further down the path towards rumination and the associated risk of depression.

Better to pass an hour or so in his hobby room, continuing his current wargame, he mused. This would be a guaranteed means of quelling any troubling thoughts which had been taking shape and assuming power in his mind.

On this occasion, he was unfortunately proved wrong, however. Mathew possessed a far from universal ability to project his pity towards not only anyone he knew or whose plight he had heard about, but also towards those living in another time and place. When, for example, he read contemporary accounts about the Peninsular War written by soldiers who had actually experienced along with their accompanying families the privations and horrors of that time, he felt no less moved than when hearing contemporary news reports about similar suffering in various parts of the world today.

Mathew's current wargame had reached a stage which reinforced rather than mitigated his growing obsession with pity. At various points in the game, his complex rules required him to carry out a morale assessment for each unit of soldiers. This was determined by a range of factors such as how severe their losses were, the casualties they had inflicted on the enemy, whether they had achieved an objective or been reinforced.

Each unit was given a morale rating at the start of 'play' from zero to three. This would tend to decrease as the action progressed. For example, if a unit had suffered up to 20 percent losses, it would have a 40 percent chance of losing a morale point which would be determined on the throw of a dice. However, if the same unit had just been reinforced by friendly forces, the chances of falling morale would be reduced to only 25 percent. Once a unit's morale fell below minus three points, they had either to surrender or at least withdraw from the action.

Whenever it came to calculating losses on either side in combat and particularly when assessing the impact on morale, Mathew experienced an emotion akin to pity. In a confident mood, he might ascribe this emotion to a rare refinement of his nature, whereas in a self-critical state of mind it appeared as base sentimentality. Either way, he would never dream of discussing this with anyone else for fear of being regarded at best eccentric, at worst borderline insane.

Mathew retired after ten and rapidly sank into a deep sleep, trusting to his subconscious the task of further assimilating his day's experiences.

CHAPTER 10. THE SLEUTH AWAKENS

Just before leaving work the day before, Theresa had warned Mathew that from now on he would be taking a leading role in interviews with various experienced agency workers sitting in to provide support and feedback. He arrived at his new workplace eager to get started on his first assignment and prove to himself that his newfound confidence in his abilities was justified. He even forgot his original plan to linger a while again at reception in the hope of a warm-up chat with one of his fellow trainees. He was taken a little unawares, therefore, when Peter walked into reception just seconds after himself.

Mathew sensed from Peter's relaxed body language that now wouldn't be a bad time for a quick catch-up, even if the setting wasn't as accommodating as the canteen with its background hub-hub of voices to mask any indiscreet remarks. In slightly hushed tones, therefore, he invited Peter to step into the right-hand corridor to exchange impressions and compare notes about their first few days at work. Peter consented readily and the two of them sat down on a conveniently placed bench about five metres down the corridor, comfortably out of earshot of the receptionist.

Peter was clearly pleased at the opportunity to share his thoughts and feelings about the agency. However, frustratingly from Mathew's point of view, he confined himself mainly to impressions of the people who had been assigned to him on the Monday and Tuesday and his banal views on the canteen food, carparking facilities and other peripheral matters. It appeared that, unlike Mathew, he had secured a full lunch break in the canteen on both days so far and was enthusiastic about the tendency for most staff to clock off well before 5pm.

More than anything, Mathew wanted Peter to reveal the type of clients he'd been dealing with and what he thought of the VETS scheme and so briefly outlined his own experience by way of encouragement. His new colleague, however, wasn't minded to disclose equivalent detail and confined himself to the professional profile of the three or four individuals he'd dealt with. Mathew decided he would have to be a little more provocative and so asked,

'Did all the prospective agency clients seem at ease with VETS and look like committing, or did they have any doubts about the scheme as far as you could tell?'

Peter just smiled and said, 'You know what they keep telling us: trust the algorithm. It predicts who's going to be drawn in with ninety per cent accuracy. So far, I've not met any of the ten per cent where it's got it wrong! I must say, I'm damned impressed with the slickness of the whole operation. When I think how in sales it was pretty much the other way round: a ten per cent success rate was considered pretty damned good.'

This still wasn't quite what Mathew was after, although it was certainly interesting to observe that Peter had supplied further evidence of his mercenary character by comparing his agency experience with his old career in sales. But no further information about the dynamics of the interviews he had been involved in was forthcoming and this was what Mathew needed in order to validate his own experience and provide the reassurance that all agency employees were working more or less to the same script.

The official working day started in three minutes' time and Mathew would have to make his next move fast. He opted for the direct approach and asked brusquely:

'Would it be fair to say that the agency uses subtle persuasion rather different from the hard-selling techniques you're used to?'

He realised even before he opened his mouth to speak that this formulation of words had huge potential for causing offence, but Peter's facial expression immediately put his mind at rest.

'The whole idea is that the algorithm selects people either because they don't need any persuading, as they are predisposed to doling out their money, or because they can easily be persuaded. So, somehow, I can't imagine the agency using any crass methods or underhand ruses.'

Like the ones you no doubt used throughout your career in sales, Mathew thought, irritated by Peter's dismissive tone which contained more than a hint of contempt for his new set of clients. With time running out, he made one last effort to tease out a little more:

'So, you mean from what you've seen so far, the whole interviewing process is a total walk in the park? Nothing's set your alarm bells ringing at all?'

'No, can't say it has, but since you seem so keen to home in on the negatives, you'll be the first to know if I do come across anything. Anyone would think you're an undercover journalist trying to infiltrate the agency and denounce it in the press.'

Although there was no hint of malice in Peter's voice, Mathew was taken aback by this last remark and tried to convince himself that it was just a good-humoured attempt at being witty, albeit not a terribly successful one.

They'd chatted in the corridor for a good ten minutes and now it was time to move off to their respective offices. As he walked to his first rendezvous of the morning, Mathew reflected on any useful insights he had gained from his chat with Peter. At least he'd established some sort of contact with his least favourite new colleague and this should make it easier to open a conversation with him in the future if the need arose.

Then Mathew had a discomfiting thought: perhaps Peter was unwittingly right and that there was an element of the investigative journalist or even detective in his own outlook. Even from primary school, he had always liked to question, probe, challenge and provoke with his comments and questions. It had become so second nature to him that he was often unaware he was doing it.

Then he was momentarily seized with a fear induced by his instinct for self-preservation: what might be the consequences if one day he let slip a seriously indiscreet comment or asked an impertinent question? May he already have done so and blotted his copybook with the agency? He immediately suppressed this fear as cowardly and irrational, but it would resurface as a vague anxiety at odd intervals throughout the day.

Mathew nevertheless approached his growing role as agency interviewer with zeal and confidence and received enthusiastic feedback from the lady, Gemma, who sat in for support. She more or less left him to introduce the sessions and ask most of the questions, making it absolutely apparent that she was taking a back seat at every stage of the interview. Her main role prior to each interview was to take him through the existing records of each *donor candidate*, as she preferred to call them, and briefly discuss them, making it amply clear how far along the 'persuasion' process each individual had travelled.

They completed two interviews in the morning session and the only new element in the procedure was a debriefing during which they discussed the outcome of the interviews and made notes together on the next stage of the process. As agency employees were expected to be proficient in all aspects of the cycle, from algorithm research and analysis right through to setting up donor payments, Mathew would need to attend a few half-day training sessions at the end of the week, after which he would be 'practically flying,' as Gemma put it.

As he walked to lunch, leaving Gemma behind to round off a few admin items, Mathew's glow of satisfaction at a morning's work well done was tempered by two distinct concerns which he was itching to discuss in the canteen, if only he could find a suitable conversation partner. The first of these made him feel a little finicky and even a little foolish. It concerned Gemma's use of the term *donor candidate*. Initially on hearing it, he had wondered whether it referred to a special category of client or to a particular phase of the persuasion process. Then he recalled the homework they were set during training to come up with their own term to describe voluntary tax contributions. It seemed logical enough, therefore, that since there was no perfect combination of words to describe the voluntary donations being made to the Treasury, agency workers were encouraged to choose the terms they felt most comfortable with, even if this meant creating their own.

His second concern, however, carried more weight, as it could potentially call into question the whole ethos of the VETS régime. Gemma had been the first to mention, albeit in passing, the guaranteed first-class health care benefits which voluntary tax donors could expect in case of need. This seemed to imply a two-tier health service. In the recent past wealthier individuals often paid for private medical care while the less wealthy made do with the creaking National Health Service, once the post-war pride of the nation. Since the 2020s, the government had pumped huge investment into public healthcare, but was there now an emergent danger of a divide between a higher and lower tier health care system depending on whether you were a VETS member of not?

As he entered the canteen, his burning desire to find someone to talk to about this was dampened by a sudden realisation of how hungry he was. He made for the hatch serving hot lunches, came away with the vegetarian dish of the day and sat some distance from, but facing the entrance. Emily wasn't yet in evidence, but he had come down quite early and the canteen would certainly fill up over the next few minutes. His decision to sit alone was rewarded, as only moments later Emily entered, quickly loaded up her tray and promptly came over to sit down beside him.

Conscious of the brevity of the lunchbreak, neither wasted time over small talk and immediately got down to discussing their latest preoccupations. Mathew, now a little more relaxed in Emily's company, dared to speak first, but kept his remarks short and to the point before seeking her opinion. She had also been a little concerned on hearing talk of the enhanced health care or medical insurance offer, but admitted she had not particularly dwelt on it.

'I suppose it's OK so long as the bulk of the population continue to benefit from high quality health care. A two-tier system is probably less acceptable where there's greater social inequality and the most underprivileged get a lousy service compared to the better off. I don't think you can argue that applies to England these days, especially with private medicine having more or less disappeared except for the superrich.'

'I'm sure you're right,' conceded Mathew, genuinely reassured by Emily's reasoning, 'on the other hand, the more people who sign up for VETS and eventually come to take advantage of the health benefits, the greater the danger that a real social divide could emerge again. Mind you, I don't think the government would allow that to happen, as they seem pretty wedded to the idea of further reducing social inequalities.'

'A good point. I'm sure they're keeping an eye on that side of things. The other benefit – being able to draw down on what you've put in if your circumstances change - is a really good idea, I reckon. It'd be hard to argue against that and after all, it's only what National Insurance used to be for. My grandad used to say that when he started working, people would give up half their pay in income tax, national insurance and pension contributions. A fair and logical system unless you happened to be one of the many without a job. Thank god it's much simpler these days.'

Mathew wanted to challenge Emily and say: *Yes, but not, when the government is forced to use devious means such as this agency to balance its books!* However, he thought better of it, outwardly agreed with her and set about bringing the conversation around to where they might meet up this evening.

'To be honest, I'd quite like a chance to talk over a few more things with you about the agency. Is there any chance we might meet up some time later this evening?'

Before he could wish he'd been even more forthright and suggested a rendezvous at the outset, Emily's reply came back with interest.

'Sure, I was thinking the same myself. Though I wouldn't want you to get the idea I always talk exclusively shop both while at work and even after clocking off! Did you have a time and place in mind? You're quite welcome to come round to mine tomorrow evening if you want. Unfortunately, today's out as I've a tricky schedule ahead when I finish here…'

'Tomorrow's fine if it suits you…,' he replied, trying to sound as matter of fact as possible while looking for eye contact in the hope of detecting a hint of romantic interest. Emily, on the other hand had slightly averted her gaze just at the point where she suggested meeting at her place. Mathew didn't need to refer to his mentally archived web page to recognise that Emily's body language was in his favour. Before he could kick himself for his unengaging response and suggest ordering them a takeaway, Emily added a throwaway invitation to tea which gave him a second chance to respond with a touch more enthusiasm.

The official lunch break was due to end in five minutes' time, so the two of them headed through the canteen to rendezvous with their respective designated agency adepts for the afternoon session.

As he walked briskly, almost strutting, to yet another different interview office, Mathew already felt a sense of familiarity, almost communion with the agency building with its long monotonous though not unpleasantly decorated corridors and seemingly interminable interview rooms. He also sensed a growing affinity with the agency staff while not yet perceiving himself to be one of them. There remained too many unanswered questions requiring further investigation before his critical and analytical nature could be satisfied and enable him to identify more fully with his newfound colleagues.

Because Mathew had been assigned to a different office for the afternoon session, he had assumed it would also be with a different agency supervisor and so didn't expect to find Gemma waiting for him as he opened the door. On seeing his surprise, she apologised and explained that the colleague who he was meant to be working with had been assigned to another role at short notice. She, however, appreciated having Mathew to do the bulk of the interviewing for the next case, as it would take the pressure off her and give him the chance to demonstrate his versatility.

The next couple were a mother and daughter who lived together and it wasn't entirely clear in whom the impulse towards public generosity had first stirred.

Both ladies fitted the algorithm for different reasons. Joanne, the daughter, despite living with her mother most of her life, was an independent well-educated thirty-eight-year-old who earned a good salary working in public health. She had never married. Her mother, Louise, had also been something of a career woman until her retirement two years ago and, like her daughter, supported a number of voluntary organisations including an animal charity and prisoner rehabilitation foundation.

Mathew had been advised that with virtually all couples, one member is nearly always the prime mover in approaching the agency or responding to its overtures. He quickly ascertained that it was Joanne who had come upon the government ad which had been strategically placed on a website she had browsed while searching for information on behalf of her mother about recent proposals for penal reform. Louise had been encouraged by the progress her campaign was making towards further reducing the prison population and it was actually she who had persuaded her daughter to respond to the ad with a view to making VETS contributions. After making a careful study of the VETS and verifying its authenticity, Joanne was happy to support her mother's wish to join the scheme.

Mathew earned an extra feather in his hat towards the end of the interview when the daughter's own enthusiasm for VETS grew to the point where she too, as if not to be outdone by her mother, signed up to the scheme.

The final interview for the afternoon produced an indeterminate outcome and left Mathew feeling a little deflated to be finishing his day on an anti-climax. Gemma, however, seeing his disappointment, reassured him that he had managed and led all the interviews extremely well and only made a couple of comments on how he might further enhance his performance next time. Tomorrow, he needed to arrive promptly by half eight, as he would be going on his first trip out to visit a client in their own home. Naturally, he would be accompanied on this first occasion, as he would have to learn new protocols. During the remainder of the day and on Friday, he would be completing a few short training modules as Gemma had alluded to earlier.

Leaving work following Gemma's encouraging pep talk and eagerly anticipating his rendezvous with Emily, Mathew felt exhilarated. He mechanically made his way to the usual bus stop and boarded a few minutes later to take up his preferred seat towards front of the lower deck. He entered a kind of contentless blissful daydream for most of the journey, almost losing track of time and place. He returned to full objective consciousness seconds before arriving at his stop and was almost thankful for the rousing effect of the cool autumn air which kept him alert during the five-minute walk to his house.

On entering his hallway, Mathew's first impulse was to share his euphoria with his friend Frank who surely would be a kindred spirit given his recent good fortune in finding enjoyable and gainful employment. Just as he reached for the phone, however, reason and self-control intervened and persuaded him to defer this pleasure until he had changed from his office clothes, freshened up and relaxed for a few minutes in front of the TV with his habitual restorative cup of tea and snack.

Two hours later, Mathew felt sufficiently rested and mentally relaxed to call his friend. Frank answered with his familiar greeting, but his cheerful intonation subtly suggested a darker emotion which immediately came onto Mathew's radar.

In fact, Frank's pet sitting experiences over the last few days had been extremely mixed. True to his old form, he made a valiant effort to provide his friend with a couple of amusing tales of encounters with various animals and their owners, but it wasn't long before he gave into an urgent need to share a whole litany of grievances and worries which his new job had thrown up.

Even when not particularly depressed, Frank could sometimes be adept at seeing only the negatives in every conceivable situation. This was clearly one of those occasions and Mathew braced himself for a rough ride ahead.

The first issue was that on the strength of one short conversation, Frank had decided that his new boss was motivated more by the pursuit of profit than a genuine concern for the veterinary staff and his human and animal clients. Mathew tried to ascertain that he had actually spoken to the owner and not the human resources or business manager. These types, he argued, always tend to talk in purely monetary terms.

But what had really upset Frank was a second-hand account from a fellow worker, Mike, about an irresponsible pet owner. This individual had gone back to their original East European home for two weeks on a family visit and left him to care daily for a whole raft of pet animals ranging from hamsters and mice to fish and reptiles. He had dutifully visited the mini zoo each day and quite enjoyed the routine of feeding the tiny mammals and cleaning out their cages, then attending to the technically trickier task of caring for the cold-blooded creatures.

All had apparently gone to plan and Mike had signed off after the fortnight period came to an end. Four or five days later, he found he was rather missing the visiting routine as well as the pets themselves and so decided to make a social call on their owner on his return from abroad. Unfortunately, he found no one at home and commented on this next day to his line manager who made enquiries and discovered that the owner had in fact not reclaimed his house keys from the company. There was nothing especially strange about this, as most people have several sets of keys for various reasons.

Mike took the keys and was given permission to enter the house to check all was in order. What he found was too horrible to relate. Suffice it to say that the poor creatures hadn't been fed or tended to since his last visit five days ago. Several had starved with some cannibalised by more resilient members of their species. While at the scene, Mike received a call from headquarters advising him that at last the owner had been contacted: he had decided to prolong his stay by a week owing to a family issue and 'forgot' to inform the company.

'I hope they reported him to the NSPCA,' Mathew interjected at this point. Frank had been told by one of the managers that they had done so, but believing he was just being fobbed off, he had reported the abuse himself to make sure. Then he went on to give his own personal account of an aggressive dog owner whose manner he hadn't liked at all when he met him briefly to receive instructions about feeding and exercising his pets. The animals were in reasonably good health, but uncharacteristically timid and unfit for their breed. He suspected that this owner like many others wasn't a genuine animal lover, but kept pets out of a selfish and cruel need for domination.

Mathew didn't doubt any of what his friend was saying, but felt he ought to steer his thoughts and emotions in a more positive direction.

'I can see how you've found some of your work upsetting, Frank, but at the end of the day, you have to take the rough with the smooth in pretty well all jobs and at least now you're on the scene you can make a difference. I remember an animal-loving friend at secondary school who used to talk incessantly about becoming a vet until one day his cat was run over. The trauma taught him that he was squeamish and couldn't bear the thought let along the sight of an animal suffering. I couldn't help thinking he was being cowardly and rather went off him after that.'

'I see what you mean, Mathew, and that all makes logical sense, but I'm just not sure I can hack it seeing all the abuse that goes on. We're meant to be an animal-loving nation still and yet at least half pet owners keep pets for purely selfish reasons. They say they are good for mental health and a cure for loneliness, but you have to ask yourself why some people are so lonely in the first place – probably because they've driven their friends and family away. And then they keep their dogs cooped up indoors all the time because they're too old or lazy to walk them....'

Mathew was becoming irritated with his friend, but managed to steel himself to make one more constructive observation: 'To be honest, I reckon you're overthinking everything. You should just enjoy the company of the animals and see the job and its responsibilities as an opportunity to grow.'

Frank muttered something indeterminate in reply signifying that his rant was over and the two friends ended their conversation by confirming their arrangement to meet up at the weekend. A few moments' reflection revealed more to Mathew about how his own outlook had shifted of late than it did about

Frank's current mindset. It was not like him to be so forthright in giving out advice, almost to the point of moralising. This disturbed him a little, not because he felt his advice just now to Frank had been wrong or risked having an adverse effect, but he because couldn't at first understand what had prompted him to step outside his usual comfort zone.

After a little closer self-analysis, however, it all became much clearer. Mathew's own confidence and sense of self-worth had grown over the past couple of weeks thanks to his new job and the prospect of romance with Emily. He had been unconsciously trying to transmit this to his friend. In his discussions with agency workers and interviews with clients he had been encouraged to adopt a highly positive and assertive tone and this was now manifesting in his exchanges with people outside his work environment. There were plenty of people in his own experience whose manner had completely changed only shortly after taking on a new role at work or entering a new relationship. Why should he be any different?

Mathew would ideally have shared a little more about his own recent life events with Frank, but had sensed at the outset that his friend's need was greater than his own and dutifully shrank back into his more familiar role of the good listener. There was really no one in his own life he could be comfortable pouring his heart out to, certainly not his mother or his sister. Andrew would have probably come closest to fulfilling this role were it not for his past involvement with Paula.

He could certainly discuss his work concerns with Rory and indeed intended to within the next couple of days, but they'd never been on close personal terms. Given Rory's personality, he couldn't see their relationship ever significantly changing, nor would he particularly want it to.

That left Emily. Mathew did a quick time check and worked out that his rendezvous with her was now barely twenty hours away. He felt rather like a child willing away Christmas Eve to bring Christmas day nearer minute by minute. And now that the evening was drawing to a close, soon he would be able to get to bed and let sleep bring the event to within grasping distance.

But as he finally retired for the night, he recalled once again how as a small child, his intense excitement in anticipation of Father Christmas' visit turned into despair the longer he lay in bed trying to force himself to sleep. It seemed the more he tried the less tired he became until at about three am he feared Father Christmas would give up on him altogether and he'd be the only child he knew not to get a pillowcase full of presents.

Thirty years on from his early childhood experience, Mathew now relived many of the thoughts and emotions of that seminal night which had taught him how emotional pleasure and pain often lie side by side. He was thankful for the enhanced perspective which adulthood had brought him as well as the autonomy and freedom to resort to a much wider spectrum of ruses with which to defeat an insomnia-inducing demon.

He now knew how to relax by listening to quiet jazz piano ballads, drinking a cup of strong camomile tea an hour or so before retiring while refraining from eating after seven and meditating briefly to clear his mind of any unsettling thoughts. Finally, when already feeling drowsy, he would read a dry scholarly book in bed to help him drift off to sleep or in case he woke up in the middle of the night.

After applying all these techniques, Mathew's consciousness faded into welcome oblivion shortly before midnight.

CHAPTER 11. EMILY

Mathew finally rose at around half six after indulging a series of intermingled dreams which had seemed connected during the experience, but totally unrelated when he began to analyse them. He adhered to his resolution and jotted down the salient features of each dream and hoped this process would help him to reconnect them in a way that his subconscious was clearly much better at doing than his conscious mind.

Even as the dream was unfolding, he had recognised a familiar theme – that of confused interactions with a female figure whose identity was perpetually shifting between first his mother and sister and then between Emily and another feminine presence which he couldn't identify. Then a bizarre scene came back to him where Emily was sitting impassively before him repeating several times the enigmatic phrase *You want to raise her. You want to raise her*. He was baffled and disturbed by these words and the quiet but insistent manner in which Emily had uttered them. Then, just as he had finished his written record of the dreams, he made the sudden and startling realisation that he knew what the phrase meant, but that this knowledge was too deep down in his unconscious mind to access at will.

As he set off on his bus journey to work, Mathew continued to muse over the significance of his dreams. For a brief moment, he concluded that he must understand them on some level, as they were after all a product of the host – his own mind. He then immediately rejected this notion, remembering he'd read in some authoritative source that the subconscious mind which generated his dreams was itself *illogical*. It communicated through imagery and probably the whole purpose was to present experiences symbolically to the conscious mind for interpretation. Dreams provided free interplay between two aspects of the mind which during wakefulness could rarely communicate, as they operated in essentially two separate spheres.

The moment that Mathew entered reception, the meaning of the mysterious phrase revealed itself to him. Who had he associated Emily with until a couple of days ago? *Theresa*, of course, when he feared he might be finding her more attractive than Emily! But how could he play a linguistic trick on himself, even in a dream and mistake *Theresa* for the phrase *...to raise her* purely on the basis of phonetic similarity? And his infatuation with Theresa had been fleeting, to say the least: In fact, he'd barely given her a thought since Tuesday when his feelings for Emily had at last dominated.

It was Theresa who met Mathew at reception for his first trip out. All he'd been told by Gemma yesterday was to arrive a bit earlier and that he'd be accompanied on this first visit. He hadn't even thought to ask about transport and for a brief moment felt culpable in case Gemma had assumed he'd driven to work and that they'd be using his car! Then he recalled that the agency possessed a couple of vehicles that could be signed out for this purpose and hoped this would be the arrangement today.

Theresa handed Mathew two folders of documents relating to their mission and asked him to follow her to what turned out to be her own car. Once he had settled into the front passenger seat he felt tolerably relaxed as though the piles of papers he was clinging onto neutralised any potential awkwardness which might otherwise have arisen between two young adults of opposite genders sitting so close together side by side.

Mathew opened the conversation in pseudo-frivolous style by asking, 'I feel I ought to be reading through the paperwork so as to be doing something useful while you're driving, only it would make me travel sick, I'm afraid!'

'I wouldn't dream of asking you to do that', she replied, 'on the other hand, I hope you don't mind if I brief you on this case while driving – it's fairly straightforward and there's no reason why once you're in the know, you can't take the lead for the interview.'

She explained that they would be dealing with two young entrepreneurs who had set up a successful health food business which had grown from a small shop employing two or three people just two years ago to four high street outlets run by over twenty staff. They would be asking the owners to pay a small VETS levy on top of the business rate which went mainly to the local authority.

True to his previous form, Mathew questioned the logic behind this, as surely it would make more sense, he argued, to get them at add an extra amount onto their VAT bill which went to central government anyway. Theresa explained that it was marginally easier and less costly to administer this way. In addition, psychologically, a levy on top of a local tax was perceived more favourably by small to medium businesses and also resonated better with the residents who used the businesses.

Finally, Theresa forewarned Mathew that she would take over the interview at the opportune moment to discuss various means by which the entrepreneurs could advertise their generosity towards the public purse. She had already sent them an agency brochure promoting this feature of VETS with businesses and outlining the different options for 'virtue signalling' such as displaying a prominent sign in their shop windows with catchy captions or indicating extra VETS amounts paid on till receipts.

On arrival, they were greeted by the two young men who were keen to regale them from their health food range. Mathew looked quizzically across to Theresa as they sat down to carrot cake and smoothies. Apparently reading his mind and or body language, she nodded back reassuringly in the affirmative, and the two of them tucked appreciatively into their treats.

The interview went exceptionally smoothly with both young entrepreneurs more or less equally engaged. Mathew sensed that the slightly older of the two was more sold on the social value of the VETS, whereas his junior member saw the benefit more in terms of kudos for their business. That was the great achievement of ethical campaigners of a generation ago. They eventually got most of the big multinationals on board with fair trade, fairer wages and environmental responsibility not so much by exposing their evil business practices as by influencing public opinion. The public at large being the consumers were then in a position to demand higher ethical standards.

Mathew was impressed by the couple's idea of encouraging their own employees to harmonise with their bosses' ethos by making VETS contributions themselves in return for higher salaries and job security. They were passing down the chain a slice of the carrot they had received themselves.

Theresa later commented to Mathew that it was not strictly the agency's business to urge their clients to promote the VETS principle to third parties, however, if they themselves raised the issue, it was agency policy to respectfully hear the clients out on this point and offer moral encouragement and advice. Mathew argued that it was more appropriate to see the employees of the health food stores not as third parties, but as integral components of the business. Theresa agreed, claiming that she had used the term 'third parties' in a technical sense and for the sake of brevity. Mathew let the matter rest there, though he mentally retorted: *Well for the sake of brevity and clarity 'their employees' would have done fine!*

It was no surprise for Mathew to learn that where businesses contributed to VETS, a similar 'drawdown' facility existed as for private individuals. In other words, if they got into financial difficulty further down the line, they could receive back a portion of what they had overpaid in business rates, though the application process was more tortuous than for private individuals, as the financial and accounting situation with small to medium-sized enterprises was obviously far more complex.

The final point discussed was the clients' wish to allocate a portion of their VETS to promote healthy eating among children. They hoped this would be delivered largely through the school curriculum by funding expertly produced teaching aids, providing teacher training and specialist peripatetic teachers. Theresa explained that VETS money would go into a global fund and couldn't normally be allocated to specific projects determined by donors. However, all practicable suggestions would be gratefully received by the ministry concerned.

During the short trip back to the office, Theresa said they would follow up today's work by drafting a summary of their discussion with the health food duo. She stressed that they would receive formal feedback on their ideas for how their contributions might be used directly from the Ministry of Education and Training. No doubt sensing by his silence that Mathew might need further convincing, she added that this was more than a courteous formality and that there had been well-documented cases of serious proposals by donor clients helping to shape government policy.

Once they had written up the summary report, the start of the official lunch break was only minutes away, so Mathew made his way down to the canteen hoping to find a quiet space ahead of the madding crowd. To his relief, only two co-workers had beaten him to it and were sitting in quiet contemplation over some reading matter. After failing to settle down as serenely as he would have liked, he changed plan and made for the serving hatch to ensure first place in the queue and before long was straining to read the vegetarian lunch options from the menu. Moments later, he was sitting back down and enjoying his third snack of the day and looking out for Emily.

Emily, however, didn't appear and Mathew had to make do with Jonathan instead who joined him looking more relaxed and content than almost ever before. A brief conversation revealed that Jonathan believed he had found his true vocation at the agency and rather boringly repeated what he'd just recently stated about the satisfaction he found in working with such amenable people – both co-workers and clients, as he chose to designate them.

Mathew was genuinely pleased for Jonathan who had initially inspired in him a degree of instinctive pity. It wasn't just his being a red head, of lanky build and visible lack of self-confidence. There was some other intangible quality which Mathew couldn't quite define. He would have liked to question him further on the type of clients who had been coming his way since they last spoke, but he needed a mental break and was instinctively conserving his energy for the afternoon session and, at least as importantly, his evening with Emily.

The afternoon was set aside for one of the promised further training sessions. It turned out to be a rather dry affair concerned with the admin side of the agency work, but it did bring the original four recruits together once again and so missing Emily at lunch merely proved to be deferred gratification. He had little time to exchange notes with her, however, as the training took the form of a mini lecture and afterwards, they all had to rush off in various directions to a final interview. Mathew's heart sank somewhat as it dawned on him that the initial relaxed work pace at the agency looked set to quicken as they approached fully trained status.

Nevertheless, by half four the interview and paperwork were done and yet another client had signed over a modest portion of their wealth to the government. Mathew was free to clock off in eager anticipation of the evening ahead with Emily. He texted her as agreed and awaited a response which came just two minutes later: She was winding up with her own client and would be signing out within the next ten minutes or so. Could he wait outside reception if the weather wasn't too bad? Instinctively, neither of them wanted to attract undue attention by rendezvousing by the ever-watchful receptionist's desk.

Fortunately, it was still only mid-October with the darker nights and cooler temperatures still some way off and Mathew was able to enjoy an aimless fifteen-minute stroll in the welcome fresh air until Emily finally emerged from the agency building. The two exchanged friendly smiles, but hers was overlaid with unmistakable preoccupation.

'What's up, Emily?' he asked simply.

'It's probably nothing, but just now as I finished writing up my case notes and moved to the door to leave the interview room, I overheard Peter's voice in the corridor. He was talking to at least two other men in what sounded a rather harsh tone, though I couldn't make out the words well enough to catch the gist of the conversation. I waited a few moments by the door as the voices moved further down the corridor and then I followed keeping a little way behind. Peter had stopped talking to the men by then, but they didn't look at all like the typical clients I've come to associate with the agency. How can I put it? They had a sullen, even surly air about them...'

'Gangsters, obviously!' quipped Mathew. 'Perhaps they've made enough money over a long career of shady dealings to be able to hang up their sub machine guns and become respectable citizens. You know, like members of organised criminal gangs the world over. Getting on the right side of the law makes for a sensible retirement plan!'

As it developed, Mathew felt his mock thesis becoming dangerously plausible. He was about to add that perhaps they shouldn't spend all evening together talking shop about work, when he recalled that the ostensible reason for Emily inviting him round was exactly that – in his own words - *to talk a few things over.* On the other hand, it was Emily herself who, within seconds of inviting him round for tea, had said something about not wanting him to think she always talked shop. But clearly this thought stream was just another case of his overthinking the situation. He would do better to let Emily direct the conversation while his overheated brain cooled down.

As they entered the agency car park, it suddenly occurred to Mathew that he'd never mentioned his decision to bus it to work. Emily would no doubt be assuming he'd follow her in his own vehicle, he thought, and momentarily slowed his pace, as if the energy thus conserved could be rechannelled into finding the words to explain. Emily, however, had learned of his travel habits from other sources and simply beckoned him over to where she'd parked her car near the exit.

'I'm sorry it's not very roomy inside,' she apologised, as he settled into the passenger seat which appeared in pristine new condition. 'I heard one of the others comment on your noble use of bus transport and, to be honest, might consider it myself once they start up that new route they've been banging on about for over a year now. When the government made the promise five years ago that no one would have to change buses more than once for a five-mile journey, I somehow knew it would take them more like ten.'

'What – ten different buses?' Mathew quipped. The joke was successful, as he made both Emily and himself laugh.

Emily confirmed Mathew's vague recollection from one of the training sessions that she lived barely ten minutes' drive from work. He was grateful for this as, despite breaking the ice with his bus joke, he was already feeling discomfited by Emily's scent which was a little overpowering and distracting in the confines of her car. He noticed he'd tensed up again while fastening his seat belt and so forced himself to relax and continuing the conversation on the impersonal topic of bus travel helped the process. He almost apologetically outlined his more superficial reasons for favouring the bus over the car before handing over to

Emily who proved reassuringly well informed about the whole subject.

While Emily expounded her theories on the benefits of public transport, Mathew enjoyed the relief afforded by his passive role in the discussion and inwardly counted down the minutes to the end of the journey. Emily stopped speaking with what Mathew calculated to be just two or three minutes of journey time to go. He decided to take a gamble and reveal his less idealistic motives for choosing bus over car transport. This clearly achieved the desired result, as Emily laughed for the second time.

'You mean to say you managed to kid yourself that you were only thinking about the environment when actually your hidden motive was to save a few pounds a week on the parking levy! I'd never have credited you with such awesome powers of self-deception!'

'Actually, I don't think it's so strange and I reckon people deceive themselves about all sorts of things pretty well all the time. I've always had quite vivid dreams which, though probably like most people's, are often wildly illogical, but nevertheless contain some meaning. It's as though we have an all-knowing sub-conscious mind which uses dreams to communicate ideas to our conscious mind that we can use in our everyday wakeful state. Dreams are a borderline state providing an interface between the two aspects of mind...'

Sensing he'd dug down into his favourite dream topic rather too deeply for a tea-time discussion, Mathew paused in a desperate attempt to come up for air. He cut his losses:

'And so, I think a similar thing is happening when people deceive themselves. I tend to see through my attempts at self-deception because the conduit between my conscious and sub-conscious mind is, well, more developed. Now that makes me sound superior!'

Emily may well have been listening intently, but as she was

mostly looking ahead while driving, she hadn't been able to signal this so well to Mathew. But she had now at last turned into her suburban close and the conversation came to a natural close as she announced they were about to roll up to her house.

Emily parked the car on her modest-sized drive and let them into her hallway without undue ceremony. She ushered Mathew into her living room while she went off into the kitchen to prepare refreshments. Mathew appreciated the unconstrained freedom to slowly cast his gaze around his new environment and take in its most salient features. In truth, there was little to remark upon. He found the furnishings and general décor to be in good taste. The colour schemes were subtle and well-coordinated.

This was certainly a room designed for and probably by someone who appreciated quiet contemplation and relaxation. The last thing he noticed just as Emily returned with tea and biscuits was the refreshing absence of a television.

'I see you've no TV. I must confess, though I'm no TV addict, I do have this ritual of turning on the news every couple of hours when I'm at home. My favourite times are first thing in the morning, when I get back from work and just before bedtime. Do you have your own domestic rituals, Emily?'

He felt almost as though he'd taken a liberty by tagging the name of his hostess onto the end of his question. It seemed he'd committed this potential indiscretion consciously yet involuntarily and at once feared an adverse reaction.

'I do have a TV secreted upstairs in my study, but you're right to imply I'm even less of a fan than you, Mathew. I've never thought of my habits as rituals, but if I had to confess to any at gunpoint, I'd probably say – cereals with half fat milk for breakfast and a large cup of decaf coffee while reading a couple of pages of a historical novel. Usually in the evening, I try to meditate, but get distracted daydreaming about what I might do with a larger house.

'Talking of dreaming – daytime or night time, I want to pull you up on something you said just now. You implied that your subconscious mind sort of knows everything and likes, usually through dreams, to transmit this infinite wisdom to your conscious mind. But in your case of self-deception, it seems to be the other way round. Your conscious mind believed itself to have innocent motives with your less noble ones were hidden in the subconscious....'

Mathew was pleased with Emily for tuning into the elaborate thesis he'd expounded earlier and that she was clearly taking his intellect seriously. He was even more pleased with himself for having a ready answer.

'It's all to do with sublimation. If our conscious or let's say everyday mind entertains an idea or motive that falls way short of our higher moral nature, we sublimate or hide it away in our subconscious which only pushes it back out into our conscious mind when we need it and can deal with it.'

This time it was Emily's turn to quip. 'I knew that. I was just testing the depth of your psychoanalytical knowledge and understanding!'

It seemed to Mathew that their conversation so far had ranged from, to use the old cliché, the sublime to the ridiculous. However, what qualified as the ridiculous - the prosaic chat about domestic rituals or the esoteric in-depth treatise on the subconscious mind – was open to question. Eager though he was to get Emily to tell him more about herself, he sensed it was now time to deal with the issue he'd primarily come to discuss: Peter and his sinister corridor companions.

'So, you say, you didn't hear distinctly anything that was said between Peter and the shady blokes in the corridor?'

'No, but I could tell they were deliberately talking in hushed voices and as I followed them down to reception their body language suggested, how can I put it? a degree of tension and awkwardness.'

'And that's not how I'd characterise Peter's normal manner. Rather self-assured, I'd say,' Mathew contributed.

'I suppose we have to ask ourselves why we're so concerned by this.' Emily continued. 'The issue for me really is that in training we've been encouraged to believe throughout that the agency's business is to gently coax decent high-minded people to generously donate some of their surplus, but often hard-earned cash, to top up the Treasury's depleted funds. All the folk you and I have met to date appear to match this profile. These two individuals just didn't seem to fit the part – either as agency staff or potential clients.'

'And I think we've both felt all along that neither does Peter really seem to blend in with the agency's avowed aim of having all staff working in harmony and almost interchangeably with a common core of compatible people. I mean with his background exclusively in sales, comments he's made about aggressive selling and just recently his evasive response when I pressed him about the profile of clients he'd been working with. He seemed unnaturally secretive to say the least. And now this latest episode. Any theories Emily?'

'Well, the most obvious answer would be that the agency works with another tranche of potential clients who are not quite as generous as the bunch we've seen and need that extra push. Peter, with his exemplary sales record over the past decade or so is the man for the job. I imagine he's good at emphasising the insurance aspect and lays it on thick with the virtue signalling opportunities and such like.'

Mathew felt the topic had been satisfactorily explored and attempted to wind it up for the time being.

'I suggest we keep an eye on Peter and consider simply asking him who the two dudes were yesterday. *You* could broach it innocently, as you've not really had a chat with him yet.

Whereas if I encounter him first, I could be more forthright and make a joke of it along the lines of: *Hi mate – I saw you slinking off with two of your new gangster friends the other evening. Care to let me in on the deal?*' He then explained how Peter had accused him the other day, albeit jokingly, of being an undercover journalist with a mission to sully the agency.

'Wow, I didn't realise you'd already had a proper tête-à-tête with him. In that case, I think I may as well leave it to you…, on the other hand, as I've not yet blown my cover as a meddlesome investigative journalist, I may be better placed to and get him to open up'

'The difficulty was that I started out questioning him what I thought was subtly, but as he didn't seem eager to reveal much, I got bolder and bolder until he made the undercover joke as if to get me to back off. You'll probably find the same resistance. Except…'

'Except that I'm a woman who had to escape his company the other day to sit by you and I, or should I say *we*, wouldn't want to encourage him again would we?' She smiled provocatively at Mathew who reciprocated, though his smile was of a more sheepish variety. Their eyes met just long enough for both to register a satisfactory measure of romantic interest, but allowing Emily to disengage gracefully without causing either of them undue embarrassment.

'Right, so here's what we need to do,' Emily continued, taking over the lead. 'Play the interrogation by ear, as he'll sense anything too staged and clam up, but keep him under observation and one of us hang about in reception till he arrives tomorrow – I'll volunteer first, if you like – and watch which corridor he goes down and try to locate the office he's working in. We can rendezvous mid-morning if we get a chance or, failing that, at lunch, and exchange intelligence. We'll also have another chance to follow him after lunch if one of us – you can volunteer this time – follows him to his PM interview room.'

'Sounds like a good plan to me,' Mathew confirmed, 'He may be seeing them again tomorrow, but perhaps more likely on Monday after they've had the weekend to reflect on their nefarious past deeds and need for redemption by VETS. Or, if Peter's been specially assigned to the agency's more reluctant clientele, as we've been supposing, he may furnish us with some more interesting specimens.'

'Yes, I'm sure playing amateur sleuths will be a bundle of fun – but we need to think about our objective in doing all this. Is it merely to satisfy our curiosity? Or to call out the agency for misrepresenting its mission? Or to convince ourselves that there was really nothing untoward going on and so we can continue working for the agency with a clear conscience?'

'It could be all or any of those. We shouldn't overthink the situation,' Mathew ventured, trying to convince himself, 'just getting to the truth should be sufficient cause.'

They talked a little longer to refine their tactics and thrash out their motivations. Mathew learned that Emily too had been briefly plagued by an anxiety that her reputation with her new employer might be spoiled if she were caught in the act of challenging the agency. Like Mathew, however, she had mastered her transient faintheartedness and said that teaming up with him as partner in crime had shored up her moral fortitude.

Emily had conducted much of this conversation while nipping in and out of the kitchen as she prepared their simple tea of home-made cheese and onion pie with salad. Mathew had brought a bottle of grape juice and box of cupcakes as his contribution and the two of them used the meal to mark the transition from their work-related discussion to a pleasantly relaxed chat about themselves.

Emily required very little encouragement to talk at some length about her childhood in a largely dysfunctional middleclass family. She and her brother, who was just over a year older, got off to a secure start in the very early years, but before Emily's sixth birthday, their parents had fallen out and thereafter their upbringing was chequered to say the least. Her mother left the family home following a seemingly prolonged period of noisy rows. She and her brother never witnessed actual physical violence, but the threat of it often hung in the air.

This turbulent phase of Emily's life seemed never ending to her at the time, though her father later told her it couldn't have lasted more than three or four months. Her brother appeared to have blotted the trauma from his memory. She believed this was perhaps because he was psychologically mature enough to manage the experience in this way. However, she later came to believe that the reason was more sinister. Being that little bit older, he had endured the added burden of feeling responsible for shielding his little sister from the upsetting domestic scenes.

Despite his own limitations, their father had remained the children's rock for the next ten years, providing them with stability and as much love, care and attention as he was able, given all the pressures he was under. They never saw their mother again and as teenagers were told by their auntie, her sister, that she had suffered from severe mental illness and, following hospitalisation in a psychiatric ward, eventually returned to live with her parents.

It was as Emily approached her fifteenth birthday that she had to face her second major childhood trauma when their father remarried almost out of the blue. Never a great communicator, especially where personal relationships were concerned, it didn't occur to him to afford his children the opportunity to get to know his prospective second wife gradually and seek their approval rather than presenting them with the sudden shock of a fait accompli as a potentially wicked step-mother moved into their midst!

Emily's initial reaction was to greet the new woman in their life with a sullen frostiness, although within weeks she had adjusted quite well and they had more or less come to terms thanks to their best mutual efforts. Indeed, she and Mary, her father's second wife, became quite close and the relationship had endured to the present day. Her brother, on the other hand, adapted less well and Emily believed this was one of the main factors in his decision to seize the first opportunity to leave formal education and work away from home. His ties with the rest of his family had remained quite weak ever since, though on the face of it his adult life had turned out quite well. He was now seemingly happily married with two small children and following a career he claimed to enjoy.

Mathew listened intently to Emily's account, seeing many parallels in his own family history. However, he resisted the temptation to interrupt and left his own input until she had come to a natural close. Afterwards, he added his own particular philosophical reflection which he felt was supported by both their childhood experiences.

'It was living through similar ups and downs as a child that I came to a formative view of life along the lines that the good and bad aspects seem to roughly balance each other out in the long run. So as a small kid at Christmas time, the pleasure of receiving all the presents along with the excitement of looking forward to it was matched by the disappointment with some of the presents, the ephemeral enjoyment of most of the others and anxiety over something going wrong, etcetera.

'This pattern has been repeated time and again in more serious aspects of life, like when my parents fell out. I remember being devastated when dad left, but then mum was happier, as the constant threat of violent rows no longer hung in the air. We felt liberated and rediscovered the joy of playing childish games together.'

'I agree and I'd add to that how well we adapt to new circumstances on the whole. When you start to look outside your own life at other people's you realise that probably most people have a similar chequered experience,' Emily continued Mathew's idea.

'Yes, but then you come across one or two extremely lucky or unlucky individuals who are exceptions to the rule.'

Emily pushed the nuance further. 'The saddest thing is that those who start out with all the bad luck to begin with – for example having two abusive parents or no parents at all – these people seem to attract misfortune right the way through life – low attainment at school, lousy or no job, dysfunctional relationships, even prison and premature death.'

'And then, of course, it works the other way too for those - what's the old expression - born with a silver spoon in their mouths?'

In order to spare Emily and avoid contradicting himself, Mathew didn't go on to relate how later experiences in his life had caused him to review his earlier conclusions that good and bad tend to balance each other out. In recent years, there had certainly been one or two longish runs of unpleasant events with very few redeeming moments in between.

With tea now well and truly over and this third or fourth phase of their conversation running out of steam, Mathew sensed that he had imposed on Emily's hospitality enough for one occasion and prepared to seize on a suitable moment to say it was time he was on his way. In a bid to pre-empt the offer of a lift, he announced:

'Well thanks for the tea and the excellent company. I think the time's come for me to leave you in peace and test out the government's five-year-old promise of a journey home using no more than two buses.'

'That was for a five-mile journey. You may be pushing it a bit, as don't you live about the same distance from the office, but in the other direction?'

They checked the distance and bus route from Emily's to

Mathew's house easily enough on *Snap-maps*. It was just under six miles all told and would in fact still only require two buses provided he didn't mind walking a few hundred yards either end. At least nowadays, there was no real need to check bus timetables, as it was only just after eight and virtually all services ran every ten minutes until about ten in the evening.

Mathew was relieved that Emily didn't protest at his avowed preference for the bus. True, he had been thinking mainly of her, as she was beginning to look quite tired, but he was genuinely looking forward to another invigorating stroll in the early autumn air and then a carefree bus ride halfway across town as dusk turned to dark.

The bus trip home threw up no surprises. The bus from the stop near Emily's house took him to the central bus station and within five minutes or so the second half of leg of his journey home was underway on a familiar service he often used to get to and from the town centre. He always found that the combination of the gentle swaying of the bus combined with the artificially lit darkness outside lulled him into a semi-meditative state which he was loath to snap out of when the time came to disembark. These effects were intensified by the growing affinity bordering on intimacy he was feeling with Emily.

It was half nine as he entered his hallway, though his body clock was telling him it was more like eleven and bedtime. He had just enough energy to check his post, get undressed and curl up in front of the TV with a mug of cocoa to catch the ten o'clock news. As usual, there was nothing of world-shattering importance to report, just a minor moral scandal around another less well-known member of the former royal family. He had a faint childhood memory, presumably just after the abolition of the monarchy, when such stories featured quite prominently in the news, but nowadays they barely registered more strongly with the viewing public than routine fallings from grace of middle-aged and almost forgotten film or music celebrities.

Mathew sank into a deep and contented sleep in the secure knowledge that his dreams would be reliable allies in processing the day's events. He would surely wake up physically refreshed and with a crystal-clear mind fit to unravel the mystery of Peter and the two wolves – as he creatively renamed them just as he crossed the threshold from somnolence into oblivion.

CHAPTER 12. FLYING HIGH

Mathew awoke with a start, immediately realising he'd forgotten to set his alarm clock the night before. He needn't have worried, however, as his most visible timepiece, his mobile, clearly indicated just 6.10 am. For once, he had no awareness of having dreamed, but his last thought before falling asleep returned more vividly: what if the two men with Peter yesterday had not been potential clients but something completely different such as inspectors or even police investigators? Just because their dress code wasn't quite up to the standard of agency staff didn't necessarily mean they were rogues!

Or, although she was unable to make out anything they were saying, perhaps he should test out Emily's feminine intuition. After all, she had had a chance to observe their body language and may have sensed the power relationship between Peter and the men and hence who seemed to be in charge. In any case, he appreciated an excuse to touch base with her again before the day started. At least now he had her phone number, so he'd call as soon as he felt fully awake and was clear about exactly what he wanted to say.

Bearing in mind that Emily would be setting off and probably getting up later than himself, Mathew waited until he was seated on the bus before calling her.

'Thanks again for the tea and chat yesterday,' he began with the niceties, 'Just a quick call to ask a question I should have thought of before: As you couldn't make out what they were saying, was there anything concrete in Peter and co.'s behaviour to suggest that he was in charge rather than the two other blokes?'

'Yes, I'd say his assertive body language. Didn't I mention that yesterday?'

Mathew confessed, 'Yes, you may have done, but this morning I woke up besieged with doubts instead the greater clarity of mind which I usually get from a good night's sleep!

She laughed, 'So much for sleeping on it! Never mind. I'll forgive you just this once for disturbing my morning serenity meditation.'

Mathew felt a degree of relief despite a twinge of guilt in case he actually *had* interrupted Emily's meditation routine which seemed quite plausible, given what he'd perceived of her domestic ambience yesterday. At least he wasn't troubled by her veiled mockery of his dream analysis, as it had gone completely over his head.

Owing to someone's oversight, Mathew hadn't been briefed on what lay ahead on today's agenda and it was only on actually entering the building that this occurred to him. He stood vacantly in the middle of the reception area for a moment until he managed to refocus his mind. He felt a shade embarrassed at becoming distracted by what was essentially a side issue. Before he could reproach himself too harshly, however, a familiar voice hailed him from some distance away. Seconds later, Theresa emerged from one of the long corridors leading off behind the reception desk.

He was to start off the day in yet another training session – this time it was all to do with the niceties of dealing with the famous awkward customer after which, Theresa reminded him, he'd be genuinely flying. *This phrase must be in the trainers' very own training manual*, thought Mathew, as he recalled Gemma using it only the other day.

Mathew welcomed this opportunity to reflect on his self-assigned mission of the day – how to catch Peter in flagrante with his suspicious associates. The session, which was scheduled to last two hours, would hopefully end well before lunch so he'd be able snoop around and perhaps gamble on being in the right corridor just as everyone began to leave their offices at the end of the morning.

If he kept his eyes peeled and possibly even dared to question a few of the agency staff on their way to lunch, he may be able to locate Peter or, at the very least, gain some intelligence. He could even message Emily letting her know where he was stationed so that she could hang about in one of the other principal corridors doubling their chances of a 'catch'.

He became so engrossed in his sleuth-like train of thought that the introductory part of the talk completely passed him by and he struggled for the second time since he'd arrived to concentrate on what he had officially come to work for. Fortunately, although the session was well presented, very little if any vital information was imparted and so Mathew had ample opportunity to message his latest plans to Emily who was sitting across the other side of the lecture room. She nodded in acknowledgement as he looked over to her for confirmatory eye contact. A further quick glance around the lecture room established that neither Peter nor Jonathan was present.

During the customary fifteen-minute break and tea-trolley treat, Mathew and Emily quickly exchanged a few words as discreetly as possible as if both were accomplices in something akin to the Guy Fawkes gunpower plot. Before coming over to chat to Mathew, Emily had used her initiative to ask the chief trainer whether there would be or had there already been another similar session for the other recent recruits who had been with them at induction. He confirmed that the other session had been held yesterday morning. She explained this to Mathew.

'That's good to know, otherwise I'd have had even greater

suspicion something fishy was going on, as I should have thought both Peter and Jonathan would benefit from this training, though for very different reasons!' Emily wanted to make more practical use of the remainder of the break now that their plans for the pre-lunch period had been settled.

'I'm just going to circulate a bit and ask a couple of random people how often they've encountered 'difficult cases', as our trainer likes to call them.'

Mathew agreed this was an excellent mini-project and set off in the opposite direction to Emily. He homed in on one male agency worker who was standing alone looking rather out of it. He chose his words carefully.

'It's an interesting theme for the training don't you think? So far as a newbie, I've only had straightforward cases requiring no persuasion. I suppose my managers have carefully selected people who have already set their hearts on the scheme.'

'Well, I suppose it's a case of learning to walk before you run, though I think it's fair to say that by the time future clients reach us, most of the work has been done. There are the occasional cases, though where someone unsuitable has slipped through the net and they can become very defensive as soon as we mention paying more tax. I'd like to bet that more often than not they've got a tax dodge on their conscience and think we're out to get them!'

It emerged that this fellow had already been a tax inspector before joining the agency shortly after it was set up. He saw the training session more as a bonding and 'feel good' exercise and agreed with Mathew that so far, he'd learned very little of practical use.

The second half lasted under an hour and involved some of the agency's favourite role-playing exercises. Mathew could see that his partner in crime, Emily, was using the opportunity to team up with yet someone else in an effort to gain as much intelligence as possible. His own attempt failed, as the few people he'd not yet spoken to were at the other side of the room and he would have felt conspicuous walking past his other classmates to reach them. He settled for the former tax inspector he'd just spoken to for the first exercise. As prescribed, they took it in turns to play the roles of the interviewer and awkward customer and the exercise passed without incident.

Mathew's hopes were again revived when the trainer asked everyone to change partners and team up with someone they'd not yet spoken to at all today. Unfortunately, however, of the dozen or so trainees present, two of the three he'd not yet talked to were snapped up instantly and he was left with a rather unprepossessing middle-aged woman who didn't look the part of someone likely to revel in a conspiratorial chat. Nevertheless, Mathew had become accustomed to take very little for granted at his new work place - from the agency's improbable raison d'être to senior staff serving the coffee - and so went straight in for the kill.

'Hi, as you've probably a lot more experience working for the agency than I do, would you mind playing the part of the difficult customer first? I'm Mathew, by the way, and you are?'

Just a few words into his utterance, he realised his social gaffe of forgetting to start off by asking the lady to introduce herself and then assuming, because she was older, that she was a more experienced worker. When would he learn? Was it just down to lack of practice in conducting normal conversations, or was it a simple matter of the nerves most people experience when meeting someone new? After all, he had become quite relaxed when talking to Emily of late.

She was called Madeleine and her name seemed all the more pretentious as she began to overact in the role of the archetypal offended client assigned to her. Mathew responded to her claims of being brought into the agency under false pretences with, he thought, good presence of mind. He explained several of the processes undertaken by the agency to select suitable members of the public and assured her that if at the end of the interview she still felt dissatisfied or held any grievance against the agency then she would be paid generous compensation for her time today.

Mathew had thrown in this last point about compensation to provoke Madeleine out of her ham acting and provide him with some new information about agency policy. She didn't disappoint:

'I'm not aware of the agency offering compensation as a kind of disturbance allowance. I've known them to pay expenses in advance for things like a few hours' child care or travel expenses in exceptional circumstances.'

'I see what you mean. I suppose it's unlikely to come up, as most clients are correctly assessed in the first place so those who come in for interview should already have a pretty good idea of what they're letting themselves in for and are probably well heeled enough not to need travel expenses.'

By the end of their short chat, Mathew was satisfied he had met an agency worker who generally dealt with the amenable type of client and this went some way to reassuring him that if Peter was involved with a different sort of client, then he – or they – were the exception, not the rule.

This did nothing to undermine his resolve, however, and as soon as the session ended, as predicted, twenty minutes early, the two of them sped off in opposite directions, each to their agreed corridor.

Fortunately for Mathew and his accomplice, all the offices used for interviews were situated off three extremely long, but straight corridors. This meant that between them, they could keep in view pretty much everything that was going on in two of them. Mathew was well prepared for his surveillance operation. In order to appear as business-like as possible, he armed himself with a briefcase in one hand and tucked a paper folder under his opposite arm for extra effect.

He walked from the office in the central corridor where the training had taken place to the end of the west wing nearest to reception. From there, he proceeded about halfway down the corridor before stopping with his back to the wall so that he could look in either direction just by turning his head to the left or right. After a few moments, he realised that he scarcely even needed to be visually observant, as the sound of any door opening and people emerging would give him sufficient and timely warning that a meeting had just ended.

Within five minutes, doors did start to open and one or two early birds began to come out into the corridor and all head the same way towards the canteen – the opposite direction from reception. Mathew took this as his cue to walk slowly in one direction or the other to avoid appearing too conspicuous. At last, he summoned up the courage to address a male agency worker who by his gait and posture didn't seem in too much of a rush to get to an early lunch. He casually enquired whether he knew where one of the new recruits had been interviewing today. It was a long shot and the answer was predictably in the negative. After all, why would an average agency worker pay particular attention to a random new recruit?

Just seconds later, however, only two doors down from where Mathew was currently stationed, three men emerged from an office and headed for the canteen end of the corridor. It was Peter with what could only be the two persons of interest Emily had seen yesterday. Mathew immediately began to follow the group and, in his eagerness to keep up, found himself gaining on them to the point where he came almost too close. He slowed his pace and fell back to within a comfortable four metres or so behind. At the end of the corridor, instead of continuing straight on along with all the other agency staff towards the canteen, Peter and company turned left.

When Mathew reached this point, he looked left to where they were heading, but didn't follow, as this would have been conspicuous. Instead, he took just one step into this small corridor and observed as the group reached a regular looking door marked *exit*. After a few moments, apparently spent bidding the men farewell, Peter shook each by the hand in a formal manner before ushering them out through the discreet exit.

Mathew stepped back into the main corridor just before Peter had time to turn back round towards the canteen. He then followed close behind and caught up with him just before they reached the canteen entrance. He'd already made up his mind to take a direct approach.

'I saw you just now showing two chaps out at that exit off the main corridor. Who were they – clients? I must say they looked a bit like private detectives or government inspectors, not that I'd know what they looked like, never having met either!' He had improvised the last bit to soften the impact of his blunt opening question. It appeared to produce the desired effect.

Peter laughed, 'Up to your usual interrogations, Mathew? I'm surprised you don't know what a private detective looks like, as you're behaving rather like one yourself, as I commented the other day!'

'Actually, as I recall, you had me down as an undercover investigative journalist – make your mind up, Peter!' Mathew was beginning to enjoy the exchange which was in a sense picking up where he last left off with Peter, but in a more relaxed mode.

By now they were standing in the canteen waiting in the longer queue for the main menu. Mathew had been content to sacrifice his natural choice of a vegetarian option for the sake of pursuing his quarry. His confidence was boosted further on catching sight of Emily who was seated alone and already making a start on her meal. All he had to do now was persuade Peter to join him with Emily once they'd been served. He used the brief pause in their conversation as they joined the queue to conceive his next tactical plan and changed the topic to suit the current context.

'I must say, most days I usually go for the vegetarian menu as the healthiest and ethical option, but it doesn't take much to tempt me to take the other path. So just for today, I'll let you be my tempter, Peter.'

'Thanks very much! But you obviously don't get tempted down the path to perdition too often. Otherwise, you'd know there's enough choice of grub here to make up a perfectly decent meat-free meal anyway!'

'Glory be – you've given me a second chance to save my soul – mind if I push in front of you to get a better view of the salvation-marked morsels?'

'Be my guest!' Peter invited Mathew to step ahead to get close to where the standard menu was displayed and even pointed out one or two options suitable for vegetarians. So now, once they'd both been served, Mathew was in a position to lead Peter to where Emily was sitting, and this proved an easy enough manoeuvre to perform.

'Hi both!' Emily greeted them. 'Mathew and I've been on another of these short training sessions. What have you been up to this morning, Peter?'

'He's been conducting secret talks with two members of the local mafia, haven't you, Peter?'

'You just won't give up interrogating me about who I've been working with, will you Mathew?'

'Well, this morning's whole session was about dealing with awkward characters or difficult customers, depending on your preferred terminology', Mathew countered.

Emily took over, giving Mathew a welcome break.

'You've both got me fascinated now so you'll have to tell us who these fellows actually were if it's not an agency or State secret!'

Peter appeared relaxed enough, but nevertheless visibly paused for thought before answering.

'You're right, Emily, they are businessmen, brothers-in-law, in fact. They're a kind of property developers. It's a familiar set-up - two couples, related by marriage, pooling their savings to buy a property near where they lived at auction, did it up, sold it on and used the profit to buy another and so on...'

'How many houses do they now own, then? And have they always bought to sell or are they private landlords too?', Mathew asked.

'The latter. I think they've sold on three properties and now have four houses they rent out, so it's more or less a full-time job for the brothers-in-law. Their wives sometimes help out doing up the houses on top of their part-time jobs. Pretty ordinary stuff, really.'

'They don't sound like natural targets for the agency,' Emily came in. 'They may be turning a fair profit, but I imagine, they'd be wanting to invest any money they make back into their business and put some aside for a rainy day, knowing the vagaries of the property market. Did they approach the agency or did the agency approach them?'

Emily had nailed it perfectly, thought Mathew. However evasive Peter might wish to be, he'd be hard put to wriggle out of answering such a direct and legitimate question.

'To be honest, they were rather a tough nut to crack and it was the agency who approached them. It's quite a complicated case actually, and I'm a bit surprised that they put me onto it, given like you I've only been in the job for less than two weeks!'

We're getting somewhere, at last, thought Mathew.

'I imagine they've studied your profile and decided you'd make a good go of it given your background and excellent track record in sales. And I suppose like with me, you've had an experienced agency worker sitting in on most of the interviews...'

Peter's reply came as something of a surprise.

'Actually, I've been interviewing these two on my own from the start, since Tuesday. The agency must have thought they'd be more likely to cooperate in a less formal setting and that more than one person interviewing might be intimidating.'

It seemed a pretty formal-looking handshake by the exit just moments ago!, Mathew mused.

'Anyway,' it was Emily's turn again. 'Did you get anywhere with them or did they prove to be the archetypal difficult customers? By the way, had you already done that training session they put us on this morning?'

Too many questions at once, Emily, keep it simple!

Peter seemed content to work backwards through her questions.

'I attended the session yesterday, yes. I suppose it was useful to share experience about dealing with awkward customers, as you describe them. I don't have a definite outcome with those two yet, but I think they'll come round now they've heard all my pitch and had time to digest it over the weekend.'

'So, was there a particular angle you took with them – the health care advantages, for example?' Mathew caught himself being predictable not for the first time today.

'I did touch on the health care aspect, but for that to really resonate they'd have to be a bit older and not so healthy! So, I pitched in more with the kudos factor of being able to advertise the fact they're part of VETS. Remember, the agency takes a long-term view. It will be worth the time and research invested just to get them paying a tiny extra amount now if that's likely to go up in the future as they make more dough.'

Mathew and Emily's eyes met, tacitly signalling that Peter had given a convincing account and that they ought to let him off the hook. Emily moved to change the direction of the conversation.

'I can see you've an inborn talent for this job, aided and abetted by your immaculate sales background. No doubt they'll keep lesser mortals like me and Mathew on the 'soft' cases.'

'Which is all *we* seem to have been getting so far anyway!' Mathew added for good measure.

'Talking of more immediate matters – you're quite right about the veggie options from the main menu. Meat taste-alike substitutes have come a long way since I was a kid, I must say.'

The rest of the lunch break was spent in similar light-weight talk. Mathew felt relief from his self-imposed burden of doubt. Emily too, he thought, looked noticeably more relaxed.

He worked on just one standard case in the afternoon, starting with an hour's case notes review with Theresa, and ending with his interviewing the potential client. For the first time, he was now flying solo, to use Theresa's words. The father and son duo fitted perfectly into the 'soft' category, as Emily had put it earlier, and Mathew would be able to report back to Theresa a case successfully closed.

As he walked down what now seemed the interminable corridor back to reception, he caught himself wondering what the afternoon had dealt his two lunchtime interlocutors. Another 'soft' case for Emily and 'hard' one for Peter? It was only reflecting on this contrast that an ill-defined unease returned. This at first seemed to be mainly to do with injured pride at being assigned to a lower operational league than his rival, Peter, but he promised himself he would return to examine the unwanted emotion more deeply later.

He hadn't explicitly arranged a debrief with Emily, but texted her once he'd reached reception to see if she was free to meet up for a few moments before clocking off. She didn't reply right away, so he sat down as far away as he could from the all-seeing receptionist and pulled out the book he'd brought along for occasions such as this from his briefcase.

The book was entitled *Working Towards an Integrated Society* by an accredited TV journalist who had authored a number of highly acclaimed studies on modern life. What Mathew particularly liked about this book was the introductory chapter about the various crises of the past 50 years or so which had shaped today's world. He'd grown up learning so little about the decades during which his parents grew up. His father left before he'd reached the age of curiosity about the wider world and his mother never encouraged his questions. Nothing worthwhile on the topic was covered at school and the history curriculum had remained buried sufficiently far back in the past as to have no obvious connection with the present.

He was half way through a chapter dealing with the drive towards greater social equality of the mid 2030s, or rather the attempt by key government agencies working together to finally put an end to absolute poverty for the most underprivileged tranche of society.

Tackling poverty was made much easier once the concept of relativism between the best and worst off within a given society had been firmly established. Income as such meant very little, as demonstrated by the old practice of comparing living standards internationally by representing wages in US dollars. Mathew's book cited the example of Cubans' average income in dollars at the beginning of the twentieth century was much lower than the worst-off US citizens, but they enjoyed much better wellbeing in terms of health, life expectancy and financial security.

The new approach, therefore, was to measure poverty *objectively* in terms of what was needed to live a healthy and fulfilled life and *subjectively* in terms of people's self-perception. This formula proved extremely workable, as once the superrich as a class began to decline, so did the number of people in surveys defining themselves as poor.

One of the main policy levers to eliminate poverty, apart from the citizen's basic income, was the demolition of the remaining 19th century slums which had survived the great post-war cull. Another target for destruction was jerry-built 'shoe box' housing hastily erected by unscrupulous developers taking advantage of lax planning laws in the late 20th and even early 21st centuries.

Millions were accommodated in hotels, guest houses and disused public buildings for up to a year at the state's expense while whole new state-of-the-art housing estates were built providing for all their reasonable needs. These needs were determined not just by arrogant architects, greedy developers and closeted town planners, but through consultation with the people who actually stood to benefit from the new housing.

Surveys revealed that the essential thing which virtually all those in substandard crowded housing estates wanted to retain was social contact and a sense of community. Unlike the wealthy middle class, they didn't aspire to lock themselves away in outsize detached mini castles surrounded by large gardens, even more expansive drives for multiple cars with the whole lot enclosed by high walls, fences and remote-controlled security gates.

In surveys, most of those termed as *cash and property poor* stated they would be content with modest living quarters. A typical wish list would consist of decent-sized rooms, high quality building and finishing, maximum energy efficiency, a rear garden and reasonable privacy. Beyond the accommodation itself, residents wanted easy access on foot to a variety of shops and other frequently-used services with reliable and affordable public transport to get them to town and back.

The most popular new estates proved to be the boldest ones where the houses had been built without drives, but larger gardens. Why should the majority of residents who couldn't afford cars have to put up with the pollution, noise and danger caused by a minority who owned them? In any case, anyone wanting or needing use of a car on a regular basis could subscribe to an affordable car pool just a short bus ride or 20-minute walk away. For those needing to make an occasional short quick trip, there were still the taxis. Who wanted all that responsibility, hassle and expenditure of car ownership these days?

A few pages into the chapter Mathew, as always when reading well-argued impassioned accounts, had begun to daydream and reflect on his own life and to what extent it was currently measuring up to his highest ideals. Just as he looked up for a moment, he saw Theresa hurriedly approaching and appearing slightly agitated.

'Hi Mathew, I'm glad you didn't rush off straight away this afternoon. It's just that I've been told Mr Hudson wants you to call into his office for a chat first thing on Monday, so could you make sure you arrive by half eight? Ask the receptionist on arrival to remind you where his office is. I think it's down the South corridor – the one you had your interview two weeks ago! I'm sure it's nothing to worry about...' But she didn't look at all sure.

That means it probably is something to worry about, thought Mathew who on catching sight of Theresa had immediately closed his book and stood up. Just as Theresa moved away slightly uncomfortably, Emily appeared. She also looked somewhat sullen.

'High Mathew. Did you get my message a few minutes ago?'

'Oh no, sorry, I was waiting for you here, but got engrossed in a book I brought with me and then must have started daydreaming a bit so didn't think to check...'

They had already walked out onto the street together by the time he finished his explanation.

'You'll have seen Theresa just then. She'd come to tell me to see, what-his-name, Mr Hudson, the recruitment chief, for a chat first thing on Monday. I'm not sure what to make of it.'

'I imagine it's similar to what I've been asked to chat to him about too...' Emily injected a hint of mock cheer into her tone. 'Are you thinking what I'm thinking – that's it's almost certainly to do with our subtle interrogation of Peter at lunch?'

'To be honest, lately I've been battling with my tendency to always assume the worst and thought I was getting somewhere. Until you told me you've also been called in, I was doing quite well persuading myself it was just a routine meeting to see how I was getting on after my first two weeks at the agency.'

Emily tried to be reassuring: 'Well it could just be that – after all, we were both recruited at the same time. My meeting's at nine, by the way, so that means the chats are due to last up to half an hour...'

'Unless you're right and they've shoved Peter or Jonathan in between us and it's only going to be a ten-minute affair.' Mathew feigned cheering up at his latest ad hoc theory, although by now he was utterly convinced that whatever Mr Hudson had planned was intended for him and Emily alone.

'I suggest we don't try to speculate too much just now. Let's get home, relax and what say I call you tomorrow when we've had time to gather our thoughts?' Emily's positivity appeared to Mathew more authentic that his own.

'Brilliant idea! I'm meeting a friend for lunch at about half twelve, so can we make it say after three?' Mathew judged the timing with a view to allowing long enough to catch up with Frank while giving himself a genuine get-out clause in case the get-together didn't go too well.

He wished his journey home could have taken a little longer, as despite the alternating accelerations and breaking of the bus during the rush hour, he found himself pleasantly lulled into a deep meditative state. Just two stops before his own, the bus suddenly slowed down at a road block. Eventually, the bus passed the scene of the accident causing the delay which had clearly involved two motorcars, though neither displayed visible signs of damage. Then, Mathew caught a glimpse of a mangled bicycle lying on its side by one of the cars and the thought of how seriously injured its owner might be sent a shiver up his spine.

When he was about thirteen, Mathew's mother decided to renew the carpet in his bedroom. While it was being fitted, he found pages of a thirty-year-old newspaper on the floor boards. He was intrigued and a quick scan through revealed a very different content to what would appear in a local newspaper today. Pride of place was be given to a number of tragic incidents in the local area. One report was about a motorcyclist being knocked off his bike and fatally injured just a few roads from where he and his family lived. Another featured a young lady who was in intensive care after taking a drug overdose at a party.

Mathew reflected on how depressing it must have been to read newspapers in those days and wondered who, apart from the immediate family of those concerned, would be interested in such tragic news. Once his mother had remarked that the national news too used to be full of detailed reports about disasters in other parts of the country and around the world. She supposed that in recent times someone must have decided that the public need cheering up with more upbeat and positive stories.

Mathew reflected on the former media habit of reporting personal tragedies. No doubt, part of the motivation was to evoke the emotion best described by the German word *Schadenfreude: taking pleasure in other people's misfortunes and distress.* Then there was the related dark pleasure of voyeurism.

If witnessing the aftermath of a road accident had roused Mathew from his slumber, the brisk walk home from the bus stop brought him back to full alertness and reminded him of his resolve to make the most of the weekend ahead.

It was only coming up to five o'clock when Mathew sat down to his usual tea time snack in front of the TV just in time for the news. However, a moment after mechanically turning it on, he switched it off again, deciding instead to make an early start on planning his evening. First of all, he needed to confirm one last time that the meeting with Frank was still on.

He couldn't remember if either of them had mentioned a venue, but thought it wiser to suggest a neutral ground in case he needed to make a get-away which wouldn't be quite so easy if he invited Frank to his place. Mathew made a quick call, confirmed his friend was still up for meeting and insisted on treating him to a pub lunch, putting down the phone before he could protest.

One down, two to go for this evening. He would call his mother for an update on her health, benefit claim and love life at about half six after he had had a chance to fully recover from work and a little while before he planned to make himself dinner. He pencilled in his sister for about eight in case he had any energy left after an anticipated long chat with his mother.

He would certainly be best leaving a serious chat about his work situation with Rory until he'd had the chance to sleep on today's events, so he settled for messaging his friend to check when he'd be available for a chat. The answer came back with Rory's usual efficiency and precision: any time between ten and twelve Sunday morning! Mathew confirmed that would be fine. He could already see that his Saturday was going to be fully booked at this rate with three appointments so far taking him potentially from ten till about four, assuming he'd be on the phone to Emily about an hour.

However, just as Mathew was beginning to feel smug at mapping out his weekend so smartly, his sister rang, completely playing havoc with his timetable.

'I've just heard from mum. She's had more test results back today and it's not looking too good, I'm afraid. She wasn't entirely coherent when she called to give me the news. I don't think she'd been drinking again. I just mean she sounded distraught and confused and from what she said I'm not even sure how bad it is. Could we could both go round and see her again tomorrow?'

Mathew's meticulous weekend planning suddenly didn't seem so clever after all. However, he thought quickly on his feet and came back with the first white lie he'd had to tell for at least a year – at least within his family circle.

'Certainly. Unfortunately, I've a few work-related issues to see to tomorrow, but I can be over to yours by about three if that's OK. We should get to mum's by about quarter to four allowing for the primary school run.'

He at once applied himself to mentally preparing a plausible account of his work issues should it be required, but his sister didn't press him to elaborate and the rendezvous was agreed painlessly. Before ringing off she confirmed, as if by way of compensation, that their mother had at least secured her extra benefit entitlement and would receive her first payment next week.

Mathew sat down to reflect and only then noticed that his heartbeat was faster and stronger. At least this was a natural response to hearing alarming news, he thought, and then wondered why his adrenalin apparently hadn't kicked in earlier on being told he had to see the headmaster first thing on Monday. Or maybe it had kicked in, but he'd not had time to register the fact, being distracted by Emily's appearance immediately afterwards.

Should he now phone his mother? And if so, would this be because he had intended to anyway and would then feel he had stuck to his timetable even if the conversations with his sister and mother had been reversed? Or should he phone her because of what his sister had told him just now?

I'm overthinking yet again! he mused. He decided the best policy would be to mull things over slowly while preparing his evening meal as planned.

If he called his mother this evening, he'd stand a good chance of teasing out of her just how serious her health condition was, at least insofar as she understood herself from what her doctor or the hospital had told her. If he left trying to get the details till tomorrow, it could be hard with his sister there as the facts could be confused in a three-way conversation. In any case, his mother may not be as inclined to be frank with both her children present at once. She had always tended to talk to her son more protectively in the presence of her daughter. One of those family dynamics.

Once again in recent weeks, he congratulated himself on not rushing to a decision or behaving impulsively. He sat down to his meal with a healthy appetite and satisfied that the best option would be to call his mother a little later on after he had carefully planned his script. It wasn't at all obvious at first in what order and in what way he should tackle all the essential points, but his mental map had fully formed by the end of his meal.

It was still only just past seven when he picked up the phone. She answered with little delay.

'Hi mum, Paula just rang. I'm glad to hear your benefit's due next week at last. She mentioned, though, you'd had some bad news about some of the test results, but didn't go into detail. We're coming round tomorrow at about three when I've sorted out some issues to do with my new job. I hope that's OK.' His gamble that this would be her cue to elaborate paid off.

'Yes Mathew, I'm not sure whether to say it could have been worse or better. Doctor Clarkson phoned to say that my kidneys are in a pretty shocking state and that I'm likely to need dialysis, but plenty of people survive many years with that. Trouble is, it's damned inconvenient and I'm hardly likely to be offered a transplant at my age. There is another procedure they're making progress with, though. They can already do it for your liver, where they just implant a small piece of the organ and it grows back – amazing!'

Well, at least she's fairly upbeat about it. He imagined that had it been terminal, the doctor would have called her in rather than phoned.

'Was it your usual doctor friend who called with the news?'

'Yes, but I know what you're thinking. It was hardly the moment for a romantic chat. His referring me to a specialist for further hospital tests seemed the most appropriate way to of spending our limited time together!'

The poignant ambiguity of the word *limited* struck Mathew and he instantly felt desperately sorry for his mother. Indeed, any idea of romance with an older patient on a dialysis machine would surely be far from doc's mind now!

Things couldn't be all that bad, Mathew thought as he put down his phone a couple of minutes later. With his mother in reasonably good spirits and having confirmed tomorrow's visit, he could theoretically enjoy the rest of the evening with his self-imposed burden of duty largely lifted.

Mathew put on his relaxing dinner jazz retro vinyl records and contemplated a late session at his current wargame in the hobby room. In so doing, he just felt a little sad that his mother hadn't responded to his calculated cue: 'after I've sorted out some issues to do with my new job'. What would it take to get her to show the slightest interest in what her son was doing with his life?

Perhaps he was being unfair on his mother. She was the one with the life-threatening illness, after all. On the other hand, why should he interminably make excuses for her lack of interest? He recalled his last hospital visit to his grandmother as a child. She had filled nearly the whole time asking him about school and his hobbies. This was no doubt a ruse to avoid burdening her grandchild with her imminent death. It felt right, all the same. However, the rules had changed now he was a mature adult and now in her vulnerable condition, it was his mother who was entitled to first consideration.

CHAPTER 13. FRIEND, FAMILY, FRIEND

Mathew awoke from one of the most bizarre dreams he could recall. His subconscious had been hard at work jumbling up a whole mish-mash of impressions into an incongruous whole. It didn't take him long, however, to recognise the origin of the various elements, as the symbolism seemed far less abstruse than in his other recent dreams.

In soldierly fashion, he was marching through a battle scene towards a distant enemy which didn't appear to be getting any nearer. This was a common frustration in his dreams – the inability to *will* himself to move. At first, he seemed surrounded by comrades, but then they disappeared imperceptibly as the action began.

The scene was unquestionably set in his wargaming period, as he could see the nozzle-loaded cannons firing away in the distance and producing their characteristic plumes of smoke. Cannon balls whizzed and whistled through the air, but he was strangely more fearful of those which were bouncing or rolling at speed along the ground, as they threatened to take off his leg. Suddenly, but without any hint of surprise during the dream itself, he found himself floating just above the ground and at last able to move forward with ease.

In the distance, he spotted a troop of approaching cavalry, but to his horror realised he couldn't tell whether they were friend or foe. In fact, it was unclear which side of the battle he himself was fighting for. He looked down at the facings on his uniform only to find they were nondescript and colourless, providing no clues of allegiance.

To add to the confusion, the cavalry was getting nearer and also shapeshifting. One moment they were French Cuirassiers in predominantly blue uniforms with tassels streaming behind their helmets, the next they were British Scots Greys in red, menacingly wielding their sabres. Whereas before, when grounded, he had been unable to advance, now he was unable to halt his floating motion which was carrying him towards the cavalry with alarming speed. Just as Mathew prepared to defend himself against whomever may fall upon him, he discovered he was totally unarmed.

A split second before the fateful impact, Mathew was transported to the more familiar environment of his agency building and found himself pacing rapidly down a long corridor until his progress was slowed by doors swinging open on all sides, especially ahead of him. It seemed as though however determined he was to progress, the end of the corridor remained at a constant distance. Finally, his interrogator, Mr Hudson's, malignly grinning face appeared. Only his head and shoulders or bust could be seen and even this image faded to a mere invisible presence, rather like the mysterious Cheshire cat in the famous nineteenth century novel.

A detached voice then imperiously urged him on toward the reception area, but the scene transitioned instead to the canteen where he found himself rooted to his armchair being starred at menacingly by Peter with Mr Hudson standing behind.

At this point, Mathew awoke, immediately aware that this was not the sort of dream he would want to drift back into. The surest means of exiting and recording the essentials was to rise sharply out of bed and snatch up his notebook before memory decay set in.

Mathew jotted down as much as he could, conscious that if he dwelt too long on the wording of particular details, other memory fragments risked being lost during the delay. When he sat down with his notebook over breakfast and reviewed his efforts, he was startled at how many incidents in the dream had appeared bizarre even while dreaming them, whereas other aspects only seemed so in the clear light of day.

He had never dreamt of being in the midst of a Napoleonic battle before, despite a twenty-five-year-old passion for wargaming in that period. He could only assume that his subconscious was opportunistically using the imagery to represent his inner conflict or ambivalence at work. Not knowing which army he was fighting for, nor which side the cavalry belonged to symbolised the potential dilemma he may find himself in should the agency's ethics be lower than he had been encouraged to believe. The cannon balls threatening to take off his legs and his floating over the ground could symbolise his uncertainty and instability. The symbolism of suddenly realising that he was unarmed against an unidentifiable enemy presumably meant that if he did come into conflict with the agency, he would have little power to do anything.

Could the violently swinging doors as he moved through the corridor signify potential punishment for his sleuthing activities which may prove unjustified and perhaps amount to mere snooping? Mr Hudson was obviously connected to what he feared awaited him on Monday. His phantom-like partial appearance, disappearance and then reappearance reinforced Mathew's uncertainty about the purpose of the scheduled meeting, but also about its outcome and the very nature of Mr Hudson whose direct contact with Mathew had been relatively brief on the very first day. Since then, he had made only fleeting appearances in corridors, offices and once or twice in the dining area and this may explain his enigmatic presence in the dream.

Mathew knew to expect more possible interpretations of his dream to come to him later in the day. Right now, he was eager to rush up to his hobby room to continue his wargame. This too might trigger more memories.

As he approached the table trying to recall whether it was the French or the Russians' turn to 'move' next, he was reminded of the drawback of his preference to conduct his wargames in solitude. This meant that he had to switch his allegiance between the antagonists at each turn. Only twice had he allowed himself a real opponent. Paula once tried to indulge her little brother by attempting to command the French army, but she soon lost patience when he failed to adequately explain his homemade rules in all their complexity.

The only other abortive attempt at sharing his hobby was with a school friend whose careless handling of his painted figures left some needing to be touched up. To add insult to injury, the climax of the battle was spoiled when the clumsy friend bumped into the table knocking over half of Mathew's best troops.

He wondered, if he eventually got together with Emily, would his wargaming interest be something to keep quiet about or confess to. He might even try to break his habit of twenty odd years and invite her to join him in battle, but this was clearly a decision requiring the utmost caution.

In the midst of this thought, he looked down at a busy section of the battlefield and glimpsed a figure which for an instant appeared to be hovering just head and shoulders above the other combatants. Closer examination, however, revealed that a French infantry figure was actually precariously balancing on the stands of two fallen comrades, in effect raising him just a little off the ground. Mathew didn't consciously recall the elevated infantryman from the evening before, but wondered if he could have subliminally registered it via his peripheral vision. This might explain his own apparent hovering through part of the dream and could well rival his earlier theory about both Gemma's and Theresa's 'flying high' prediction.

It may even be a synchronistic fusion of the two causes. He had once read an anthology of the writing of Carl Jung, one of the earliest practitioners of psychiatry whose mystical bent starkly distinguished him from his mentor, the better-known Sigmund Freud. Jung may have hypothesised that the lady trainers' words and Mathew's hovering soldier formed a meaningful, hence synchronistic, coincidence despite not being causally related.

After a while engrossed in this train of thought, Mathew required an effort of self-discipline to bring his musings to a close. However, before resuming his wargame, he took the 'hovering' soldier and marked a large M under its base. This would represent himself in the battle and would be his little light-hearted experiment in synchronicity to see if the soldier's fate in any way paralleled his own as events unfolded over the next few days.

As he looked down at his phone to check the time, he noticed he'd received a message from Rory apologising that something had come up and he was no longer free to chat after ten this morning, but could he make it after seven in the evening instead. Mathew confirmed the new time and was secretly relieved, as it meant he had more headspace to prepare for his non-work-related meetings with Frank, sister and mother.

An hour and a half later, two full phases further on in his Franco-Russian skirmish, it was time for Mathew to leave the hobby room with the figure representing him still intact, but at last grounded again and 60 yards or so closer to enemy positions. In connection with other aspects of his recent dream, he could not as yet discern any imminent threat from the enemy's cavalry.

Mathew had given himself at least half an hour to dress appropriately for a pub venue and mentally prepare for his encounter with Frank. He socialised so rarely with friends, that when a meeting did take place, it tended to cause him considerable nervous excitement during the hours leading up to it.

He had purposely named a pub which he knew to be an easy bus ride from where Frank lived and no more than a ten-minute drive from his own house. Almost as soon as he set off, Mathew was besieged by a vague sense of guilt and was kept occupied during the rest of the journey trying to work out its origin. The best he could do was narrow it down to something he should have done, but not done or at least not completed. Being so conscientious, he was pursued by a residual sense of guilt about any number of things whenever he departed from his strict routine. Daring to meet a friend was just one of these departures. Spending longer than usual engrossed in his wargaming hobby was another frequent source of guilt.

Of course, he could reproach himself for spending an excessive amount of time on his current wargame, though he did have the good excuse for this morning's session that he needed to 'crack' his most recent dream. Indeed, he probably should have given more thought to preparing for his forthcoming chat with Frank. On the other hand, hadn't some of his recent phone and face-to-face conversations proved that he was at his best when speaking impromptu? In any case, it would probably be counterproductive to second guess what he might have to deal with. He told himself he ought to have learned by now that trying to plan in detail what he was going to say or even writing scripted notes did not generally produce the best outcomes.

Mathew pondered for a moment on how this habit had originated and become established over the years. He didn't have to try too hard to unearth the relevant memories of fraught situations at home as he grew up where so often a heavy price was paid for choosing the wrong words or even the wrong moment to bring up a subject with members of his family. This childhood experience of walking on eggshells had carried through to his school life and no doubt contributed to restricting his circle of friends.

At university, he relaxed just a little as he attempted to emulate the apparent ease with which most of his peers entered into conversation around him. He achieved limited success, however, and had probably made more progress in 'chilling' in social situations in the past two weeks than over the previous ten years. Long may the process continue!

As Mathew stepped out of his car in the pub parking area, he still felt slightly nervous. There was always the chance that Frank had had one of his 'bad dos' since their brief chat last night and cried off at the last minute. He wasn't always the most reliable communicator and had been known to stand Mathew up in the past.

Mathew got to the pub comfortably ahead of half twelve to be sure of getting in the first drink so there would be no renewed ambiguity over who was treating whom. He carefully studied the menu too to minimise potential fuss and awkwardness around ordering when his friend turned up.

Mathew had been standing deliberately with his back to the bar and so captured the moment that Frank entered the pub on the stroke of half twelve. He hailed his friend over and quickly accomplished the ritual of ordering drinks and lunches for the two of them.

Frank had followed Mathew's lead in settling for a non-alcoholic drink and also accepted his suggestion from the menu giving them the option of picking and mixing from a total of four different small dishes, a practice which had become increasingly popular in recent years.

Mathew opened the conversation simply and naturally enough, 'So how have the last few days gone at the vet's?'

Frank was clearly in a better mood and feeling more optimistic about his new job than when they last spoke and described the most colourful of his recent assignments with his usual wit. He enjoyed the variety of animals he was working with and hadn't experienced any really upsetting scenes over the past week. What was more, his attitude towards the people running the outfit appeared to have softened. He even took back his earlier criticism of the boss being out for profit more than the animals' welfare. Frank's reports of cruelty by some of the pet owners or comments about how the business might operate better had actually yielded some positive results and he was now beginning to feel an appreciated member of the team.

'It's early days yet, of course. They may be just humouring me until they find someone else less inclined to cause trouble. Still, I'm trying to follow your advice and be positive. I met an old bloke the other day who really doted on his German Shepherd, but I could tell from talking to him that he didn't have the slightest clue about how to look after it. When I told him what he needed to do for his dog he really took note and promised he'd try everything I suggested about exercise, diet and play. That's the trouble with too many people who claim to be animal lovers. They just see things in terms of how their pet responds to them and fits or fails to fit into their own self-centred routine. They rarely stop to consider how they might need to adapt to meet their pet's needs.'

Mathew felt it was an opportune moment to suggest to Frank that with his understanding of the animal kingdom and growing confidence, he might consider setting up a pet minding service on his own. Over time, he might expand like the business he was working for and even employ his own staff whom he could educate into his way of thinking. Frank's eyes lit up at this prospect which clearly hadn't occurred to him and Mathew immediately began to worry in case he'd been too hasty in planting the thought in his friend's mind.

Now more at ease in his own world, it appeared that Frank had the capacity for demonstrating a little reciprocal interest in Mathew's new job. In answer to Frank's questions, however, Mathew was careful to confine himself to giving a factual and objective account, as he feared a more earnest exposé of his concerns about the agency risked upsetting Frank's delicate and hard-won equilibrium. In any case, all his own misgivings were speculative and may well prove ill founded, so wouldn't it be hypocritical to be lecturing his friend on being positive about his own new job and giving his new boss the benefit of the doubt, if he himself wasn't prepared to do the same?

On parting company with Frank, Mathew felt a glow of satisfaction for his contribution to the meeting going so well. His friend was clearly in better shape from every point of view than he had known him for at least year, certainly since he lost his last job at the zoo. His initial worry about potentially encouraging Frank to rush into going solo soon receded. His friend had never been the entrepreneurial type and the idea of setting up on his own might have appealed to his ego, but certainly not to his temperament.

Returning to his car, Mathew looked at his watch. It was not yet half two so he had ample time to pick up his sister and get them to their mother's house by three. He reflected a moment on his habitual obsession with minute-budgeting which had resurfaced in full force last weekend as he shuttled his sister and mother between their various homes. While chatting to Frank for nearly two hours just now, he had barely glanced at his watch more than a couple of times, however. Whether this was largely a cause or effect of his being relaxed for once hardly mattered, but it was certainly worth trying to keep up the good work through the rest of the afternoon. He took off his watch and set off to his sister's.

As he rolled up, Paula was waiting for him outside her front gate. Mathew's reflex action as he put on the handbrake was to glimpse at his watch, but he stopped himself just in time. Then he recalled he'd removed it in any case. Paula sat down in the front passenger seat looking as sullen as could be and scarcely cast Mathew a sideways glance. It was almost five minutes into the short journey to their mother's before any meaningful words were exchanged between them. At length, Mathew ventured:

'In case you didn't know, I talked to mum almost straight after you called me with her bad news. I just needed to get a sense of how she was taking it and also to reassure her we'd be visiting pronto.'

'That's only natural and what I expected you to do. It didn't occur to me at the time to consider how you'd react. Even if I had, I wouldn't have wanted to say you should or shouldn't do this or that. For me it was just a matter of needing to tell you as far as possible what she'd told me. I imagine she spoke quite differently to you, as always...'

'No doubt you're right, but with the two of us together in a moment, she'll have to adjust her account to suit us both. That way we might get a fuller and more accurate picture.'

He hadn't chosen his words particularly well, but he felt them to be reasonably apt.

Paula spent the remaining five or so minutes of the journey updating her brother on her work situation. She felt she'd been snubbed by her seniors and that her innovations in her new role hadn't been sufficiently appreciated. Mathew suggested this might be because they were jealous of her success and feared she was upstaging them in some way, especially if they were men, as he supposed they mainly were. Sitting sideways on to Paula, he couldn't tell how Paula was reacting. This was frustratingly similar to what had happened last week when he had been concentrating so much on his driving that he was unable to get an adequate sense of how the others were responding to what he was saying.

Mathew restricted himself to one further comment about Paula's work, suggesting she ought to try to compartmentalise a little more and switch off once she left the office. He really wanted to talk to her about how things were going with Andrew, but there was no time to do that topic any justice, so he decided to leave it till their return journey. If ten minutes or so proved insufficient, she may just possibly invite him in afterwards for a coffee.

Talking of compartmentalising, Mathew noticed that he was beginning to mentally apportion time too readily again, but at least he was managing to refrain from perpetually glancing down at his bare wrist.

They arrived at their mother's. She was already at the front door to let them in as they came up the garden path. Only now did it occur to Mathew that neither of them had thought to bring a small gift with them such as flowers, a cake or some chocolates. But this was hardly surprising as this just wasn't done in their small family circle. In any case, he consoled himself, breaking with the usual practice would have felt a bit like visiting their mother in hospital even if the custom of bearing gifts of flowers or grapes to patients had long since fallen victim to ever stricter hygiene rules.

'Hello mum,' Paula set the ball rolling with the niceties, 'how about I put the kettle on and make us a cup of tea to start with? And it's ages since I last had the chance to raid the biscuit tin – where do you keep it these days?'

She's broken the ice brilliantly, thought Mathew, appreciatively. As his own relationship with Paula had rarely been warm, he'd forgotten that she generally felt more at ease with their mother than he did. While his sister was in the kitchen, he knew he had a brief opportunity to chat to his mother alone about her illness, but suddenly he lost courage and became tongue tied. The best he could do was to start talking, of all things, about the uneventful drive to her house. Then, just as suddenly and inexplicably, he regained his courage and asked the all-important question.

'How serious is it mum?'

'It's serious enough, but liver disease can be cured, as I was saying the other day, and my doctor has confirmed that I could in fact qualify for a transplant if need be. As for the kidneys, well they may be able to repair one and save it, so dialysis isn't inevitable. Also, even if I had to go down that route, the process is much slicker than it used to be. The trouble is, I may have pancreatic cancer into the bargain, but even though the prognosis for that can be very poor – death within a couple of months, A – it's not absolutely certain yet and B – as they spotted the problem early when they were scanning my body for other stuff, my chances, if it is cancer, will be better than even.'

So, all in all, things looked neither good nor desperately bad. Paula heard the business end of the conversation as she returned with the tea tray and biscuits. At least their mutual concern that their mother might not be straight with them had proved unfounded. It struck Mathew as paradoxical that he had never felt more at ease in the combined presence of his mother and sister than now, despite the objective gravity of the situation.

His mother's refreshed outlook on life since becoming abstinent undoubtedly accounted for much of the tension-free atmosphere she had succeeded in generating in her children's presence. She had clearly absorbed much of the philosophy of the Alcoholics Anonymous group she had been attending lately, and was adeptly applying the core principle of taking life a day at a time. Having progressed beyond the stage of having to battle hourly with alcoholic compulsions, she assured them, she was now free to focus on tackling just one or two issues each day.

Concentrating on her health would be her main priority from now on and she was fully aware of the healing power of positive thinking and visualisation. This would be much easier to achieve now that she'd resolved her financial situation satisfactorily and would maintain her until all the medical diagnoses and treatment plans were in place.

Mathew also observed a change in his mother's tone of voice which had become mellower and less suggestive of self-pity. This sense was reinforced when she pleasantly surprised him by asking about his and his sister's work and other life events.

A couple of hours later, at the start of the short journey home, Paula told Mathew that while he was in the kitchen washing up, their mother had mentioned in passing that her doctor was being extremely supportive and had called round a few times, but just as a good friend. Mathew strongly suspected that Paula had in fact elicited this information, but felt no need to interrogate his sister on the point. Clearly, his mother had been happy to provide an update on this aspect of her life or else he would have sensed a degree of tension as he returned to join them.

It was now his turn to question Paula on how things were with Andrew, but he judged it wise to leave this till they reached her house. She would surely invite him in and feel more relaxed on her home turf. Instead, he let her fill him in on a few more details about her dissatisfaction at work, though she had pretty well covered most of the ground in their earlier chat and subsequent three-way talk with their mother.

As Paula continued to present herself as one of life's victims, Mathew felt his overdeveloped capacity for pity stir once more. The involuntary emotion was so strong that he felt it well up within his solar plexus area to the point where it actually began to cause physical discomfort.

A torrent of negative thoughts immediately followed: how sad it was that his sister had such an unappealing personality to go with her unprepossessing physical appearance. Her posture, gait, fixed gloomy facial expression, the dreary tone of her voice - everything about her seemed fine tuned to repel any sympathy or empathy in others. What did Andrew see in her after all? It was a miracle he was still interested in her given how stubborn and inflexible she was. Had she not been his sister, wouldn't Mathew have been advising his friend against intimacy with so someone possessing so little promise?

Surely at work too, her colleagues must perceive her as a joyless whinger, an arid egotistical pedant with ideas way above her station. If only he could be blunt and knock some sense into her in a way that family members rarely dare to do except in melodramatic soap operas.

At last, Mathew's worst excesses of pity-cum-anger subsided and little by little he returned to a less intense and more objective appraisal of Paula's more positive redeeming qualities. When they finally arrived, he felt almost ready to engage her in the conversation he had been planning for last few hours. But Paula didn't invite Mathew in as he'd hoped, so he quickly had to get into gear for an improvised, but incisive doorstep chat.

'By the way, give Andrew my regards when you next see him. Wasn't it this weekend you were going to meet up with him?

'To be honest, I'd arranged to see him for lunch today until I heard about mum and couldn't face two visits in one day. He understood, of course, so we've rearranged for tomorrow instead. Yes, course I'll pass on your regards. I know you two get on well.' Paula smiled ambiguously, but it was all Mathew needed to put his mind at rest: at least *something* appeared to be heading in the right direction.

Paula continued, 'Sorry, I can't invite you in, but the place is a tip, and I really do need to catch up on the housework this evening. I've obviously been expending too much time and energy on my new job lately. And then there's worrying about mum which has knocked me out of kilter. I'm sure I'll get everything back into proportion before long!'

Mathew was reassured by his sister's confession. It suggested more insight than he generally credited her with and made him feel not a little guilty for mentally massacring her earlier.

Albeit by implication, however, Paula had told him what he wanted to know and he was content to drive home with a sense of a day's work well done. Of course, this was the weekend and, ideally, he shouldn't be regarding his Saturday in the same way that one might review a day at the office. Perhaps one day he just might learn to relax in the company of his mother and sister as naturally as he had just managed to achieve with Frank.

Although to be fair on himself, today's contrast was more down to the difference in circumstances. A meeting with a witty and moderately cheerful friend could hardly be compared to one with his possibly terminally ill mother.

Back home, Mathew had roughly an hour to fill before the time he'd agreed to call Rory. He decided it would be best to prepare himself a light meal while considering as calmly as possible how best to phrase his concerns about the agency in order to elicit the most constructive response possible from his intellectual friend. For the sake of his ego as much as anything else, he desperately didn't want to come across to Rory as panicked and irrational.

Having been treated to cakes and biscuits at his mother's, Mathew felt the need to atone and so settled for a simple snack based on organic vegetables and a tiny portion of rice. He disciplined himself to sit down to the meal in the dining room rather than take it into the lounge on a tray and wolf it down in front of the TV. He then drank half a glass of water and spent the remaining half hour before the call to Rory noting down the key points he wanted to make, resisting the temptation born of habit to formulate a complete script.

All Mathew succeeded in doing during these final few minutes was to tie himself up in knots. He at last conceded defeat in his attempt to find a halfway house between a spontaneous and hyper-scripted strategy for tackling his overbearing friend in conversation. He would meekly submit to abject humiliation and retreating from the encounter with a battered ego, but with at least the forlorn hope of salvaging some sound advice.

However, just seconds before the sparring match began, Mathew was blessed with a sudden rush of inspiration. This told him to completely switch his focus and direct the conversation towards Rory, asking him for an update on his latest step up the career ladder and then, emboldened, dare to ask for the latest instalment of his romantic adventures. After all, only a week ago, Rory had owned up to disappointments in both departments.

Rory accepted the opening gambit and obliged with a brief, but incisive and matter-of-fact account of the adjustments he had had to make in order to accommodate to his new role at the super clean energy company. The narrative contained the following essential points: His colleagues, both his new professional equals and subordinates, were largely dolts, but meant well and had proved amenable to his logical approach to doing things. That was Rory all over – a self-professed breath of fresh air, bringing order and reason to all around him. People just needed to be patient and listen in order to see the light!

If this was the old Rory whom Mathew recognised so well, then it was quite a transformed one who spoke next about his unaccustomed soul-searching and heart-wrenching break-up with his most recent girlfriend. Last time they spoke, Rory had acknowledged his shock at being ditched by his latest conquest, but clearly interpreted this as an unwarranted blow to his ego rather than a reflection on his own attitude and behaviour.

However, over the days that followed, he had come to realise that his feelings for the young lady concerned ran deeper than he was used to experiencing and he had even begun to examine his own responsibility for the relationship breaking down. This was a far cry from when Rory the university student would jokingly refer to any female he was intimate with as his 'bit of fluff' or, in strictly male company, his 'current shag-piece'.

Emotional distress could be a great leveller, it seemed, and by encouraging his friend to reveal a vulnerable side to himself, Mathew anticipated that he would feel much more at ease when it came to sharing his own worries. At last, Rory appeared to have exhausted his capacity for keeping up his role of the heartbroken lover and paused pensively just long enough to provide Mathew with an entry point into the hitherto one-sided conversation.

As Rory's near monologue was coming to an end, Mathew had

briefly entertained the idea of confiding a little about Emily. He dismissed this idea, however, on the grounds that anyone crashing out of an affair is hardly well equipped to listen supportively to a friend travelling in the opposite direction. It would also have seemed rather as though he was betraying a confidence. Instead, therefore, he chose the wiser course of thanking Rory for supplying him over a week ago with the pragmatic questions which had stood him in such good stead towards the end of the training process.

When at last Mathew began his agency update, he was careful to keep his emotions in check and present his concerns in an equable and matter-of-fact manner. This had to be the surest way to extract the soundest possible advice from Rory whose rational qualities, he was confident, would not be compromised by the emotional turmoil of his love life.

Rory took a little longer than last time to respond with concrete suggestions, but Mathew hardly found this surprising given the more serious nature of the issues involved. Once Rory got underway, however, he adopted his usual authoritative tone and there was no interrupting him.

'Adding what you've told me just now to what I already knew about the agency from last time, I'd say there are a couple of key issues you need to raise or be prepared to tackle in case they raise them with you on Monday. There's still a good chance that you and your colleague are simply being called in quite innocently to see how you're getting on, so be prepared to give a straightforward account, while still ensuring you get to ask the questions you want answered. I wouldn't be at all afraid to mention your colleague who appears to be getting the tougher nuts to crack. Mention that you've spoken to him amicably and are just keen to better understand how the agency operates.

'If, on the other hand, you find you're being challenged over your recent secret agent-like tactics, it could be because your mercenary friend has denounced you and you'll need to be cautious. Or someone may have overheard you talking to, what's her name, Emily, and it's got back to management. As it's a government agency, though, I wouldn't be at all surprised either if they employ their own spies to keep tabs on new recruits. From your mentor's reaction, it sounds as though she was just the messenger and not a chief instigator.

'Ultimately, you should regard yourself as on a fact-finding mission, getting as much information about the place as you can so you're able to decide whether you want to make a career with the agency or not. You're clearly not beholden to it and from what I know of you, you can walk out at the end of the day if it doesn't meet your own high ethical standards.'

'That's always supposing I still have the choice by the end of the interview and I'm not sent packing!' Despite his flippant-sounding observation, Mathew was secretly grateful to his friend. There had been no hint of irony in his words *high ethical standards* and he had clearly acknowledged Mathew's principled stance vis a vis the agency.

The two chatted for a further ten minutes or so. Rory fully understood that the government was forced to use various ruses to squeeze extra revenue out of more affluent citizens in order to fund public services, in particular, the Citizen's Universal Income. His father had been vehemently opposed to this, believing it would encourage over half the population to be idle and live off the backs of the toiling minority. However, Rory himself, despite this parental influence and his own strong initial reservations, had come to accept it as the only effective way of giving people the financial security they craved and which society as a whole had come to see as entitlement ranking with basic human rights. Rory volunteered on the subject:

'There's no denying the crime rate has drastically fallen since the CUI was introduced and the levelling up effect it's had. I must admit, like the government, I was late in recognising the value invisible and unpaid care workers bring to society. And to the economy too.'

He also accepted Mathew's point about how the country's happiness rating had shot up once people, especially the young, dynamic and creative, were free to pursue their dreams almost unfettered by material pressures. It had been almost an economic miracle that all this had been achieved without the huge tax burden which CUI detractors had predicted would be imposed on people's 'honest' earnings.

'But all good things come at a price, and if a big part of that price is the agency you now have the honour to work for, perhaps you'll have to temper your stringent ethics with a touch of realism.' It was a pity, Mathew thought, that Rory had to conclude his lecture on so sententious a note!

Following the customary niceties, the two university friends ended their phone chat with both avowing their intent to meet up later in the year. Rory had essentially merely confirmed Mathew's own way of thinking, which was really all he needed in order to face Monday's interview with confidence. His Saturday now felt nicely rounded off and he could afford to devote at least another hour or so to his wargame before turning in.

Immediately upon examining the battlefield, Mathew realised he had lost track of the figure which fate, with a little help from his own imagination, had elected to mirror his own fortunes over the next few days. Every set of military miniatures usually contained between four and eight duplicates for each pose. The hovering figure representing him was one of at least three with identical poses in roughly the same position on the table depicting a charging infantryman with musket angled aggressively towards the enemy.

He could of course resort to lifting each figure in turn to reveal the one with the letter M under its base, but on reflection decided to leave things as they were. Casualties were removed from the field so he'd know surely enough if and when his hero came to grief. In some respects, not knowing exactly which figure represented him would render the game more exciting.

Two phases later when Mathew called it a day, his unit had advanced with no further losses to within a hundred yards of enemy infantry which would be firing their first volley at the start of the next phase. Then the real action would begin.

* * * *

Mathew had a well-earned lie-in, finally getting up around nine o'clock and relieved to have been spared the usual assortment of disturbing dreams, at least ones he could recall. With no more social and family meetings, phone chats or any other planned engagements he could look forward to an agenda-free Sunday. He felt no need to include as an agenda item his anticipated pleasurable and relaxed chat with Emily. Moreover, she had invited him to call at any time that suited him, which, he dared to hope, suggested she was quite looking forward to talking.

He devoted the morning to domestic tasks which he generally treated as therapy rather than chores when free of urgent business. He felt mid-afternoon would be the optimal time to call Emily and confirmed this with her by text.

Needless to say, Mathew devoted a good couple of hours to his wargame, still eager to plot how his designated representative on the table might fare and how this would compare to his own fortunes in the real world. The game had now reached a high level of complexity with over half the forces on both sides having joined each other in combat. It was quite a pleasantly time-consuming operation to work through each group of units on his chart, deciding who was to move wither and who should be firing at whom, though the most deadly and labour-intensive hand-to-hand mêlées had not yet begun in earnest.

By the time Mathew left the battle field, there were four figures in the same combat zone sharing his figure's pose, any one of which could represent him. One of them had fallen victim to an enemy volley in the very latest phase, but fortunately did not bear the dreaded M under its base. He would live to fight in one more phase at least. In real life, that phase would be tomorrow morning's interview! Would he dare to tempt providence by completing yet another phase before the interview or would it be wiser to do this on his return home with Emily after the interview?

He gave Emily the agreed mid-afternoon call. Their chat ranged over several topics before they got down to consulting on a proposed action plan for tomorrow's interview. Unlike Mathew, Emily didn't have a friend whom she felt comfortable confiding in and so hadn't discussed her ideas and feelings with anyone but Mathew himself.

She reacted positively to what he told her of Rory's comments and advice and was fully prepared to adopt an approach similar to Mathew's during the interview. Emily was almost as relaxed as he was regarding her future with the agency or lack thereof in case things turned sour. Thanks to savings she'd made during her previous well-paid employment, she enjoyed financial security, had no family responsibilities and held firm to her original outlook on the new job as an adventure above all else.

'Besides', what's the worst that could happen?' she joked, using the expression which gained in popularity following a film of the same name at the turn of the 21st century. The phrase rapidly became a cliché before finally evolving into an ironic means of denoting a decision or action which actually did carry serious risks.

They arranged to meet up after work to compare notes, but this time it would be Mathew's turn to offer his home as the venue. This would mean his driving into work so he could bring Emily to his place and then back to the agency building where she would pick up her own car. This seemed a reasonable compromise between spending half the evening travelling hither and thither by bus and making at least two unnecessary car trips.

Mathew had one last hurdle to overcome before tomorrow morning. He knew that however much he may try to convince himself that he was totally relaxed about the interview process and its ultimate outcome, in reality he was not a little excited if not downright apprehensive. He knew that spending the rest of the evening poring over his wargame would only lead to greater excitement, especially in view of his own symbolic participation in the heart of the action. This would either mean he'd struggle to get to sleep or else be likely to wake up ridiculously early, probably with his head spinning with unsettling and bizarre dreams. He, therefore, took the wise decision to defer the next phase of his battle till tomorrow evening after the day's labours were done.

One wholesome pursuit he'd neglected of late, certainly since staring his new job, was physical exercise - whether by working in his back garden or taking brisk walks around the neighbourhood. Mathew knew all about the importance of physical fitness as a contributor to general mental health and wellbeing, but was among at least two thirds of the population who found it incredibly difficult to motivate themselves to take exercise purely for the purpose of keeping fit and healthy.

Mathew recalled an instructive session with an enlightened GP about ten years ago when he had first been struggling with work-related anxiety and sleeplessness. The doctor had explained that we homosapiens have carried through into the modern world a biological and psychological need for regular sustained vigorous exercise from the days when our ancestors subsisted in the wild as hunter gatherers. The bulk of modern humans lead a largely sedentary lifestyle and tend to overlook this basic instinct which is at the root of many physical and mental health problems. Mental fatigue from a hard day's work at the office only goes so far in providing a substitute for primordial physical exhaustion, at least insofar as promoting wholesome sleep is concerned.

In the past, Mathew had volunteered delivering newsletters for a local environmental campaigning group. This pursuit, in addition to taking part in periodic local litter picks, had provided the motivation he needed for purposeful exercise. He only wished he had kept it up. However, this evening, so strong was his desire to tire himself out that he had no difficulty in persuading himself to get out into his back garden in order to make a full inventory of every conceivable job that needed doing.

Unfortunately, he had not allowed for the time of year. With autumn barely yet underway, there were very few leaves to rake up and tip into a composting bin located at the bottom of the garden. For want of anything else practical to do, he filled a further half hour roaming up and down the lawn, attempting to recall which flowers had blossomed last spring and summer and the order in which shrubs, bushes and trees had come into leaf. Finally, he pulled out a deck chair from his small shed in order to contemplate the modest work he had completed and remembering to breathe in the fresh air as deeply as possible. All this, he hoped, would contribute to an effortless and sound sleep later.

One more hour of moderately vigorous activity, Mathew figured, should round off the natural fatiguing process. He considered a brisk walk to the local late opening shop and back, but rejected the idea on the basis that the mental activity needed to prepare a shopping list risked producing the opposite effect to what he wanted. At last, he settled for a good long 'pointless' walk during which he would attempt to clear his mind as far as possible and enter into a more meditative state.

Arriving back at his house after a fifty-minute brisk stroll, Mathew was confident he had achieved his goal. It was nearly ten o'clock and, whereas normally he would interrupt his evening routine to catch the latest news, on this occasion he was happy to throw off his shoes and coat in the hallway and head straight for the bedroom. His success at tiring himself out was so complete that he quite forgot about his final planned activity which would have been to listen to half an hour of dinner jazz piano.

Once in his bedroom, like a lazy or rebellious teenager, he stripped off the rest of his clothes, dumped them on the floor and, finding just enough energy to set his alarm for six thirty, collapsed into bed. Two minutes later he entered a deep sleep.

CHAPTER 14.
MINDING ONE'S AS TO DS

Mathew awoke just five minutes before his alarm was due to go off. He took this as a good sign, as from experience, it meant that he was well rested and ready to spring into action and deal with whatever lay ahead. The fact that a mysterious inner sense had somehow enabled him to pre-empt his alarm clock confirmed that he would remain alert and be well served by his intuition throughout the day.

He was relieved to have avoided his worst fear - failing to get to sleep at all until the middle of the night and then fitfully waking at regular intervals to check how much time remained before his alarm was due to go off. Thankfully, in recent years this had only happened to him on the eve of an event which he was really dreading, with or without good cause.

He had also avoided the lesser troubled sleep syndrome which more commonly occurred before a moderately stressful event such as today's interview. Here, he would get to sleep with no or little trouble well before midnight. But then he would awake at least an hour before he needed to, feeling wide awake and with a racing brain. If he then tried to go back to sleep or doze, he would just end up ruminating and worrying more about the event to be faced as well as his sleep deficit catching up with him later in the day, probably just at the most inopportune moment. So, on such occasions, he had learned to get up straight away and go about his business in order to dismiss any residual anxieties.

Another encouraging sign was that the details of his dreams had all faded beyond recall. He was simply left with a vague awareness that they had involved all or most of the women in his life – certainly his mother, sister and Emily, but also with Theresa, Margaret and Gemma somewhere in the background. The dreams being just out of reach was actually quite a relief, as he would have had little time or inclination to dissect them on this particular morning.

The journey to work by car proved a little more stressful than the bus travel routine he was already accustomed to. However, having given himself a large safety margin to allow for traffic, he was able to park inexpensively just five minutes' walk from the agency building and get there with a good twenty minutes to spare. In order to collect himself fully for the interview ahead, he decided not to enter right away in case someone had the bright idea of ushering him in early. Better to pace up and down for a while outside cultivating a confident body posture and positive aura.

He entered reception at eight twenty-five and was immediately directed to the very first office he'd been interviewed in by Mr Hudson. It now seemed an eternity ago, though in fact it was just nineteen days since a rather casual browse on his computer had launched him onto his new life path. As he approached the door with the name plate, he fleetingly wondered what the P initial before Hudson stood for. Patrick perhaps? Surely not another Peter? He was about to find out.

'Good morning, Mathew, Paul Hudson,' he said holding out his hand. 'I trust you recall our first chat at the initial testing just a few weeks ago. I hope you didn't mind too much being asked to make a slightly earlier start and it didn't worsen that notorious Monday morning feeling. Mind you, I have to say most of our staff here don't complain too much about the hours we keep. We seem to have got the length of the working day just about right.'

'I'd second that,' Mathew jumped in at what he felt was an opportune moment. 'Eight thirty was just a normal start time at my last job, though that seems an age ago now.'

'I appreciate it's all happened so quickly. That's what most of our new recruits say. Of course, much of it's down to our highly honed recruitment, induction and staff training procedures. Though none of it would be possible without you talented and dedicated people on the receiving end of it all.'

Hudson's highly demonstrative feel-good opening quelled any fears Mathew may have entertained about being dismissed forthwith for thought crime against the agency. Clearly, he would have to work much harder to blot his copy book unless this was all a trap to lull him into a false sense of security.

'Anyway, we like to touch base with you new colleagues once you've been through the whole training caboodle and drawn first blood, as it were, working with our clients. We find it's useful to get feedback at this stage before memory decay sets in. Obviously, your trainers and mentors have reported back to us on a regular basis on how you've reacted to our programme and I must say that all the feedback we've had on you has been most impressive. Admittedly, this hardly surprises me given how quickly you grasped the cheeky algorithms we used to get you here and in the bit of testing I subjected you to. Some recruits seem to feel they'll be penalised for asking awkward questions, but initiative and self-belief are what we value above all else here. After all, it's understanding human psychology that allowed us to find you in the first place and what allows you to get through to the clients.

'Curiosity is an admirable quality too. Knowing the whys and wherefores of a system and the rationale or philosophy behind it is what keeps the system itself robust. Now, from what everyone tells me – Miss Bentley (you probably knew her as Margaret), Theresa and Gemma, not forgetting Roger in the early days – most if not all your questions were answered as they arose. But do tell me if there's anything at all that has occurred to you since, or perhaps you've been afraid to ask?'

Hudson had been so disarming in his opening remarks that Mathew struggled for a moment to recover his presence of mind and ask even the most innocuous of the questions he had prepared for the interview. Nonetheless, as on previous occasions when under pressure at the agency, he slickly and gracefully switched over to automatic pilot mode:

'I recall some of my most interesting chats were with Theresa, a consummate professional if ever there was one. It was she who first introduced me to the acronym VETS – Voluntary Extra Tax … Scheme (he almost called it 'Subscriptions', though surely that wouldn't have been a sackable offence!) and I don't think I ever got round to asking why the term wasn't used in training….'

Mr Hudson was not slow on the uptake.

'It was one of our course designers who removed all the acronyms in the first draft of our training materials, saying they either confuse people or cause them to switch off. I agree that initials fine when used as a lazy form of shorthand for people who know what's behind them, but they're no good when introducing people to new ideas. They take away the personal factor, which is what we're all about at the agency.'

It was time again for Mathew to provide a supporting argument:

'That makes complete sense. Acronyms are also an effective way for so-called experts to make themselves sound clever or to shut out people of their private intellectual circle…'

Hudson clearly liked the direction their chat was taking.

'And some initials don't even work as shorthand. My grandfather served in that farcical Falklands war in the nineteen eighties and was amused by how they referred to the Argentine prisoners of war as POWs. Shorter in print, but just as long to say: *P O double Us* or *prisoners of war*!

Hudson, Mathew thought, was enjoying passing the time of day and didn't look like subjecting him to the third degree. Nor did he appear to anticipate any difficult questions. Surely, he wasn't saving up a killer blow for the end of the conversation? Mathew needed to act now before his courage ebbed.

'The other thing I was going to ask you was why, if you select all your recruits using a similar algorithm, are we recruits all so different? I mean, I've got to know all the other three members of my induction group and although we have financial services as a common background, our personalities and attitudes seem quite diverse...'

'You may have to quiz Roger on that, he's the real psychology boffin, but it's important to remember that we're only looking for key common features to determine people's suitability for our agency's work. There are many other personality factors recruits may have which are irrelevant to our cause, as it were. Don't forget, our clients too, even though they share a common generosity and concern for the public good, differ from each other in many other character traits – just not ones that matter to us.'

Finally, Mathew dared to ask a more searching question.

'I fully get all that, though when you say clients share a common generosity, I have witnessed and heard talk of some whose generosity towards the public purse has to be teased out more than others. Are these the ten per cent the algorithm has failed to rule out or are you pushing the boundaries a bit?'

Hudson smiled appreciatively:

'That's actually a very good way of putting it – *pushing out the boundaries*. In truth, it is still very early days for the agency and it certainly made sense to start with the 'soft' cases. Once we'd gained expertise in identifying this group and training our staff to interview them to good effect, it was a natural step to broaden our scope. The huge government deficit isn't sustainable for ever, so we need to stay dynamic and draw in an ever-wider circle of people. I look forward to the day when it will be the norm for all citizens with a public conscience to sign up for VETS.'

Seeing the discussion was going well, Mathew continued:

'I gleaned that side of things from my first trip out with Theresa. One of two entrepreneurial brothers-in-law seemed sold on the idea of being able to advertise the fact the business contributed to VETS. He must have been looking ahead to the future, as I very much doubt many of his customers would have heard of VETS yet, but I sensed he felt it was a cool thing to do in terms of gaining kudos for his business.'

Buoyed by his apparent success in engaging Hudson, Mathew went on to comment on his reservations about the health care promise, simply signalling his concern that this could lead to VETS being perceived as a scheme like any other to tempt people to buy into a privileged care plan unavailable to those on a lower income. Hudson claimed he and many of the senior agency staff were mindful of this potential pitfall and were considering the best way to approach this in terms of 'comms' and even the possibility of abandoning the idea altogether.

Mathew finished his main contribution to the conversation by approving of the draw-down facility for scheme members should their circumstances change. He spent the final few moments as Hudson wound up the interview with a series of good-natured platitudes scouring his memory banks lest he'd missed out anything vital. He remembered just in time to comment on how busy Mr Hudson must be having to interview all the new recruits in such a short space of time. In confirmation he received the response he was fishing for – that all his fellow inductees did in fact have an appointment with Mr Hudson in the course of the morning. Given that Emily's slot was quite late on, he felt it was safe to assume that she would be the last in.

Mathew left Mr Hudson's office greatly relieved to have got the ordeal over with, but as yet unsure as to whether he'd really achieved his goal. Indeed, as the interview progressed, his goal had strangely become less distinct, no doubt thanks to Hudson's disarming manner!

It was only just after a quarter to nine. As Mathew wasn't due to pick up his first case study of the day till nine, he took the opportunity to make his way to the canteen area to gather his thoughts. Even before getting there, he had managed to convince himself that the interview had been broadly successful and almost certainly served to reinforce his good standing with the agency. He would now use the spare ten minutes or so to message Emily with what he'd ascertained and his feelings about the experience.

Although they had discussed their combined approach in some detail, he felt it safer to remind her to ask a few questions of her own and share her individual thoughts and experiences with Mr Hudson. It would be foolish at this stage to set alarm bells ringing by presenting too obvious a double act. For one fleeting moment during the interview, Mathew had felt himself slightly flush as Emily came into his mind while he was talking about other members of his induction group. This was accompanied by the thought: *What if he guesses now or already knows we're becoming close?* He was pretty confident now that Hudson wasn't aware of this, but Emily may provide him with a second chance to pick up on this vibe…

Having sent Emily a concise message just a couple of minutes before his first work assignment, he noticed his mood changing from relief to one of deflation. He put this down to a natural hormonal process as his adrenaline level dropped back down towards normal and he was soon on an even emotional keel again once he'd started poring over the file of his first client of the day.

What Mathew really needed now was the reassurance

of an unremarkable model agency client ready to leap unquestioningly into VETS. By the time he had finished making notes, however, he felt uneasy despite the fact that the potential client's file contained nothing to suggest anything untoward. He now had a further quarter of an hour or so in which to ruminate on his renewed negative feeling which now felt more like disappointment and undeniably related back to this morning's interview.

Then the truth suddenly dawned that his earlier sense of deflation had actually been well founded. His completely unexceptional conversation with Mr Hudson had subtly disappointed the sleuth within him which had always been there lurking under the surface, eager to latch onto any hint that his worst suspicions about the agency were justified. Some of his disappointment, however, may be explained by his own lack of sufficient daring to prod Hudson a little harder.

With this awareness, Mathew hoped he could transfer his need for excitement and intrigue onto Emily's imminent interview. Perhaps he should encourage her to ask a searching question or make some provocative comments, then he could sit back and await her account of the fallout. But that would be selfish on his part, as then she, not he would have to face the consequences. In any case, Emily may well do just that without any urging from him.

But it was Mathew's first case of the day that provided him with a perfectly legitimate question he would have asked himself had it come his way before the Hudson interview.

The young woman concerned seemed at first sight an exemplary candidate for VETS. Her file indicated that she was a budding professional in her late twenties. She was a qualified History teacher with six years' classroom experience behind her at the same secondary school where she had become second in a small department. Her salary was more than ample for a young lady still living with her parents and so her disposable income was a legitimate target for the agency.

On meeting Joanna, however, Mathew was assailed by severe misgivings. The most obvious cause for concern was that she had heard about VETS from a colleague who was an existing contributor. She looked very intelligent and somewhat older than her years – more like thirty-five than twenty-eight – and somehow seemed vulnerable. She projected a confident and austere persona which enabled Mathew to visualise her managing perfectly well a classroom filled with less-than-angelic teenagers. And yet there was something about her which troubled him.

Joanna deftly outlined her eligibility to be a voluntary tax donor and made an impassioned speech explaining why she felt she needed to give extra financial support to the State education budget: The more intellectually demanding subjects such as her own, History, had lost too much ground in the curriculum in recent years and she feared a dumbing down of educational standards. Mathew jumped in to explain that her VETS donations, while they could be directed towards the education budget, were unlikely to be used for the specific purpose she had in mind.

Once he had challenged Joanna on this premise, it became easier to summon the courage to play an even greater Devil's Advocate role and virtually try to talk her out of the scheme. As he was unfettered by an experienced agency colleague breathing down his neck, why not use this opportunity to find his own voice and act with impeccable integrity?

He launched his offensive, making the following points: she was comfortably off now, as she was still living at home, but wasn't she saving for a deposit on a house of her own? Was her job secure, given what she had said about subjects likes hers being squeezed within the curriculum? May she have been unduly influenced by her colleague who may be in a stronger financial position?

What he actually found himself thinking was: *Shouldn't you be thinking about getting married and needing to maintain your own financial independence? Do you think there's much of a future for teaching History in schools and may it not go the same way as religious studies and be phased out of the curriculum altogether? Perhaps your unconscious motivation for applying to join VETS is to compete with your colleague.*

Mathew had prefaced his questions and comments to Joanna by expressing his appreciation of her generous intent and that he only wished to make her aware of any pitfalls which she may not have considered. Nevertheless, he sensed by the end of his pseudo assault that he had no doubt crossed one or two boundaries and apologised in case he'd come across as abrupt. Joanna did indeed look rather taken aback and crestfallen, so he relented further by pointing out that even if she went ahead with VETS, she would not be obliged to continue if her circumstances or outlook changed.

Joanna recovered her composure, said she appreciated Mathew's honesty which had only served to strengthen her resolve to be a 'member of VETS', as she put it. She would join at the entry level of contributions with a view to increasing them over time.

Mathew felt vindicated by the outcome of the interview and was by now wishing that an agency colleague had been present to observe the scene and praise him for his prowess. Nevertheless, he wondered if all agency workers would have been so attentive to the client's interests as he had been.

During the break, he took a few moments to message Emily with his new inspiration for a question to Hudson. *Emily, just had interview with young lady who may have volunteered for the wrong reasons. It turned out OK, but got me thinking. Ask Hudson if agency has a policy on warding off individuals who may be delusional or suffer from psychological condition which makes them vulnerable, over suggestive and not competent to decide on joining VETS. Are agents – are we – trained to look out for this and respond accordingly?*

Then, with his mind at rest, Mathew headed for another interview room where his was due to meet Gemma for his second interview of the day. He refrained from mentioning to her his morning chat with Hudson or his handling of Joanna, sensing that it would be wiser to allow himself incubation or assimilation time in case he inadvertently came out with any remarks he might later regret.

The session with another archetypal elderly couple proved unsurprisingly straightforward and Mathew was free to head off towards the canteen just after noon for a welcome lunch and catch-up with Emily.

On his way, he checked his messages and found Emily had sent him one just ten minutes ago to say that she was about to attend her appointment. On this basis, Mathew calculated that assuming the interview lasted roughly as long as his own, he might catch her coming out just before the end of his lunch break. It was no good messaging her now, as she would probably already be in with Hudson and he feared she might be distracted at a critical moment even by receiving the faint vibration announcing a missed message or call. Better to be patient and choose a moment when she was less likely to be tied up.

As had so often happened over the past two weeks, Mathew was almost alone in the canteen with the lunch break not having officially started yet. No doubt owing to this morning's extra excitement, he had little appetite and felt no particular desire for company other than Emily's. He decided, therefore, to pick up a sandwich and take a stroll through the agency building corridors.

The downside to the job so far was that it was predominantly sedentary. His day was spent sitting first thing poring over client files, sitting at interviews and then sitting again at lunch with the same routine repeating in the afternoon. The only variety so far had been his one day out which had merely entailed sitting in

Theresa's car and then sitting again at the health food shop! He certainly wasn't getting anywhere near the recommended ten thousand daily steps required for good cardio-vascular health. This was an ideal excuse to pace up and down the agency corridors and add a few hundred more steps to his daily output.

Mathew set himself the task of returning to reception and from there walking the full length of the building down the North corridor, then coming back towards reception via the central corridor and finally going up and down the left-hand corridor, which Emily had referred to as the South corridor. As he set off, he took care to walk moderately slowly and listen and look out for absolutely anything of interest on either side rather than stare straight ahead towards the corridor's end.

Mathew found it immensely difficult to be observant while walking, as he had become hard wired to consider walking simply as a means of getting from one place to another. Every fifty paces or so, he realised he had been accelerating and had to stop in order to start off again more slowly. By the end of the first corridor, he had at last conditioned himself to pay more attention to his surroundings.

Coming back down the central corridor towards reception, he instinctively slowed down just before reaching the point where Emily had followed Peter and the two men whom they had since dubbed the *gangsters*. He remembered to look out for the side passage just before reception which led to a discreet exit point. Who knows – perhaps some even more colourful and sinister characters had congregated there ready to slip out of sight following a secretive briefing by an agency on 'special operations', Mathew mused.

However, twenty yards or so before this point, Mathew faintly heard some masculine voices to his right which increased in volume as the door of one of the offices slowly opened. As a reflex action, he withdrew towards the doorway of the office ahead of the one the voices were coming from. As he lent lightly on the door, it gave way into the office. He followed the door going inside leaving it slightly ajar. A quick look around confirmed he was alone and he began to listen intently to what was evidently two individuals who had just emerged into the corridor and were chatting quietly, though clearly not aware they were being overheard.

The sleuth in Mathew relished the excitement of listening in to what was probably going to be the first earnest conversation he'd actually heard between two experienced agency colleagues. To date, the only real talking he'd properly heard or taken part in was between one established agency worker and one or more newbies and between two or more new recruits. Whatever these two were discussing, he would surely gain a further insight into the agency's inner workings. But what ensued proved to be another cautionary lesson in not jumping to hasty conclusions.

'Thanks again Simon for your reassuring feedback on category B clients. Clearly, the agency has developed its capacity to assimilate these into the main programme. I always said it would just be a matter of time once we got well established with the As.'

The second voice came in, slightly less confidently:

'I hope I've not given the impression we resent having to deal with category Cs or Ds getting into the system. It's just unnerving sometimes when people produce significantly lower scores here than in the initial algorithm. We have a few skilful staff who handle the Cs well once they've been alerted to the lower scores and have had a little time to adjust their interview techniques, but...'

The other man helped him out:

'I know it's damned difficult to distinguish here between the Cs and Ds, but it seems pretty clear that once you get them through the door or, in some cases through *their* door, you can gather enough basic data to pass on to us so we can take over.'

With that, the two men began to make their way towards the corridor and Mathew couldn't make out what, if anything, they were saying. He made sure he gave them enough time to move away to a distance well beyond earshot before exiting the office, carefully closing the door and following them tentatively towards reception. He was keen to avoid provoking the slightest suspicion that he may have heard what they were saying just in case either of them turned round and saw him trailing along behind.

There was still ten minutes or so to the end of his lunch break, so Mathew decided to nonchalantly walk through the reception area and step outside, ostensibly to catch a breath of fresh air. This might enable him to pick up a few more clues as to what had been going on between the two men just now, assuming that the apparent visitor would still be there taking a few moments to sign out. He was not mistaken in either respect.

Both men were in reception and as Mathew passed them, deliberately looking straight ahead as he went for the door, he overheard the more diffident man thanking the other – a Mr Jenkins – for his visit and wishing him a safe journey home. This confirmed the different status between the two. Mr Jenkins had called the other by his first name just moments ago and had plainly been on an official, possibly even an inspection visit.

It wasn't hard to guess roughly what the categories under discussion referred to. *A* was clearly the so-named 'soft' clients, *B* – the ones Mr Hudson and others had owned up to as those requiring a 'nudge'. He could only assume that *C*s and *D*s were far from the standard fare of the agency and evidently represented something of a grey area, with the *D*s possibly verging on black. Mathew's impulse was to try to summarise this in a quick message to Emily, but he quickly thought better of it and reassessed. She may still be finishing off her session with Mr Hudson and, in any case, they were due to meet up after work where they would be able to exchange notes uninhibitedly at his house or, if neither could wait – during the short car journey.

Mathew had two clients to see in the afternoon. The first was a straightforward interview on his own with a middle-aged lady who had already committed to VETS and just wanted to go through the finer details. The second required a little more preparation and involved teamwork with Theresa, but didn't throw up any particular challenges or surprises. He was free to sign off shortly after four o'clock and, as Emily had already messaged to say she would be ready around half an hour later, he went back to the canteen rather than risk drawing attention to himself by hanging around in the reception area.

There was hardly anyone around with it being a little while before the official end of the working day and no doubt most other agency workers who had finished their casework early would have made the more natural choice of setting off home. Mathew allowed himself to slip into a contemplative mood and in so doing noticed a subtle change in his attitude as compared with even a week ago. Greater familiarity with the agency's environment, routines and ways of working was beginning to breed in him a sense of ownership, though if challenged, he would be hard put to define quite who was the owner and who the owned.

Rather enjoying his momentary sense of belonging, Mathew scanned the canteen area for anyone to engage in a chat unlike just a few hours ago when socialising was the last thing on his mind. As the only two other people there were sitting too far away and looked engrossed in their own inner worlds, he defaulted to pulling out his copy of *Working Towards an Integrated Society* again and waited for Emily to show up. The next chapter dealt with pay differentials, but before he had even read the introductory paragraph, Emily messaged that she was due to finish earlier than expected and would be on her way to meet him directly in the staff carpark in about ten minutes' time.

Mathew decided to set off right away even though the car park was only a few hundred metres away, as he was a little nervous about finding his car. He had been so preoccupied and distracted on his morning drive into work that he had not made a conscious note of where he had left it.

Similar situations had caused him anxiety in the past. The worst occasion must have been in a multi-storey car park at Manchester airport soon after he'd got his driving licence. He could remember neither which level he had parked on nor even roughly whereabouts on whichever level it was. No doubt this was because, as an inexperienced driver, all his attention had been on driving safely and getting his passengers to check-in on time.

On entering the staff car park he felt rather foolish: It would have been almost impossible to 'lose' his car there in such a small area, but he told himself it was better to feel a little foolish in private than be painfully embarrassed in front of Emily had she got to his car first! The spare five minutes proved most useful, however, as Mathew suddenly remembered that he'd forgotten to tidy the inside of his car in Emily's honour.

He spent the time frantically opening all the doors, plucking out the items which lay strewn over the seats and on the floor, from windscreen scrapers and de-icer sprays to a spare coat and jumper. These he deposited in the boot, then quickly brushed down the passenger seat by hand, pulled out the mat, hastily shaking out the grit and other unwanted contents before replacing it. Finally, just seconds before Emily arrived, he slammed all the doors shut again. As she approached, Mathew discreetly wiped his dirty hand on the inside of his jacket before greeting her and chivalrously reopening the front passenger door for her.

As she got in and they drove off, Mathew meant to speak first, but found himself tongue tied and it was Emily who soon broke the silence.

'I'm bursting to tell you how I got on,' she began in an ambiguous tone, 'but if I tried to blurt it all out now in one go, I wouldn't do it justice and would risk distracting you from your driving and get us both killed.'

Mathew was both amused and puzzled by Emily's eccentric and enigmatic way of dealing with the issue and, taking his cue from her, agreed they'd both wait until they got to his before sharing their testimonies. They talked instead about their casework, coming to the conclusion that on that point at least, there was nothing worthy of discussion and before they had exhausted their next topic – the dull autumnal weather – they were already at Mathew's house.

Unlike his car, Mathew had given some thought to making the interior of his home presentable for Emily and his downstairs rooms had at least benefited from a thorough monthly vacuuming. It was only just after half four and so too early for tea. Nevertheless, he thought it best to leave his guest in his tidied sitting room while he rushed off into the kitchen to put on the kettle and cover a plate with a variety of biscuits. These he tactically served up in the sitting room before going back into the kitchen just as the kettle boiled. This toing and froing served to minimise the time Emily was left alone and avoid encumbering himself with too much to carry at once.

He had to make two trips for the tea, as he was not quite able to squeeze everything onto his solitary serving tray in one go. He managed the tea pot, cups and saucers in the first shift, but his sugar bowl and tiny milk jug and teaspoons had to wait until the second trip.

Meanwhile, Emily had picked up his coffee table book on impressionist art, unsurprisingly, perhaps, preferring this to his other two – one on 18th century naval warfare, the other on Napoleonic military uniforms. Mathew had considered removing these two books before setting off for work, but on second thoughts decided to leave them there, as if Emily did choose to comment on them, it would provide him with an easy lead into discussing his wargaming hobby. If their relationship blossomed, he wouldn't be able to conceal it from her indefinitely.

'I must confess, when we came in, I almost handed you the remote, but then remembered that you've banished the TV from your living room!' Mathew joked as he sat down on the sofa with Emily. He continued, 'I hope the choice of biscuits doesn't disappoint. I was wary of offering anything too enticing and filling so as not to spoil our tea later on, though I'm easy about what time we eat. Do you have any preference or set routine for eating in the evening?'

'Well, provided I don't eat too many of your biscuits, I'm sure in a couple of hours would be fine, though it might depend on how lavish a meal you're cooking up for me...' Emily teased.

'Hopefully, we won't need all of the two hours to exchange notes on today's intelligence, but whether we'll still have much of an appetite afterwards remains to be seen...'.

'OK, then, let's get cracking. Shall we draw lots or is it lady guests go first? I feel it's only fair to warn you....' she paused for effect, 'that I don't have anything earth shattering to announce and wouldn't want to be the one to produce an anti-climax!'

'In that case,' Mathew saw his opportunity to sound decisive and delightfully enigmatic, 'I suggest you go first. As you rightly pointed out, you *are* the lady guest and I *do* have something potentially earth shattering to tell!'

Emily gave her by now familiar understated reaction:

'I'll be brief then so we don't use up our whole first hour before dinner beating about the bush. Actually, I did discover a couple of new interesting facts chatting to Mr Hudson which you may read more into than I did first hand.'

The format of Emily's interview appeared very similar to

Mathew's, though he got the impression that it may have been slightly shorter. This may have been because Mr Hudson was tiring towards the end of the morning or just that he had been less interested in talking to Emily as a female, being, as she suggested, something of a chauvinist.

However, the first interesting fact she unearthed through direct questioning and thanks to Mathew's texted prompt was that the agency assumed that all potential donors coming through the algorithm and preliminary interviews were of sound mind and deemed capable of making unclouded judgements regarding their own financial affairs and interests. Predictably, Hudson stressed that the algorithm's embedded deep psychology would weed out people who were emotionally unstable.

The second revelation was that the agency deliberately teamed up male and females at the mentor stage, as this had been proven to be the best combination in a number of studies. Strong evidence to support this had originally emanated from experimental societies during the last century such as the Soviet Union where boys and girls were typically paired up for mutual social and educational support in classrooms.

Obviously, this gender pairing wasn't possible for the training. When asked for her honest opinions, Emily had commented that the first two inductors had been male, whereas the main trainers had been female. She had, therefore, charged the agency with being unconsciously sexist with men at a senior level and women lower down the pyramid of authority.

Hudson, and this is why she labelled him as chauvinist, claimed that men demonstrably cut better figures in the highest positions, as they inspire greater trust with the population at large, whereas women fulfil a more nurturing role which is compromised if they occupy the most senior roles. In response, Emily had actually directly accused Hudson of old-fashioned sexism to which he smiled condescendingly and said that, given the agency's egalitarian pay policy, notions of seniority had very little relevance. Emily was tempted to push her argument further, but judged it wiser to adopt a more conciliatory approach in the closing stage of the interview.

At the outset, Emily had stressed to Hudson how positive she felt about her experience of the agency in general, thereby earning the right to ask the odd awkward question or make a challenging point later on. By the end of the process, she felt more or less vindicated in her approach.

Mathew congratulated Emily on her brave attempt to dig a little deeper into the inner workings of the agency. Now it was his turn.

Emily listened intently as Mathew shared his own experience - from his innocuous interview with Mr Hudson to his intriguing and, to her mind, amusing eavesdropping episode. He slightly spoiled the impact of his final revelation by dwelling pointlessly on the way he agonised over how much, if anything, to reveal to Emily when messaging her from the canteen. However, despite his poor delivery, there was no doubt between them as to who had won the contest to haul in the biggest intelligence catch of the day. Emily may have won in the interview stakes, but Mathew had eclipsed her in the sleuthing league.

'But what were the chances of your happening on such a revealing conversation? You could have been in any one of a hundred different places on any of the three corridors. It's almost enough to make one believe in fate or divine intervention.'

'Unless there were a dozen such chats going on all over the place because it was an annual inspection or 'open doors' day or something.' Mathew had intended this as a joke, but on reflection, a posse of inspectors periodically descending on the agency was at least plausible. He recalled that as a child at primary school one such inspection struck terror into the hearts of his teachers and disrupted normal education and lessons for him and his classmates for several weeks. Thankfully, such intrusive government raids had ceased by the time he reached secondary school.

'What we should do,' suggested Emily, 'is draw on what we know for sure and what we can infer from what you overheard. I'm sure we can broadly define the four categories of people the agency seems to be dealing with.'

'Yes, and while I still remember who said what to whom, we might try to assess what the agency's role is in processing the different groups and whether what it's doing or the way it's doing it is ethically above board or not.'

'I suspect in order to carry out a meaningful ethical health check, we'll need to get in to see Roger who, according to Hudson, is likely to be much more au fait with that side of things.'

Mathew could not disagree with Emily on that point. Without further ado, he took a sheet of A4 paper and the two of them produced a table as follows:

Category A – model clients – wealthy and generous, require little or no encouragement to join VETS.

Category B – need a gentle nudge and/or incentive. May respond to kudos or other psychological appeal of VETS.

Category C – may be dishonest, looking for a cover for dodging basic taxes, personal or business rates, etc. though their actual line of work is not dishonest or at least not illegal (they may be working more for profit than altruistic purposes). In some cases, may be easier for agency to turn blind eye and gratefully receive 'extra' tax contributions. In others, better to refer to HMRC for tax evasion prosecution.

Category D – Strongly suspected of or definite perpetrators of criminal activity. May be expedient to let them think they have hoodwinked agency into believing they are straight and letting them contribute while tipping the wink to the police, fraud squad who will determine whether to pursue criminal prosecution.

Once they'd agreed on a final draft of the four surmised categories, the next step was to consider how or whether to take their investigation further. Emily was the first to address this:

'I don't know about you, but I've found all the anticipation through the weekend and today's interview itself quite stressful and wonder having got this far, if I'm really up for pursuing this further right away. Perhaps we should take a break?'

Mathew was keen to strike while the iron was hot, but, as tea was in the programme in any case, he didn't mind bringing it forward a little this evening in the hope that Emily would then feel sufficiently restored to resume the all-important strategic discussion.

The vegan meal he'd prepared the evening before needed heating up for fifteen minutes, so he quickly nipped in and out of the kitchen to turn on the oven and came back with a bottle of chilled grape juice as an aperitif. In order to avoid any further allusion to work-related issues, he asked Emily whether she had any hobbies or pastimes.

'That's an interesting question.' Emily replied. 'Not the question itself, but the way you phrased it, as though there is a real distinction between hobbies and pastimes. I suppose all hobbies are pastimes, but not all pastimes are hobbies. I think that's an example of a syllogism!'

'Sorry, Emily, I didn't mean to overcomplicate the question, but I see what you mean. I read somewhere that both these words have been steadily dropping out of use in recent decades and young people today often don't recognise the noun *pastime*, originally from the French *passe-temps*. They only understand if the verb is used in a phrase like: *How do you pass the time?* But nowadays, nearly everyone says *spend the time* and time itself rarely *passes*, but *goes* for most people.'

Emily assumed a thoughtful air, 'But it can still *fly*, of course, especially when defining a simple question like: 'What do you do in your spare, free or leisure time?'

Mathew was touched by her good-humoured way of guiding him out of the pedantic mode he had been slipping into and waited for her to answer his question which she had so nimbly re-phrased.

'OK then, so rather than just laboriously tell you how I spend my time outside working hours besides what you've already learned from when you were at mine last time...'

'Like not watching TV and reading historical novels.' Mathew interjected, proud to have remembered another golden rule: *Demonstrating that you've listened to what she has said is another key way of impressing a lady!*

'Yes, I wonder if I could say that reading is my pastime and that learning about social history is my hobby? I mean not an academic interest, but a genuine passion for reading contemporary first-hand accounts from people who lived in different times and came from different walks of life.'

Mathew saw his opportunity and seized upon the historical link to his own hobby:

'So, we do have the history connection in common then, as my passion is wargaming, particularly (he lied: exclusively) the Napoleonic era. I've painted hundreds of miniature plastic figures from the period and spend hours playing with them in my hobby room upstairs.'

He stopped to catch his breath and take stock of any fallout from this sudden release of dubious information about himself, but there were no outward signs of shock or disdain on Emily's face. Quite the reverse, in fact. As her expression transitioned from neutral to intrigued, she made a request Mathew could have hoped for only in his most bizarre dreams.

'I don't suppose you've got one set up at the moment, have you?

If so, I'd love to see it.'

'As a matter of a fact, I am in the middle of a pretty large-scale battle. After dinner, I'll take you upstairs to the hobby room and show you it, if you're still interested.' He was glad he'd not omitted reference to his hobby room.

'Absolutely, I'd be bitterly disappointed if you didn't and I can't think of anything more likely to take our minds off agency business than a historic battle. I've read a few famous journals of soldiers who took part in the 1812 invasion of Moscow and Battle of Waterloo. I've got quite a photographic eye for uniforms too so I'll be able to check how accurate your painting scheme is.' Emily's tone gave away she was teasing him regarding his painting scheme, but she was nevertheless clearly intrigued by his hobby.

However, dinner was now ready and the Napoleonic interlude would have to wait a little while.

Mathew produced his vegan pasta bake with a sense of pride and satisfaction at its simplicity and yet guaranteed success. It was also remarkably easy to serve up, required the minimum of crockery and cutlery and was heartily consumed by the two of them within fifteen minutes over a relaxed conversation about nutritional preferences. The ice cream desert was even more straightforward and gave them just enough time to exhaust the nutrition topic before coffee. In his eagerness to engage in battle, Mathew suggested they take this upstairs to his hobby room.

Emily, who had been looking forward to languishing a few more minutes after the meal, put forward the more sensible option of withdrawing with the dirty dishes to the kitchen first, washing up and then finishing their coffee there – a better plan than spilling it all over the stairs.

Finally, hands completely free, they marched up to Mathew's hobby room. As he opened the door and Emily looked inside, she couldn't resist teasing him:

'Of course, if we *had* brought up what we hadn't managed to spill of our coffees on the stairs, now we could put our cups down on this splendid wargaming table and cause havoc among the ranks! Although, if, as you say, the battle has been raging for two weeks, I suppose some of the troops might be ready for a cuppa by now!'

Mathew was too absorbed in admiring Emily's wit to even consider being hurt by her bout of sarcasm. In any case, immediately thereafter she changed her tune, congratulated him on the fantastic military display, demonstrated a little knowledge of the period and, far from challenging him on the accuracy of his colour schemes, asked him to explain the rules and the current state of play.

Mathew disciplined himself to provide Emily with as brief an outline as possible, desperate to avoid a repeat of the scenario all those years ago when he had bored his sister close to tears. At least now he had acquired the self-awareness and linguistic sophistication to achieve this goal. He did, however, dwell just a little on the current phase of the game.

'So, we're up to phase fifteen of a maximum of twenty phases with the Russians about to fire on French positions and engage in a mêlée or hand-to-hand combat, as you can see here where the opposing forces are levelled up against each other.'

He inwardly hesitated here. Was this the right moment to confide to Emily about his little mystical experiment of posing as one of the combatants? Or, as she had taken his first gamble of revealing his wargaming hobby so well, would it be foolish to risk spoiling it now with a gamble too far?

Emily had been following his account intently and, as if on cue, when he'd finished his extended exposition of where the game was up to in terms of phase fifteen, she responded in a manner which went beyond his wildest dreams.

'After all the effort you've put into explaining your intricate rules, it would be churlish of me not to ask if you wouldn't mind enacting this crucial phase fifteen here and now so I can test whether I've grasped any of it. How does it work – if I take part, am I meant to come in on one side or the other, or do we just make all the decisions for both sides together?'

Mathew had a spontaneous brain wave. Rather than deciding for himself whether to let Emily in on his gaming secret, he would play out this phase with her and let the outcome itself determine whether or not the full extent of his pseudo insanity would be revealed.

'I don't think it would be fair to make you compete as a total novice, so I'll take all the decisions and move the pieces, explaining the whys and wherefores as I go along. I'll assign you the duty of removing any casualties from the battlefield, otherwise known as gaming table, and you can also place them back in their rightful boxes.'

'That's rather like when my uncle used to do DIY jobs for us and allowed me to help him by passing the tools or handing him the nails and screws.'

'Not quite,' continued Mathew, 'there is a bit more to it than that. Before returning the bodies to their boxes, you need to check under their stands for any special messages. One carries a very special marking! I'll also let you roll the dice for the side of your choice, and if you prove competent at that, I may give you a casting vote on any agonising decisions I have to make.'

'I can conceive of no greater honour! Why are we waiting? Let's get started!'

All that remained was for Emily to choose which side she wanted to be on for the purposes of rolling the dice and removing the casualties. The defending Russians always started each phase and so she took the possibly wise decision to assign this side to Mathew to enable her to observe the order of play. It struck her as terribly unfair for all the defending units to make the first move and fire the first shots in every part of the battle field, beginning with the artillery, then the infantry, ending with the cavalry. Mathew tried to justify this esoteric aspect of the game, but with limited success.

As the phase began, Mathew became engrossed in one meticulous process after another: assessing range, calculating hit probabilities, a series of dice throws followed by further calculations to determine which soldiers had been hit. Suddenly, he became painfully aware that he risked in Emily's case a reenactment not only of the battle of Borodino, but also of the scene many years ago where his sister had reached the limit of her patience, abandoned her role as general and stormed out of his bedroom.

He began periodically to look up somewhat nervously at Emily to assess her engagement levels. So far so good, it seemed, and he was relieved once the casualties started mounting and she was able to assume her role as chief mortician. He noticed her excitedly checking the base of each fallen soldier and the slight flicker of disappointment across her face as she failed to find any markings.

The Russian phase was over at last. It had taken nearly half an hour and cost over twenty French lives from artillery and musket fire. Now, after troop movements had been determined, Emily would increase her involvement by rolling the dice for each time a group of French units fired. Depending on the probability calculations, different dice were used for each operation: four-sided, eight-sided, twelve-sided, twenty-sided and even percentage dice, as well as conventional six-sided dice.

This aspect of the game enthralled Emily. She confided to Mathew that she had a particular interest in probability as a branch of Mathematics. After all, skill and understanding in this area had served her well in her previous incarnation as a mortgage broker. For example, it had enabled her to almost instantaneously spot impossible figures produced by her computer owing to data input errors, usually committed by her colleagues rather than herself, of course.

The French firing phase lasted barely ten minutes, as most units had been advancing towards the Russians at a pace which didn't lend itself to accurate volley fire. However, artillery shot and howitzer fire had brought down about a dozen Russian infantry and cavalry. Emily began checking the bases of these figures too as she removed them, but Mathew, feeling it to be unduly cruel to send her down a blind alley, admitted that none of the Russian figures were marked. Noting another glimmer of disappointment flicker across her increasingly attractive face at his latest attempt to manage her expectations, he found himself on the verge of making a full confession.

But Emily helped him out again:

'Mathew, you look as though you're either bursting to tell me something or desperately trying to hold in a … May I guess it's something to do with what's marked on any of these soldiers' bases?'

Mathew was left with no choice now that Emily had directly challenged him. He only wished he'd planned on telling her at some point anyway and had prepared his mini speech. But then he recalled the lesson he had learnt of late that more often than not it was his spontaneous responses that yielded the best results.

'OK then, I'll put you out of your misery. You've earned the right to know by stealthily observing my behaviour and accurately interpreting it. I've marked the base of one of the French soldiers with an M for me, or Mathew, if you like, so I can pretend I'm actually taking part in the battle. I just thought it would be a laugh and add a little more spice and excitement – waiting to see if I got killed or not! I hope you don't think I'm terminally stupid and childish and unworthy of being your fellow ingenious sleuth at the agency….'

Emily gently replaced the dice she had been handling in their correct place on the table and nimbly walked over to where Mathew was standing. She embraced him tightly and, gazing squarely into his eyes, declaimed:

'Stupid, certainly not! No stupid person could devise such complex and intriguing wargaming rules. And childish only in a good way - that you've kept your inner child alive. You said I'd earned the right to be let in on your secret, well I'll let you in on one of mine to level the playing field – a rather eccentric hobby of mine. But only after...'

With that, she kissed him squarely on the forehead.

CHAPTER 15.
THE ENDGAME APPROACHES

Mathew awoke as usual in good time for work – this time a mere three minutes before his alarm was due to go off.

The excitement of yesterday would normally have sent his mind racing and made normal sleep nigh impossible, but he could only assume that the myriad impressions he had taken in had tired him out both physically and mentally. On top of that had to be considered the unusual multiple pressures of a stressful work interview, an impromptu eavesdropping session, a pseudo romantic dinner followed by an intense and potentially fatal wargaming stint with the new woman in his life. At least his alter ego on the wargaming table had survived to fight yet another day, hence its fate had so far coincided with his own in the real world of agency intrigue.

Emily's affectionate kiss on the forehead had undoubtedly been the culminating point of Mathew's evening. In fact, when he was driving her back home, he was so lovestruck that Emily's promise to reveal her own eccentric hobby completely slipped his mind. They used the remaining time they had together that evening outlining their strategy for the next couple of days at work.

Tuesday, now today, they would lie relatively low in order to give themselves longer to assimilate what they had learnt so far, reduce the risk of arousing too much suspicion and plan a more specific course of action. In the late afternoon, Mathew would book an appointment to see Roger alone on Wednesday or as soon as he was available. Emily would keep out of it as far as possible so that if things went badly and Mathew was forced to leave the agency, she would still have the option of staying on if only to continue her own investigation.

They had agreed to delay a full-blown romance until the agency business was resolved, but the possibility of cohabiting to reduce their living expenses had occurred to them should the worst come to the worst and Mathew lost or had to give up his job. It was conceivable too, of course, that Emily could be dragged down as Mathew's accomplice if the agency did indeed conduct its own clandestine surveillance operations. Or she may simply feel impelled if not compelled to resign if the agency's work practices fell below a certain ethical standard.

Following a relaxing bus journey, Mathew arrived at work several minutes before his official start time, as usual, and looking forward to his morning's casework. At reception, he was given the relevant folder and told which office to go to, but for some reason, he wasn't briefed as to whether he would be working solo or accompanied. Even before he began to scan through the documents, he knew he would prefer to be operating alone on this occasion. Until he had been in to see Roger and cleared the air one way or another, he wouldn't feel entirely at ease with another agency worker observing his every move.

The case before him was straightforward in certain respects, but the background to it was particularly interesting. The gentleman he was about to interview had written a lengthy and moderately literate statement of about one thousand words in which he outlined his criminal past during which he had dishonestly accumulated a substantial fortune through fraud. After being caught, tried and convicted of several offences, he served three years of a six-year prison sentence. Before his release, he had declared himself a reformed character and committed to handing over the majority of his ill-gotten wealth to the State.

A number of questions arose in Mathew's mind. Had his early release been dependent on convincing the authorities he had reformed? If so, shouldn't his offer to donate the money in the form of VETS be regarded more as a response to bribery than as a strictly voluntary act? Shouldn't the State in any case have recovered the 'proceeds' of his crimes, as they were legally termed? Mathew couldn't find any allusion to this in any of the documentation and felt conflicted as to whether or not he should bring this up during the interview. He would have to play the situation by ear.

Mr Walter Saunders, as he was called, in fact proved to be extremely obliging and eloquent in filling Mathew's information gap. He at once explained that thanks to good conduct, he was due to be released once half his sentence had been served and that his decision to return most of his stolen wealth had been totally unsolicited. True, restorative justice had been mentioned to him by a visiting magistrate just a week before his discharge, but he had been introduced to the concept long ago. There had been no strings attached to his release apart from six months' probation. Making financial amends was not put to him as an option for paying back his debt to society to reflect his change of heart probably because all concerned believed him to be penniless apart from the universal income he would receive in due course.

A decision had been taken not to pursue Walter's proceeds from crime, as these amounted to only tens of thousands of pounds and didn't justify the costs likely to be incurred. Walter also explained that he had initially undertaken to return only about three quarters of the defrauded money, as he would need the rest for financial security – rent and living expenses – until he got properly back on his feet and found employment. Then he would pay back the rest.

Mathew made a snap almost involuntary decision to follow this case through to what he saw as its logical conclusion.

'It's very laudable, I'm sure, to want to make amends to society for the crimes you committed in your past life. Do you mind my asking what kind of fraud you committed? I mean, there are so many different types and defrauding elderly people out of their life savings is generally regarded as more morally reprehensible than, say, tax evasion where no particular individuals are targeted.'

'To be honest, I did used to be what people call a conman. I used various ruses to cheat people out of small or larger amounts of money, but never their life savings!'

'So that means when you were caught, some of these people who came forward and could demonstrate that you'd conned them could have claimed under the State compensation scheme. But many others who couldn't prove you were the culprit or who were too afraid to come forward would have lost out for good.'

'Well, that's true, I guess, but I had no control over that.'

Mathew continued to press his case home:

'Then, of course, if you were looking to put a figure on how much your crime actually cost society, you'd have to factor in the cost of the police investigation, which is exceptionally high for fraud, the trial and the huge cost of keeping you in prison for three years. Did you manage to calculate all that and include it in the amount you say you wish to donate to VETS?'

Walter's face had by now fallen and he was struggling to maintain his composure.

'To be honest, I'd not really tried to work out all the cost to society and the taxpayer, I was just trying to be realistic in offering to pay back what I could. As I said before, as soon as I get fixed up with a job, I'll try to pay off what I can on top of the ten thousand or so I'm able to fork out right away.'

Mathew was taken aback by the relatively small amount Walter was envisaging which wasn't indicated in the briefing notes, and was sorely tempted to reveal the quick calculation he'd made using his mental arithmetic skills and general knowledge: three years at approximately £1000 per week = £150,000. However, as he observed the increasingly crestfallen reformed criminal before him, he relented as his anger gave way to pity. He smiled, tapped Walter on the upper arm in an attempt to reassure him, saying no one could expect him to pay back everything to society in financial terms; besides, there were other ways of making amends such as community work and just being a good citizen.

The subdued man spent the last few minutes of the interview time laboriously, but eagerly completing relevant agency forms. As he moved his head gently from side to side, the tip of his tongue protruding slightly from the left corner of his mouth, Walter reminded Mathew of not-so-bright fellow pupils in his primary school classes. His pity grew steadily into a more profound emotion of compassion along with a sense of self-reproach.

As Walter proudly handed him the completed papers for proofreading, Mathew thanked him warmly and apologised for the harsh line of questioning he had subjected the poor man to just moments before.

Upon further self-examination, Mathew concluded that his initial aggressive stance towards Walter may have been a reflection of the stress he was undergoing and would continue to undergo so long as the 'showdown' with Roger lay ahead. It had been unfair to vent his frustration on Walter and he was left with a residual twinge of guilt despite his efforts to make amends immediately afterwards.

It was too early for lunch so he spent the rest of the morning preparing for his next interview and reflecting on how he would be expected to step up his caseload in due course as he became more experienced, though even with three or four interviews a day it seemed a relatively cushy number compared to other jobs he'd had. That was all assuming, of course, that he would be sticking around.

He headed for the canteen at midday, feeling inclined to enjoy a little company. Given the concerns he and Emily had about whether or not or to what extent they were under surveillance, they had agreed to ignore each other just for today and so he was glad to see a few familiar colleagues already standing at the serving hatches or sitting down to an early lunch. He would join one of them.

Only when considering what to have for lunch did he realise that he hardly had any appetite. Was he still suffering from nervous tension? He opted for a salad sandwich and sat down by Jonathan who was also tucking warily into a light lunch. Mathew wondered if Jonathan's temperament would ever allow him to relax at this time of day and sit down to a proper meal and enjoy a lively chat with the more gregarious agency members. At least, he seemed pleased that Mathew had joined him.

'In our fourth week, aren't we? How's it going for you so far?' Mathew opened the conversation conventionally.

'It certainly seems much longer than that, though I've noticed that each week seems to go faster than the last – a common psychological phenomenon by all accounts.'

'Indeed. It happens over the longer term too. My mother warned me when I was about eighteen that time would stream by ever faster from now on and that I needed to get on with my life so I wouldn't end up with huge regrets later on.'

'I think I may have lived long enough to notch up a few regrets already!' said Jonathan plaintively.

Mathew took this rejoinder as a signal that Jonathan was about to launch into a self-pitying lament, but as the follow-up never came, he took the initiative with a brazen attempt to cut to the chase.

'I know we're meant to be on our break, but d'you mind if we talk shop a bit? What's been your toughest case so far then Jonathan?'

Predictably, Jonathan paused for a few moments. His expression suggested he was torn between two or more close contenders, but Mathew suspected this was a weak attempt to display bravado. After all, Jonathan could only have taken part in a handful of interviews since they last talked. On that occasion, if remembered correctly, he'd been too tired or distracted to pump him for intel on his most recent clients. At least this was only a minor regret on Mathew's part in contrast to the life-limiting ones which Jonathan claimed to have 'notched up'.

Jonathan finally revealed his most awkward case so far was where an elderly Asian gentleman wanted to donate towards international aid, a budget which had been cut by successive governments, but which had become an increasingly popular cause among idealistic citizens in recent years. This in itself was not the problem, however, it was that his wife sitting by his side appeared to have only very rudimentary English and Jonathan seriously doubted whether she understood what her husband was signing up to. Early on in the interview, Jonathan had invited the gentleman to explain to her what was being discussed, but this offer was rejected.'

'I had a strong conviction that he ought to be outlining the key points to her, but at the same time I had no right to interfere in their relationship and desperately didn't want to come across as culturally intolerant.'

'Did you take it up with your mentor – Denise isn't it? I mean, did you ask if there's an agency house rule whereby if more than one individual is involved, both or all parties have to show they're fully aware of what they are signing up to?'

For the second time of the day, Mathew felt a degree of remorse for fielding a question which the other man was almost certain to struggle with. But what could he do? He had to use every chance that came his way to gain more intelligence about how the agency functioned.

'I can't say I did in the end, though it did cross my mind to. I suppose I could still check with Denise. Surely, it's worth the Agency's while to enlist an interpreter in cases like that.' Jonathan's reply came just as it occurred to Mathew that he was missing the most obvious opportunity.

'Emily and I had our settling-in interview yesterday with old Hudson. Have you had yours yet?'

Jonathan said he had and that nothing of any consequence came up except he'd made it clear how much he was enjoying his new job – much more than his previous work. This was just the 'wet' response Mathew had expected and couldn't resist:

'That's great, though I suppose that would have been the time to bring up the concerns we just talked about...' but, as usual, he relented: 'Of course, it was a bit of an intimidating situation, not knowing quite what the purpose of the interview was...'

Jonathan gratefully expanded on Mathew's get-out clause:

'It certainly was, though I was confident by the end that .... he didn't have any hidden agenda. He also mentioned that various people had fed back to him that they thought I'd been getting on pretty well.'

'Did he mention anyone else you might want to talk things over with in case you had any specific concerns about your work or the agency?' Mathew knew he was pushing his luck now and may just be flogging a dead horse.

'No, he just said there'd be another catch-up session scheduled in about a month's time.'

'That's interesting, he didn't mention that to me. Mind you, I think I was first in yesterday and perhaps he hadn't warmed up properly. Anyway, I'm glad I had this chat with you so now I'll know what to expect.'

Mathew left his interrogation of Jonathan at that, satisfied that he'd gained at least a little more information, though probably more about Jonathan than about the agency. Was it not a common feature of timid folk like Jonathan that they avoided showing any interest in others for fear of inviting unwelcome questions about themselves?

Mathew made his way to reception towards the end of the lunch break, having decided that putting off booking an appointment with Roger till later was risky, as he couldn't be sure that he'd have a convenient opportunity between his afternoon interviews. In addition, once he had made the appointment, he would be less anxious and better able to concentrate on his work.

One of the regular receptionists half-greeted him by almost looking up as he approached. He tried to ask to see Mr Jameson in a tone which was at once business like, matter of fact and respectful. He had obviously overdone it, as the result came out so fast, quiet and garbled that he had to repeat the whole sequence to make himself understood.

'During my settling-in interview yesterday, Mr Hudson suggested I might want to follow a few things up with Mr Roger Jameson. I wonder if I could make an appointment to see him sometime this week?'

'How long an appointment do you think you'll need, Mr Bryant?'

He'd not given any thought to how long an in-depth discussion with Roger would be likely to last and so floundered for a few moments.

'Well, my interview with Mr Hudson must have taken about half an hour, so, I should imagine that would be about right....'

CHAPTER 15. THE ENDGAME APPROACHES

He hoped he wasn't sounding too casual or disrespectful, as he had absolutely no idea what view the receptionist had of his status vis a vis that of Roger. Had the agency's avowed principle of equality filtered through to her? Might it be that certain staff members, such as those employed at reception, were excluded from the egalitarian circle?

'OK, I'll just see if I can catch him in his office if you don't mind waiting a minute.'

Mathew nodded assent, as he could see that she had already entered Roger's number on her phone and was awaiting an answer which came with lightning speed.

She smiled and began nodding as Roger spoke.

'He says that's fine and asks if you can outline what you'd like to see him about unless it's something private.'

'Oh no, of course, …. Just tell him I have a few questions following on from my interview with Mr Hudson yesterday.'

She relayed his message almost verbatim to Roger who immediately came back with a suggestion.

'He asks would tomorrow at about half three be convenient. He says he'd be happy to arrange for you to be kept free at that time.'

'That would be marvellous.' Mathew replied, relieved beyond measure, but trying to retain a composed demeanour in front of the receptionist.

Mathew set off to his office for his afternoon casework with a spring in his step, mentally applauding himself for not procrastinating over booking his appointment and feeling so relaxed he didn't care what sort of client he was destined to encounter or whether he was due to fly solo or with a co-pilot.

It was Theresa who joined him again for the preparation work. She apparently needed to explain a few details surrounding the background to the case in hand, but thereafter, he was left free to conduct the interview unsupervised.

It was another ordinary middle-aged high-minded couple who ran a successful restaurant business and a simple matter of helping them decide which of the voluntary payment options suited them best. Mathew caught himself spontaneously mentioning for the first time to his clients that agency employees all donated a portion of their salary to VETS. When he reflected on this later, he realised he had been guilty of pure virtue signalling, as the couple had not required any persuasion.

It was only just after three as Mathew accompanied the new clients back to reception with a sense of another job well done. He had at least resisted the temptation to extend the interview unnecessarily by divulging more than was necessary of the agency's philosophy. However, sooner or later he was bound to be quizzed on this and so, a practice run explaining the deeper values of the agency probably wouldn't have been such a bad idea.

It struck Mathew as odd that he had become increasingly comfortable in his role as an advocate for the agency while simultaneously entertaining serious doubts about its practices. Until he was sure that its ethics were sound, was his urge to inspire his clients with confidence and trust in the agency not hypocritical? This was why it was so important to be able to clear the air with Roger tomorrow so that one way or another he would be liberated. Free either to continue working for the agency in good faith or to resign and apply his good will services elsewhere.

Mathew didn't have another interview in the afternoon, but there was another case to prepare for tomorrow morning. He settled down to this immediately on returning to his office which fortunately had been allocated to him for the whole day. He had digested all the relevant background paperwork by about four o'clock and had made a few notes for the interview. He now found himself in a quandary as to what to do next. It would feel a little awkward clocking off early for the second day running, but reading for half an hour from his *Working Towards an Integrated Society* on office time would seem a bit of a cheek.

No sooner had he resolved to thoroughly review his notes than the desk phone rang. He had not yet received a call while at work and assumed the call must be a misdial for a colleague. Finally, after the phone had rung persistently the third time, he picked up a pen and pressed the answer button, preparing to take a message. The call, however, was for him.

'Hello Mr Bryant. It's Jeannine here at reception. Earlier today, we arranged an appointment for you to see Mr Jameson tomorrow afternoon. Mr Jameson has just called me saying that he is free now in case you are available to see him. Apparently, you only had one interview this afternoon and have already seen the clients out, so he's hoping you will be free.'

Mathew froze and then felt physically sick. Trust Roger to be so readily available when he himself was unprepared! Yes, he knew roughly he wanted to say, but was banking on having ample time to formulate how to say it and certainly needed to run through his plan with Emily first. He was also spooked by the fact that Roger had taken the trouble to delve into his work schedule for the day and had actually noticed his previous clients being ushered out half an hour ago.

These thoughts, however, flashed through Mathew's mind with lightning speed and after barely a pause, he found himself agreeing to the impromptu interview and promising to be along in just ten minutes. He rose smartly from his desk, slowly packed his things away into his briefcase and purposefully made his way out of the office into the corridor, all the while assessing his unexpected situation and psychologically slipping into fight mode – flight and freeze no longer being open to him.

He was reminded of an incident at school when he realised moments before an examination that he had misread his timetable and had to cram all his History revision into just ten minutes. However, his solid underlying grasp of the subject matter combined with the sudden rush of adrenaline enabled him to rise to the occasion. This time too, Mathew told himself, with the benefit of life experience and the advantage, unlike in the examination, of setting his own questions, he would be in control of the situation and surely acquit himself well.

Mathew found that the regular motion of pacing down the long corridor helped him marshal his thoughts and bolster his resolve and he soon recovered his equilibrium. It was not unlike how he imagined it would feel to be an archetypal soldier marching towards an enemy to the rhythmic sound vibrations of drums and buoyed up by a belief in the justice of his cause. He smiled at his own melodramatic imaginative invention, while rapidly formulating his plan of action which in normal circumstances would have required not minutes but half an evening.

As he entered reception and came into view of Roger's office, he knew what he needed to do. He would stand outside the door for just two minutes in order to assume the confident and powerful persona which he need to project and remain in control throughout the conversation ahead. He must not allow Roger, himself possessed of a commanding aura, to dominate.

A few years ago, Mathew had been strongly influenced by a short lecture on MyTube in which the speaker emphasised the impact of presenting one's argument by way of three related, mutually reinforcing ideas. This was what he would do today with Roger. Far from having to request a follow-up interview, which Mathew would undoubtedly need in order to complete his mission, Roger would be left so intrigued by the discussion that he would suggest a further meeting himself.

Feeling fully composed, Mathew knocked squarely on the office door and was invited to enter at once by Roger who came forward to greet him with a handshake.

'Great to have another chance to chat, Mathew, do take a seat. Paul Hudson warned me you might want to clear up a few points with me after your interview with him yesterday. I always take it as a good sign when our new employees exhibit an interest in delving a little deeper into what we're all about here at the agency.'

Mathew could see that Roger was bidding to take command and subtly lay out the ground rules for their forthcoming engagement. He needed to set out his own stall before he lost the initiative and so began by slightly misrepresenting his dialogue with Hudson.

'Yes, I appreciate Mr Hudson's purpose was essentially just a catch-up session and that he had quite a few of those to fit in yesterday with my fellow novices, so I felt it only fair to let him off the hook and pester you instead.'

Somewhat taken aback at the interruption, but disarmed by its gentle irony, Roger gave way and allowed Mathew to summarise the main points emerging from the Hudson interview. As much to remind himself as to impress Roger, he set about a two-minute three-pronged résumé. He alluded to the positive feedback he had received via Hudson from trainers and mentors including Roger himself, how reassured he was that the agency encouraged enquiring minds on the part of employees, and how refreshingly different his fellow recruits were in terms of personality and temperament, despite all being a product of the same algorithm.

Mathew had calculated that this opening salvo would be likely to put his interlocutor at ease and make him more receptive when it came to the more provocative points he intended follow up with. Indeed, Roger responded with the anticipated complaisant platitudes which prepared the ground for Mathew to step up his assault.

He began the next phase by appropriating the observation Emily had made during their second teatime conference. As they were in league together, he was confident she would approve and he would take care to present the case as impersonally as possible.

'One point I forgot to raise with Mr Hudson yesterday was the way the agency nearly always teams up its new recruits with a member of the opposite sex. I'd assumed it was purely by chance that my mentors always seemed to be ladies – Gemma, Theresa and Margaret – until I got talking to the others over lunch in the canteen. They had also noticed this and wondered if there was some profound psychological principle involved here.'

Mathew hoped he had more than adequately camouflaged the source of his intelligence.

Roger, who now seemed resigned to handing over the dominant role in the conversation to Mathew, took visible pleasure in answering this first question.

'You are absolutely right. I'm not sure how profound the psychology is, but it certainly is based on sound evidence that pairing up males and females tends to produce better results than members of the same sex. I seem to recall it is to do with reducing the tendency for mentors and mentees to engage in a subtle but generally unproductive rivalry. Also, pedagogically it was demonstrated back in the 1950s that learning tends to be more effective when students are placed in opposite gender pairs. A brighter female will help a weaker male to better understand something out of a nurturing instinct, whereas a brighter male will support an intellectually weaker female at best out of chivalry and at worst from a desire to show off. Either way, the desired outcome is achieved.'

Recognising that Roger's explanation mirrored Emily's reference to twentieth century Soviet research, Mathew couldn't help expressing his enthusiasm for the theory.

'Yes, a win-win situation, as people used to say before it became a terrible cliché!'

Mathew was tempted next to broach the agency's move towards courting the less amenable clients, but then thought better of it, recalling his planned tactic of gradually stepping up the ante in order to effect as smooth a transition as possible to the controversial questions.

'I did mention both to Margaret, I think it was, and also to Mr Hudson yesterday that the health benefits which came along with signing up to VETS might be seen as a bribe with a potential to create a two-tier health care system. So, I just wondered if you had any thoughts on that personally. I believe it's been the subject of considerable debate within the agency.'

Roger handled this question too as confidently as the previous one about gender pairing. True, he had been asked for a personal view and on a more complex and contentious issue at that. Roger's personal opinion, however, contained surprises, however. Yes, a case could be made that some clients were being incentivised to join VETS through potential health benefits, though he wouldn't call this bribery, as the topic wasn't brought up automatically or with the express aim of persuading people to join. And no, this would not be allowed to evolve into a two-tier health service, as there was strong public opposition to this and a political consensus not to allow it to happen.

Mathew resisted the temptation to dissipate his energies by engaging Roger in a prolonged debate on this question alone, as he knew it was time to escalate the challenge and launch the third and most provocative of his questions.

Had he not been so concerned to keep Emily out of his inquisition, Mathew might have begun with her account of the shady individuals she had observed leaving the building via a side exit. Of course, he could have pretended that it was he who had been the observer, but concluded that honesty was the best policy. He would assail Roger directly with his eavesdropping caper.

As Mathew neared the critical part of his account, he realised that there was little point in claiming that he had overheard the revealing conversation in the corridor purely by chance: It had been too long and involved. He therefore decided to own up to his penchant for fancying himself as a part-time sleuth and be as frank and accurate as possible. When he came to relating the discussion of the different category types, Roger's expression perceptibly changed from benign complaisance to one of deep concern. Mathew had anticipated a significant effect on Roger, but for the first time in their conversation he had no notion as to what his reaction would be.

Mathew summed up his conclusions from the talk about categories thus:

'I'm not at all concerned about what they referred to as the category B clients. I've encountered a few of them myself and discussed with agency colleagues. I fully accept the notion of what might be termed the 'hard' or 'harder' clients as opposed to the 'soft' ones. What I understood from the conversation I overheard, however, is that the agency is letting potential clients go through to the interview stage even after your assessments here indicate they are significantly less suitable than the original logarithm suggested.

'It wasn't clear from the conversation how many of these low scorers there were and how readily the agency is allowing them to come through to the interview stage. What I heard certainly suggested they had been picked up before they got to interview otherwise why would the agency worker have talked about the *few skilful staff capable of handling the Cs,* as he put it?'

'It's pretty clear to me that if category Cs are not really suitable to be clients at all and only just capable of being dealt with by a minority of our agency staff, then category Ds, who definitely can't be dealt with by our agency and need to be reassigned, are likely to be serious tax evaders if not out and out criminals.

'I'm not sure exactly how to frame my question here, but could start by asking whether the agency has a definite cut-off point where it is unable or refuses to deal with clients. If so, how is this determined and what other agency or agencies are involved in dealing with those that are deemed beyond the pale as far as this agency is concerned. I can only assume that at the extreme end of the spectrum, law enforcement must be involved, for example.'

At this point, Mathew paused, realising he had he had given Roger more than enough to chew over and respond to. Roger had shown no signs of wishing to interrupt Mathew at any point during his exposé and proved quite content to listen intently while gathering his own thoughts. At last, he began his reply.

'Thanks for taking the trouble to delve into all that. You've probably gained a deeper insight into the wider picture than most of the staff who've been working here since the start. I fully understand your suspicions given what you've heard and observed and hope I can clear a few things up. As you'll expect, I have great faith in the agency having been in on its inception and having seen its operations grow from strength to strength in a short space of time. I also believe it must and will continue to progress and expand its scope.

'There are some among us who would like to see the agency grow faster than others. I must admit I'm one of the more cautious. At present, we liaise with various other agencies proactively in order to deal with the small minority of distasteful clients who come our way. Other agencies such as HMRC typically tackle those you heard referred to as category C and you quite rightly inferred that those termed category D who slip in under the radar are generally dealt with by the police.

'We don't like referrals, especially when we feel it's clear that people have approached us or responded to our ads in good faith. Once we've handed people over to other agencies, we rarely get any feedback on how their cases have been dealt with and so we have a couple of staff who advise people if we suspect they may have been breaking the law inadvertently. We suggest ways they can set their affairs straight and avoid fines or prosecution. We can't afford to create an atmosphere of distrust around the agency if we are to continue to grow. I'm sure Mr Hudson touched on how we hope to promote an appealing image so more people will come forward to join VETS as the cool thing to do.

'Also, there is little point in our existing if we become perceived merely as a branch of HMRC or an adjunct to it. We will only continue to operate meaningfully so long as the principle of voluntary donations remains popular among the political elite. The fact you need to be aware of is that the country can't afford to maintain the current low tax regime for much longer, at least not if as a society we wish to continue to provide services at the level we are used to enjoying today. So, we need to develop the role of the agency in two principal ways. One: step up the rate at which we're recruiting A category donators and two: branch out into proactively attracting a much larger group still from the B category. It's like with any movement – it starts with a small nucleus of highly motivated individuals. Their influence radiates outwards and draws more and more people in.

Mathew had been patient for the past couple of minutes, but couldn't resist coming in at this point:

'If this doesn't work as planned, could income tax and business rates not be raised to make up the shortfall in government income? I mean if there were a consensus among the main political parties even though it wouldn't go down well with the public at large.'

'The trouble is that a move like that would probably cause such widespread popular resentment that it could fuel a return to the old rivalries between political parties who would be tempted to court public opinion by reviving the divide between low and high-taxing ideologies. Then, of course, with a return to higher compulsory taxes would we'd risk losing us the support of many voluntary contributors who would feel the rationale behind VETS was lost. So much of our good work would be undone.'

Mathew knew It was time to draw his challenge to a close.

'Well thanks a million for taking the time to discuss all this fascinating stuff and clarifying so many points. I realise now that half an hour could never do justice to all my questions....'

Roger reacted as Mathew had calculated.

'I'd be delighted to continue our chat tomorrow at the time we'd originally arranged, if you don't mind. I'm sure there are other issues you'd like to talk through. In fact, I'll try to get another colleague in who may be able to fill you in on some aspects of the agency's operations that I'm not so au fait with...'

All had gone according to the plan that Mathew had conceived during his five-minute walk on the way to Roger's office. He was more than satisfied with the outcome of his three-pronged attack. It felt rather like a troupe of skirmishers in one of his wargames: He had harassed the enemy and unsettled his formations without taking any losses. He could now withdraw and prepare for the full-fledged onslaught to come later.

The analogy was far from perfect, of course, given that Roger had behaved much more like a strong ally than an enemy. Mathew hoped he wouldn't turn out to be one of those fickle powers that changed sides as the tide of the war turned against Napoleon following his disastrous invasion of Russia in 1812. Mathew preferred this analogy until it dawned on him that it was he as the wavering employee, not Roger, who best fit the role of the potentially fickle ally of the agency empire.

On his way from Roger's office and out through reception, it didn't even occur to him this time to wait for Emily or even pause to send her a reassuring message in the safety of the street. He felt a need to get a good distance away from the agency building contacting her, though the impulse was more as a precaution than out of any real sense of being followed or observed.

During the bus trip, Mathew took out his phone briefly, but immediately returned it to his pocket, preferring to mull over the acutely interesting events of yet another day at the agency. Getting up from his seat as his stop approached, he felt that his adrenaline levels were at last returning to normal. The short remaining walk to his front door enabled him to fully relax and look forward to his usual cup of tea and snack in front of the television.

By six o'clock, Mathew felt fully refreshed and, with his thoughts in order, at last he phoned Emily to update her on his latest agency experience. It was only then that he remembered that she would have no idea that he had already completed his interview with Roger.

'Wow, that must have been a bit of a shock! I think I'd have chickened out and tried to think of an excuse not to be put on the spot like that! I can't wait to hear how you got on. As soon as you're done, I may have a few things to tell you too... .'

'Perhaps you shouldn't have told me that, as I'll be distracted now, anticipating what you're going to say!'

'The same applies to me, so, as we can't sensibly talk at the same time, I suggest you go first as we'd both kind of assumed you would originally.'

Emily's promise of interesting tidings actually had the opposite effect - that of concentrating Mathew's mind so that he was able to summarise his discussion with Roger economically within five minutes or so. He omitted the earlier surprising interview with Walter the ex-convict, promising himself he would come back to it later on if time and energy allowed.

'So, you didn't unearth anything really new, then. But it was at least interesting that Roger seemed to be playing with a straight bat and, far from wishing to hide anything, is keen to have you back for a second round tomorrow.

'Now for my contribution. It may be nothing, but the last week or so, I've been looking at and trying to take in as many faces as possible. I've noticed there are a couple of people I've seen a few times in the corridors who appear to be involved in interviewing clients, but who I've never encountered in the canteen. They have a different feel about them somehow and project a subtle aura of not really being part of the place. It occurred to me they might be coming in from outside and perhaps not part of the regular agency payroll.'

Mathew seized on the opportunity for a play on language. 'You mean agency staff working for the agency. Surely though, in order to fit into the routine and ethos of the place they'd have to go through the basic induction and training. Then, in a sense, they'd be as good as regular agency staff. I mean, it only took a week or so for us to go through that rigmarole, so what would be the point?'

'Call it feminine intuition, if you like, but there's something not quite right about them. I got a similar feeling on espying those gangster-looking men we saw with Peter the other day, only this time instead of fishy clients its fishy agency staff. I reckon you should ask Roger and whoever he brings along tomorrow whether they ever use staff with a different background and if so, why. Now weren't you saving up something else to tell me?'

Mathew recounted his bizarre experience with *Walter the Wayward,* as he spontaneously called the ex-offender in a feeble effort to entertain Emily, feeling that it was about time he lightened the atmosphere. He'd not yet had leisure to analyse the situation properly himself and so examined his feelings about this particular encounter as he went along.

'So, what I had trouble believing was that Walter could convince the agency through its usual channels – the algorithm and follow-up confirmatory assessments - that he was genuine about wanting to donate to VETS and that it was for the right reasons. Also, since the money he was offering was stolen in the first place how could this count towards VETS? And he was holding some back for living expenses in any case.'

Emily, who had been listening intently, summed up her reaction:

'Well, it sounds as though you, like the agency staff who had assessed him thus far, gave him the benefit of the doubt in the end. I'd like to guess they are just casting the net ever wider as an experiment to see who they can haul in. At the end of the day, if Walter fails to live up to his promise or disappears, it will be no great loss. The people who he'd robbed have been compensated long ago by the State and if he does cough up in full and, as he claims, and goes on to better things, then it will be a real success story both for the agency and the restorative justice movement.'

'I'm sure you're right, Emily, but I think I'll raise this tomorrow along with everything else I'm going to mention. As Roger is bringing along a back-up buddy, I ought to get you in on the interview too for moral support. Why shouldn't I have someone to lean on? But I suppose it's a bit much to expect them to release two new staff from their normal duties for the second time in a matter of days ....'

The two of them then spoke for a few minutes more about which points to raise tomorrow. If Mathew still didn't feel he'd got to the bottom of everything at the end of this second phase, Emily could always make an appointment to mop up any issues. They decided that Mathew would mention early on that one of his colleagues had a few questions to ask in case Roger and co made a spontaneous offer to invite her to join them.

Having put down the phone, Mathew quickly ran through in his mind the other people in his life who appreciate a call at this time of the evening, but then decided to cut himself some slack. He'd been dutiful enough for one day – a reasonable amount of routine work at the office, an impromptu potentially stressful and high-stakes interview followed by a searching analysis, first with himself and then with Emily.

Come to think of it, Mathew mused as he prepared himself dinner, *how many people have thought to phone me of late for a catch-up call or take the initiative in arranging a meeting?* It was a rare occurrence indeed as far as his mother and sister were concerned, unless something was amiss. With his friends too it tended to be he who made the first move in getting in touch periodically. As he sat down to eat, his subdued and deflated mood harmonised with the blander than usual meal he had prepared himself.

After eating, Mathew found his spirits were reasonably restored and his thoughts turned to the next and potentially decisive phase of his war game. Just as he was on his way upstairs to his hobby room, a knock at his front door brought him back down again. It was Andrew. He immediately invited him in, his pleasure at seeing his friend more than compensating for the minor irritation of being thwarted in the pursuit of his childish pleasure. Andrew lived the nearest of all his friends and family, so it wasn't a great surprise for him to drop in unannounced, though in the days when he was with Paula, he hardly made a habit of it.

'I hope I've not caught you in the middle of anything, Mathew. I was just passing and wanted to let you know in case you'd not heard from your sister that we're kind of seeing each other again. Largely thanks to you, I have to say.' He smiled and added. 'Obviously, I had my suspicions it might be more to do with her needing to share her worries about her mother and problems at work with someone, but I'm pretty sure it's more than just that.'

Andrew's news merely confirmed what Mathew had been expecting to happen in the fulness of time, but right now he was more concerned to tease out of his friend what he knew about his mother in case there had been any developments during the last couple of days since his weekend visit.

'That's great to hear! I don't suppose when you spoke to her last Paula mentioned if her mum, that is, our mum had any more news. We both saw her at the weekend and I was going to call her this evening or tomorrow at the latest in case there'd been any more developments, but since you've no doubt spoken to Paula since the weekend...'

'No, she mentioned the weekend and I think she'd have said if there'd been anything since. To be honest, we spent most of the time talking about her new position and how she feels her colleagues are resenting her and making her life difficult as a result. I'm sure she's gone on about this to you too. The trouble is, we're only getting her side of the story and I'm just dying to tell her to relax and not let it get out of perspective.'

'Well, you'd only be saying what I've already told her. If she hears it from both of us, hopefully she'll take notice and just get on with it...' Mathew found himself responding somewhat irritably. But Andrew smiled magnanimously.

'It's good that we're both on the same page with her over that. I think it's the same with most of us – we need someone to offload to when we get home from work, so we probably shouldn't read too much into it. Talking of which – you've not told me how you've been getting on in that area....'

Mathew replied that he wasn't unlike his sister in that respect and had he not got so much preparation to do before tomorrow morning as well as make a couple of calls, he'd love to offload to his friend. He didn't go as far as to mention that he'd acquired a new love in his life to offload to. That could wait for another occasion.

'That's fine. I'd better get off then. No doubt we'll have a chance to catch up at the weekend if not before. And don't worry – I won't be making a habit of dropping in on you unannounced. I just knew you'd appreciate hearing about me and your sister. I know she can be a bit coy...'

Andrew was right in every respect and Mathew felt even more worthy of his much-anticipated spell at the wargaming table as he made a second attempt to ascend to his hobby room.

Mathew recalled that he had completed the fifteenth phase with Emily last night and, given the advanced stage of the action with virtually all units engaged, it seemed unlikely that all five

CHAPTER 15. THE ENDGAME APPROACHES

remaining five phases would be required before a clear victor could be declared. There were six more or less distinct zones in the battle which he had to work through, going through one at a time to determine casualties. He made a quick calculation as he came to the group of soldiers in which his own figure was engaged in hand-to-hand combat.

Each soldier had approximately a twenty per cent chance of becoming a casualty in each phase. There were three remaining soldiers with his figure's pose. A weaker mathematician than he would have calculated the chance of one of these falling at 60% or three times twenty. However, he knew that to calculate the chances of all of them surviving, he had to divide four squared by five squared. This came out at 51.2 per cent, hence the chance of one or more falling was 48.8 per cent, just under evens.

This calculation was totally unnecessary, but Mathew performed it anyway for the pure fun of it. When he came to roll the dice for each of his three key figures, however, he felt a bizarre sense of foreboding. He would need to throw percentage dice with a score of twenty and under being fatal. The first throw produced sixty-seven. The second throw - eighty-nine. The final throw came out as seventeen – a kill. As he removed the third figure, he almost flinched on turning it over to check the underside of the base. It was unmarked. Yet again, he had survived to fight another day.

Total casualties on both sides were now considerable – around twenty per cent of the defending Russians and nearly thirty per cent of the attacking French. It therefore looked even less likely that the battle would require all four remaining phases to reach a conclusion. The odds were broadly in favour of the Russians beating off the attack, as the morale ratings of the French had fallen perilously low to the point of undermining their combat effectiveness despite their numerical superiority.

With Mathew's hero in the heart of the combat zone and facing at least a twenty per cent chance of falling at each phase, his own personal fate in the game seemed destined to be played out very soon indeed. In fact, as he and his comrades were now outnumbered at a ratio of about five to four in this particular combat zone, his chances of coming to grief in the next phase would be even higher at about thirty per cent.

With at least two hours of the evening left, he now had to decide whether to use most of this time to complete phase seventeen – possibly the penultimate one – or choose another form of recreation. It was now too dark for his other natural alternative choice of gardening, though he would probably have benefited from a breath of fresh air rather than remaining couped up in his hobby room. He had already internalised his plan for tomorrow's interview scenario and decided to leave jotting down the list of key points he intended to make until the morning before work.

A brainwave came to his aid in resolving the present quandary. In order to expedite the next phase of the battle so that it would not devour the whole of the rest of the evening, he would use the simplified hand-to-hand combat rules for each of the broad six zones into which the battle had resolved itself. This simply meant calculating the overall casualties for each group of fifty or so soldiers instead of throwing the dice to decide the fate of each individual combatant.

This process took a mere half hour until he came to the final zone in which his own soldier was engaged. He had guessed right: a quick calculation confirmed that the outnumbered French soldiers in this zone each had a 30% chance of falling. This worked out at a forty-nine per cent chance – just under fifty-fifty that both he and his fellow figure with the same pose would survive.

Now with so much time to spare and in order to heighten the excitement, he decided to revert to the painstaking method of rolling the dice to determine each soldier's fate. So, just over an hour after a similar torturous process at the end of phase sixteen, he again prepared to roll the two percentage dice for the first of the two figures. This time, however, a score of between one and thirty would signify a kill. The throw came out at twenty-two. Killed! The second throw produced fifty-seven. Survived! So, now he stood exactly fifty per cent chance of falling at what, given the current state of play, looked like being the end of the whole game, only to be confirmed by a final calculation of overall French losses and morale.

Mathew brought back to mind how this childish game had begun a week or so ago and his more recent whim to pretend to align his own fate with that of the soldier he had found 'hovering' following his bizarre dream. On the strength of this, he realised that if he removed the fallen figure to find that he had survived the battle, this would give him a fillip, albeit it irrationally, for his follow-up discussion with Roger. If, on the other hand, it revealed he'd been 'killed', then it could have the reverse effect.

After a little reflection, he concluded that safest option would be to defer inspecting the base of the final fallen soldier to his return home from work tomorrow. He could then safely check whether the fate of the soldier aligned with the outcome of his interview. The most sensible thing now was to go back downstairs and spend the remaining hour of the evening doing something to take his mind off both the wargame and what tomorrow held in store for his future career.

Mathew's conscience at first dictated that, prompted by Andrew, he ought to call his mother again to check how she was. However, from what Andrew had said, there didn't appear to be any further developments and, as he wouldn't normally speak to his mother more than once a week, phoning now could appear conspicuous and invite a longer and more involved conversation just when he needed to avoid stress and undue nervous tension.

He decided that quiet relaxation listening to his music was preferrable to any sort of human interaction during this last hour before bed. He selected a recording of dinner jazz numbers by assorted artists which he hadn't played for a while, but knew would have the desired calming effect.

Mathew found that by half ten he was ready to retire for the night having all but banished from his mind any further thoughts about his current wargame or the forthcoming interview. He effortlessly slipped into unconsciousness and entered a familiar but ever shifting dreamworld where his unfettered psyche began to synthesise recent experiences, turning them into lurid and unpredictable patterns.

CHAPTER 16. SHOWDOWN WITH HENDRICKS

Had Mathew been challenged to guess what was likely to feature in his dream during the previous night, he might have predicted a chaotic pastiche of random elements from his incipient role at the agency mixed in with tense battle scenes from his current wargame. He would have been completely right about the work component. In an archetypal anxiety dream, he was trapped in Roger's office and subjected to a torrent of words he was unable to interpret, aware of two other entities in the room but unable visually to discern them or appeal to them for support. Emily seemed to be one of these presences, but she was invisible.

However, contrary to the normal tendency for Mathew's dreams to be connected to the themes he had been most focussed on before retiring, his wargame had been completely absent. The best explanation he could find was that by deliberately pushing the imminent ordeal at work to the back of his mind in the evening, he had left it to be dealt by his subconscious in the dream world. By contrast, his decision to deal consciously with his wargame and defer the final phase until after the final agency interview meant that his subconscious had nothing more to say to him on the matter.

As uncertain as his theory was, at least it would do for now and the sense of entrapment and lack of control in the boss's office required no dream expert to interpret.

With his accustomed excellent timekeeping, Mathew hurried through the door into reception soon after eight. It only occurred to him at the signing in desk that being so preoccupied with the session scheduled for the end of the day, he'd not given a thought to the casework he was actually employed to deal with. Therefore, he was somewhat taken aback on being handed his usual instructions folder. Quickly regaining his presence of mind, he asked:

'While I'm here, could you just confirm for me with Mr Jameson that we're still on for continuing our discussion at three thirty? He mentioned yesterday that he may be inviting another colleague to join us and I was wondering if it would be alright to bring along one of my fellow recruits too, as she's shown an interest in the issues we'll be talking about. It's Emily ….' He paused momentarily before realising he'd never picked up her surname. 'Obviously, she'd need to sign off a little early in the afternoon too if that can be arranged. I appreciate it's a lot to ask and I'd understand if it proves unpracticable.'

Mathew had rehearsed this mini-introductory speech quite carefully on the bus journey into work and although his performance was fluent, he feared his tone may have come across as a little too assertive at the start and yet verging on ingratiating towards the end. The receptionist didn't take the trouble to look up to make eye contact at any point, but wasted no time in calling Roger and confirming this would be perfectly fine. At the last minute, he had thought better of asking her to find out from Roger who the unknown entity might be. It would have risked sounding paranoid and, in any case, what could he have done with this information? They would find out soon enough.

He had the usual fifteen minutes or so to himself before he was due to start work in the office which he'd been assigned for the morning. His first priority now was to message Emily before leaving reception that all was in order and, in case they were unable to catch up at lunch time, to meet outside Roger's office just before half three. It was something of a relief to be able to carry out this small operation in full view of the receptionist for a change, even if by force of habit, he felt a fleeting sense of culpability as he furtively tapped the message onto his phone screen.

When Emily confirmed receiving his message a few seconds later, he immediately sent her another, enigmatically asking her surname and wondering whether she would guess why. Her reply came back shortly: *Coates – What's yours?* He in turn replied: *Bryant. I would have told you, only ladies first!* Emily came back: *Don't like the sound of Bryant and Coates makes us sound like a crime-busting duo like Cagney and Lacy or Starsky and Hutch. You and I are finished!* Now his turn for a bit of wit: *Can tell you've been at great grandad's Vintage TV collection. Never mind, it'll be simpler once we're married...*

Mathew's increasingly frivolous messaging with Emily had caused him to stop and start on his way down the corridor and had drawn not a few bemused glances from passing colleagues. By the time he arrived at his appointed office for the day, it was already officially time to start work in earnest.

When he opened his folder in order to skim through his morning assignments, he said a silent prayer that they would be straightforward and so not risk throwing him out of kilter for the big event of the afternoon. As much as he wished to seize every opportunity to gain a better understanding of the agency's goals and practices, now wasn't the right time to discover shocking new truths and force him to revise his 'script'.

At least that was Mathew's initial defensive instinct, but as he began leafing through the papers, he felt a deep inner confidence that he would be able to handle pretty well anything which fate might have in store for him through today's casework. Neither of the two clients' profiles suggested anything radically different from the cases he'd dealt with to date and this was soon borne out by the interviews which he again had to conduct unaided by any of his former mentors.

This fact brought to mind a simple question as to what was at play when it came to deciding whether or not a recent recruit needed back-up from a more experienced worker. Did anyone assess the prospective clients' profiles with this in mind or was it simply a matter of senior colleagues determining at what point new staff could be trusted to be competent and left to their own devices? However, this was a largely an operational issue and not a question of sufficient significance to raise this afternoon.

Mathew's prayers were answered, as neither of the morning's cases presented him with any dilemmas, nor did they provide the least evidence of nefarious practices by the agency. This was welcome in a sense, but at the same time, he was wary that such an uneventful session risked undermining his determination to carry through his planned robust interrogation of his new employer's principles. It was such a relief at this stage to know that Emily would be there by his side for moral support and also capable of making her own incisive contribution to any discussions, and, if need be, launch her own offensive.

Mathew met up with Emily in the canteen a little later than usual and so quite a few agency staff were already there. The two complicitly and tacitly found a place to sit together just outside earshot of anyone else against the background hubbub of voices. On all previous occasions, it had been Mathew's first impulse to cast a quick glance around the canteen in search of other fellow induction comrades, but now, and for different reasons, Jonathan and Peter were of no interest to him. Jonathan would never be one to challenge the agency or even dig down into its modus operandi, while Peter, possibly entrusted with some of its darkest secrets, was certainly one to avoid at this time.

Emily's morning too had been largely uneventful with, as she jokingly described it, two category A clients. She was supervised or at least 'sat in on' by one of her mentors, Patrick, for the second session. Half way through the session, he slightly surprised Emily by asking the question: How would you describe your motivation for considering VETS? The lady's answer was quite specific and detailed: *Because I know the Government is running out of options for raising money. It can't keep borrowing for ever: even Premium Bonds are public loans to the Treasury which could be called in at any time. So, if we want to continue improving public services without total reliance on artificial intelligence, we're going to have to volunteer more support.*

Both Mathew and Emily immediately understood the reference to Artificial Intelligence. About ten years ago, there had been an irreversible popular backlash against increasingly intrusive AI in providing social care. A striking example was the revolt against the proliferation of advanced robotics to service the complex needs of an ageing population. It seemed that society at large had concluded that certain technology designed to make care of the elderly more humane was beginning to have a reverse dehumanising effect.

Referring to VETS, Mathew remarked:

'It just shows that somehow the message is getting through to the wider public. Perhaps we should ask Roger if yet another special agency is in charge of the comms'.

'I suppose there must be, as they don't seem to do it here and I've never seen it advertised on the TV in public information broadcasts or read about it online'.

'Well, you have in a way, as you were targeted by the algorithm just as much as I was a few weeks ago! Of course, we weren't directly introduced to VETS, but enticed into a job promotion rather like advertisers used to indirectly introduce consumers to their products. That might be another thing to mention later today', Mathew added half-heartedly feeling again that the agenda was already overloaded.

Both fell silent for a while deep in thought. It emerged that they had a very similar work pattern in store for the afternoon: a set of case notes to read followed by an interview scheduled to finish before three o'clock. This should leave them ample time to write up their paperwork and then prepare for the 3.30 'showdown' with Roger.

Inspired by their playful descriptions of the two shady individuals they had seen with Peter a few days ago, Mathew and Emily had devised a light-hearted form of entertainment which entailed thinking up different terms each time to denote this afternoon's meeting. 'Showdown' was just the latest in the series which had included 'shoot-out', 'duel', 'last battle', 'mortal combat' and several others. This childish game, inspired by his wargaming hobby, seemed all the more ironic to Mathew given that despite their best sleuthing efforts, they had so far failed to find any real evidence of anything untoward going on at the agency.

As he and Emily left the canteen for the afternoon's assignments, Mathew reflected once more on his sleuthing aspirations. He questioned whether he wouldn't be just a little disappointed if his and Emily's investigations merely served to prove the agency to be ethically squeaky clean. Before parting their separate ways down different corridors, the two reconfirmed their plan to meet just before three outside Roger's office.

Back at his desk, Mathew felt himself slip into automatic pilot as soon as he began to study the files for the next client. He was grateful to have a normal caseload to occupy him before the three-thirty appointment, as the need to concentrate was the surest way to prevent him from ruminating. His worst ever job interview was when he was left in error alone in a room for over an hour before finally being summoned into the interview room. He had misused the extra prep time to obsessively rehearse his 'script' and only succeeded in tying himself up in knots and becoming almost completely tongue tied throughout the

CHAPTER 16. SHOWDOWN WITH HENDRICKS

encounter.

As expected, the face-to-face session with his clients came to a natural and relaxed end soon after half two, leaving him half an hour to write up his notes. There was nothing out of the ordinary to record and so soon he was able to begin the process of mode switching.

The difficulty was that unlike the previous mode switch, this time the process did not occur spontaneously. Mathew realised that this was hardly surprising, as he was stepping into the unknown: A relatively informal one-to-one chat with Roger with whom he was already acquainted was a far cry from a four-way conversation ranging over much wider and deeper subject matter and with one of the participants as yet an unknown quantity.

Mathew decided the most appropriate mentality he could adopt would be to anticipate a free, dynamic and earnest discussion in which he would find the courage to probe as deeply as possible for answers while minimising the risk of sounding churlish or causing offence. He had by no means prepared anything like a script, but took care to jot down prompts for the two or three issues he feared might slip his mind in the course of a heated debate – or at least those which had done in rehearsal with himself and Emily over the past forty-eight hours.

As he slowly walked towards his rendezvous with Emily outside Roger's office, Mathew calmly ran through a broad outline of the issues he needed to raise. Turning into the corridor towards the reception area, he immediately saw Emily already waiting for him and trying to look as natural and relaxed as possible. As he sidled up to her, they briefly squeezed hands and exchanged glances for mutual support. Emily then nodded and Mathew, after a quick time check, knocked forthrightly on the door.

On hearing Roger's voice, Mathew momentarily agonised over who should enter first. He was torn between the opposing impulses of wanting to exhibit his dominant role on the one hand and chivalry on the other. His compromise was to step just inside the office, but hold open the door for Emily to fully enter ahead of him. Letting the door go, he then strode to catch up with her as they were invited to sit down together at a large table which had appeared since Mathew's last interview with Roger. True to agency house style, the table was set out with plates of cakes and glasses for a modest range of cold drinks. Mathew mused: all they needed now was for a couple of their mentors or trainers to turn up for the waitering.

However, it was the new person in the room who bade them tuck into the refreshments. Roger introduced him as Mr Hendricks, a civil servant working for HMRC whose job it was to liaise with the agency and who had been involved in setting it up a couple of years ago. He would, Roger claimed, be just the person to address regarding any particularly complex issues they may wish to raise. In order to get the discussion underway, Roger summarised the points covered so far.

Throughout Roger's summary, Mathew could see that Emily felt under pressure to give every outward sign of following intently as if she were hearing it all for the first time. Her performance, however, struck him as unconvincing given that both men could easily surmise that she would have had ample opportunity to talk over these points with him before. He only hoped that her body language could just as well be interpreted as an effort to satisfy herself that there were no substantive inconsistencies between what he, Mathew, had told her and what Roger claimed to have covered.

Mathew himself was grateful for the summary and couldn't help but be impressed by Roger's precision in conveying the content of the Hudson interview: from the discussion about the benefits and drawbacks of acronyms such as VETS to the progress already made by the agency in widening the circle of VETS-ready clients, as he creatively expressed it this time, and the pitfalls of a perceived two-tier health system. Indeed, Mathew recalled that

Roger had been quite open about the detailed feedback he'd received from Hudson about the interview as well as from all the trainers and mentors he'd worked with to date.

Before moving on to discuss his own interview, Roger finally mentioned the points which Emily had brought up in her own Hudson interview regarding gender pairing of experienced with novice agency workers and the algorithm's purported ability to weed out psychologically unstable candidates in order to ensure that all VETS donors had full cognizance of what they were committing to. These references initially caught Mathew by surprise before he realised with a fleeting sense of guilty chauvinism that Emily's interview deserved no less consideration than his own despite its lesser content.

Perhaps out of modesty or because it was more recent and less likely to have faded from memory, Roger produced an even briefer précis of his own interview with Mathew. In this he covered how he had attempted to address Mathew's concerns about the agency's taking on less-than-ideal clients in the C and D categories and reasserted the agency's alignment to the voluntary principle as opposed to functioning merely as an arm of the Tax Office. Roger wound up by stressing the severe fiscal gap existing in the country between so-called 'regular income-based taxation' and money which the State raised by other means.

'And now', at last Roger declared, 'I think it's time to hand you over to Mr Hendricks who, I am sure, will be much better placed to deal with the issues raised in greater detail and also broaden out the discussion to the more philosophical issues which I'm sure you both want to get your teeth into....'

Mathew detected a slightly overweening air of deference in Roger's air as he looked across to Hendricks at this point, a fleeting impression which quickly faded away as he switched his attention exclusively to the new speaker in the room.

Hendricks began:

'I must say it's not every day that we get two members of a recruitment cohort taking such a keen interest in the esoteric aspects of the agency's work and its raison d'être. But, as I hope we've already proved to you by the very fact that we're sitting here now and having this discussion, we're anxious to get our employees fully on side with what we're trying to achieve. Part of that process is being transparent and responsive to all our staff concerns.

'I think the most useful starting point would a brief excursion through time – at least over the past fifty years or so. The history children study at school goes too far back and is too superficial to allow them to see how events in the past helped shape the world they live in today. It was certainly like that when I was at school and no doubt the same for your generation'

Mathew felt this to be a fair comment regarding the generations: Hendricks looked to be in his late fifties. The point too about a disconnect with history as taught at school was confirmed by his mother's reaction when he complained to her years ago about the irrelevance of much of the history curriculum at secondary school. The more relatable social and economic history seemed to be the preserve of university students.

'We really need to go back to about fifty years ago when a general perception began to emerge that governments around the world were increasingly being held to ransom by the big corporations. Some of the multi-nationals and trans-nationals, as they came to be known, owned more assets than many smaller developing countries.

'With the effective fall of Soviet communism in the early 1990s, capitalism with a new human face appeared unchallenged and supremely capable of evolving to meet contemporary conditions. It had proved capable of bringing higher living standards, or at least the promise of them, to an increasing proportion of the world's population. But the so-called 'trickle down' effect even in the developed richer countries failed to reach a growing tranche of citizens who formed a disaffected subculture cut off from the rest of society through poverty...'

Hendricks paused for a moment and, as if rousing himself from a daydream continued:

'And by the way, I can wax lyrical ad nauseum about this sort of background stuff, so do feel free to interrupt for any reason – whether it's because you want me to clarify a point, challenge something I've said, or because you've heard or read it all before and just want me to shut up!'

'No, do carry on. I think we've both read up a fair bit on recent history on the internet, but it's good to hear the government's official viewpoint.' Emily interjected looking across to Mathew for a nod of approval which he duly gave, though in so doing he realised that each such acknowledgement provided a visual clue to Roger and Hendricks as to his and Emily's complicity.

A less focused man would have struggled to pick up his thread, but Hendricks resumed seamlessly:

'While liberals had been making the case for decades, it became apparent to even the most reactionary and conservative of political minds that whereas relative poverty may have been perceived as a necessary evil in a meritocratic capitalist system, extreme social inequality had become the single greatest threat to the establishment itself. Civil unrest was reaching alarming proportions which threatened to overwhelm law enforcement agencies and clearly a radical solution was called for.

'Advances in technology were ultimately only meaningful if people from all walks of life could enjoy the benefits, whereas the wealth and power generated was being concentrated into ever fewer hands. At the same time, traditional employment for the masses was disappearing on a huge scale with very few quality jobs being created by way of compensation in the 'gig' economy.

'Fortunately, brave social and fiscal experiments conducted in a number of smaller countries had proved that where the political will exists practical ways can be found to eliminate the worst aspects of poverty and inequality altogether. The most successful policy proved to be the introduction of a citizen's or universal basic income. In countries and sometimes regions where this had been carried through, evidence abounded that the vast majority of people who had previously lived below the poverty line responded positively to this initiative. It appeared that once their essential needs were met by the State, people were usually keen to work in order to further enhance their standard of living. Counterintuitively, very few seemed content to sit back and live off the State and, even among those who did so, the crime rate rapidly declined.

'Various sociological surveys revealed that when people were freed up to work as much or as little as they liked, far from depressing the national economy, it was given a boost. A highly plausible theory to explain this phenomenon is that when people enjoy the freedom to be active in whatever domain that appeals to them and where earning money isn't the primary motive, they apply themselves with greater energy and creativity. The sum total of this unleashed human effort and talent results in a more harmonious, happier and ultimately wealthier society.

'Apologies if I've given rather a lot of emphasis to this aspect of the historical narrative. It's a particular hobby horse of mine!' Hendricks said this in a manner which invited no comment and so he continued without further intervention from either Mathew or Emily.

'Now this is where the historical narrative merges with the present and becomes directly relevant to the agency. Governments around the world realised that the big tech companies were getting, as it were, too big for their boots. While they had a vested interest in ensuring the majority of the population had enough income to provide them with a steady and growing stream of customers, they didn't have a stake in society overall, despite all their efforts to project a benign image. Their answer to alarming signs of social unrest was to invest in ever cleverer technology to combat it at all levels – whether by supplying excessively rich individuals with state-of-the-art security systems or gaining contracts with repressive regimes facing increasingly frequent large-scale riots.

Too many powerful individuals running the multi- and transnationals fancied themselves as avatars with a God-given right to use their financial might to shape the world they operated in as they saw fit. And the populace could too easily be manipulated by unscrupulous exploitation of the net by unethical media.

To cut a long story short, governments knew they had to act in order to regain political control and retain national sovereignty. Leaders of Western democratic governments didn't like to admit it, but many took inspiration from the manner in which, following the fall of communism, the second Russian president took on the emerging class of oligarchs in his country at the turn of the present century.

History would eventually come down on his side as the first democratically elected leader to use his authority in order to successfully challenge a powerful economic class in a manner which led to a more socially just society while avoiding bloody conflict in the process. The multi- and transnationals, however, could only be tackled by international concerted action and the urgency of tackling them overcame traditional geopolitical boundaries and enabled governments of the G12 – the biggest international players - to win back the power to shape their countries' destiny.

Almost overnight, the status of the big tech and multinationals changed from calling all the shots to being in harness to governments which were free again to determine public policy.'

Although engrossed by the monologue, Mathew sensed it was

time to shift the initiative away from Hendricks by daring to make his first genuine impromptu interjection.

'But in the Russian case, surely it was before the internet had become such a potent means of forming public opinion by subverting much of the mass media. It had been the government itself that had controlled the media under communism to minimise public debate and criticism of the authorities.'

'Yes,' continued Hendricks, not at all knocked off his stride, 'but just as the subverted media, as you aptly put it, a generation later became such a powerful negative force, so too could it be turned to good effect by the government once wrested from big tech companies and the trans- and multi-nationals whose interests they were serving.'

'That's always assuming that the government knew best and always had the interests of the people in view.' Emily came in at last.

'I'm afraid that's an assumption I have to make, being a government official myself, but I think it's fair to say that broadly speaking, unless they are run by totally corrupt individuals, governments right across the political spectrum generally do have their citizens' best interests at heart. It was quite an exceptional event when establishment politicians and the more radical elements came together to compromise and create a more collaborative and transparent coalition. And by so doing, they turned their backs on, or at least suspended, the adversarial and polarised political culture which had dominated the country for around two hundred years. Only by joining forces could they stand up to and eliminate a growing threat posed to the very foundations of democracy and even the most rudimentary notion of sovereignty.'

Emily jumped in again:

'So, you mean the establishment joined with political radicals in order to avert the collapse of society thanks to the big tech companies and transnationals which were causing jobs to disappear and widen the between rich and poor?'

'That's about it. In the past, governments could afford to be laissez-faire about commercial interests manipulating the masses. After all, the process generated economic growth and wealth which up to a point benefited all, but excessive commercial wealth threatened excessive influence over and ultimately control over political power...'

Mathew had heard enough on this theme and was determined to avoid a Hendricks lecture swallowing up the whole of the time available to them.

'So, let's bring us up to the present. The government, in other words, you, have seized control from big business like the Russian president accomplished fifty years ago with his oligarchs, though let's admit, it's a very rough analogy. You are working within a successful coalition of the various political parties which is quite effective in ruling by consensus. Now, what else about society had to be changed once this arrangement was reached? And, for that matter, what still needs to be accomplished?'

Far from being discountenanced, Hendricks seemed quite relieved by Mathew's cut to the chase:

'The powers that be, whatever their political complexion, always have to meet the conflicting needs of the masses who clamour for security, a good standard of living and services while at the same time wanting to pay as little as possible for the privilege. This contradiction is almost always at the root of tension between the government and the governed. Now how to square this circle?'

'Whereas in the past, a government daring to raise taxes was liable to fall to the opposition at the next election, this ceased to be the case once political parties had agreed not to campaign against each other on this basis. So, a strong coalition government can buy time with its finances, borrowing money in the short and medium term until the broader population can be educated to understand the benefits of higher taxes in the long term. This is essentially what we're doing today: through old fashioned means such as the national lottery and premium bonds, we've been borrowing from the public for decades. VETS, the newest initiative, has the difference that we're getting a select tranche of citizens to actually gift us extra money until this becomes the norm rather than the exception.

'In the past, commerce got away with often highly unethical psychology in its advertising methods in order to create needs in targeted consumers, thereby amassing huge profits. And over many decades of the twentieth century this practice passed almost unnoticed, as it apparently served most people's interests. It took a growing impoverished underclass and extreme environmental degradation to make governments wake up to the long-term dangers of excessive consumerism. But why shouldn't a government, with the public interest at heart, employ similar psychological methods to nudge people towards the cultural change needed to fund their legitimate needs?

'We know that over half a generation with the right messaging we can get at least half the population on board with contributing a higher proportion of their wealth to government in return for peace, security and a guaranteed minimum standard of living. In the early days, true, a degree of authoritarian coercion was required to overcome resistance to what at the time seemed daring policies such as the universal basic income. But within ten years or so, this became the accepted norm and provided that first pillar of a stable society – financial security for virtually everyone.

'We also realised that had the government acted sooner to address the situation, probably an authoritarian approach could have been avoided altogether. The consensus allows us to plan more collaboratively for the long term and be much more proactive than reactive. So, we're not forced to tackle crises as they arise, but more often able to pre-empt them...'

Although Mathew was uneasy about the lecture format Hendricks was doggedly adhering to, he was relieved that they at last appeared to be entering the present day. A slight pause in Hendricks's monologue had to be taken advantage of, however.

'You're implying then that the government is to be more trusted than business interests, because although it employs similar techniques of persuasion, it uses them for the public good and not commercial gain. That's all very well and good, but how can we be sure that the government will make the wise choices and that any mistakes will be challenged, given the cosy political consensus these days with all parties working collaboratively? After all, part of the role of the opposition in the 'bad old days' was to hold the incumbent government to account. Who can be relied on to carry out this function effectively today?'

In his peripheral vision Mathew glimpsed Emily's goading body language, though, just like their trainers, mentors and, most recently, Hudson and Roger, Hendricks appeared completely unfazed by this most daring challenge so far.

'I don't wish to suggest that government error can be eliminated altogether, but I do believe that the key to avoiding the vast majority of mistakes is to ensure as much consensus as possible at all levels of society. We recognise that having wrested undue control of the media from big business, a centralised government will not automatically create heaven on earth for its citizens. That's why over the past fifty years so much power has been devolved to regional and local authorities with the steady development of citizens' assemblies. Grass roots democracy and the debate it engenders keeps central government firmly grounded.

'There were a few events beyond the government's control, of course, which helped along the way to a more just and less resource-guzzling and pollution-producing society: the 2020-21 virus which slowed down many of the highest-consuming economies. The drastic reduction in the jet setting holiday culture of half the population of the richer countries came much more quickly than its growth from the 1990s, but people came to terms with it remarkably serenely.

'Imminent climate disaster had already become a general concern several years before and so progressive governments seized the opportunity to reinforce trends which were already becoming mainstream: better work-life balance, improved diet, exercise, wholesome and creative leisure pursuits, much less travel by private car. The consumerist society was the deliberate creation of an ideology fostered and controlled by the capitalist elite in order to perpetuate itself and consolidate its power over the masses.

Benevolent control of public education and the media has gone a long way already to reversing this process. Who nowadays aspires to own a private car and then upgrade it every two or three years – replacing it with a newer more fashionable model? The same goes for so many items which had become a 'must have' in the space of a generation or so for the vast majority of the population. Another good example is the fashion industry – one of the greatest polluters – which lost its grip on the popular imagination within two or three years of carefully targeted messaging, backed up by legislation too, of course.'

It was Emily's turn to contribute once more:

'Certainly, the benign role of government seems to have grown over the past couple of generations, though in the past, from what I've read, it tended to follow some way behind more enlightened public opinion....'

Hendricks was ready as ever with a tailored response:

'That's precisely it. Until the 1980s the government cashed in on ruinous lifestyle habits like smoking and was almost as bad as the tobacco industry itself in promoting it for the sake of ensuring a steady income. But anyone could see that in the long run treating people for the long-term consequences was costing the National Health Service as much as the revenue tax on cigarettes was bringing in. Not to mention the misery caused through ill health and the fact that indirect taxes hit the poorest most.

'It's probably fair to say that up to the twenties, the government was still dragging its feet somewhat and playing catch up with an exercise and diet conscious generation. But again, the political consensus helped defeat the big business power of, for example, huge fast food chains, by imposing punitive taxes on any processed foods that fell short of the highest nutritional standards. Research had proved by the mid-twenties that after air and other forms of pollution, junk foods were the next most significant driver of poor physical and mental health.

'The government had to take the lead in tackling childhood obesity as, putting aside the moral imperative, by the thirties too many people would be reaching middle age with a host of health problems from diabetes to heart conditions which were becoming unsustainable for the National Health Service to treat. There were also a number of food terrorist acts that no one would have dreamed of until they occurred, for example, the unforgettable case of the famous ex-footballer and presenter being lynched for appearing in advertisements for junk snack foods. Ten years before, who would have predicted a ban on producing foods such as beef burgers and crisps!'

Mathew, who had foreseen the gist of what Hendricks would say up until now, had become so absorbed by his narrative that he almost lost sight of his desire to control the discussion. At last, he snapped out of his trance:

'I must say Mr Hendricks, you're making the government sound like a saintly institution, steadfastly guiding the humble populace towards the light. Do I detect a gradual drift towards totalitarianism?'

'Indeed: such a drift towards a form of benevolent totalitarianism has been the theme of virtually all states in the modern era. As I've stressed earlier, if states had not acted to seize the power of technology, it would remain firmly in the hands of exploitative commercial concerns. And latter-day totalitarianism, if that's what you wish to call it, has naught to do with the abortive and malevolent forms of dictatorship which sprang up over a hundred years ago in several European powers.

'Let's take the example of violent crime which ample research revealed long ago was closely linked to TV, cinema and, increasingly from the 1990s – digital violence. Once laws had been enacted to prohibit all but the mildest images of violence through the media, an abundance of evidence showed that the mental and moral health of the nation dramatically improved, despite much damage having already been done.'

Mathew felt himself blush slightly at the tenuous connection with his wargaming hobby and couldn't resist a rueful sideways glance towards Emily who complicitly smiled back. He also reflected on how unlikely he would have been to acquire an interest in gardening as a teenager were it not for the benevolent state-sponsored propaganda as expressed through the school curriculum and the frequency of green-fingered TV programmes broadcast in the early evening on at least two channels. Even his mother had once commented there was something unbecoming in anyone under the age of forty taking such a keen interest in growing vegetables.

'And with the public interest at heart, we could have justified even greater manipulation of people or redirecting their energy into more desirable patterns for the benefit of society as a whole. However, we were mindful of the ethical concerns of persuading or coercing people into giving away more of their privacy. Certainly, people grew sick of the intrusive behaviour of big tech companies and mandated government to take control of the technology which enabled this, but there was no question of removing it altogether. The potential to influence hearts and minds is the key to power in the modern world and the government was not going to relinquish it readily. The ultimate question has always been who will lay claim to this power and wield it for better or worse.

Mathew interjected:

'I read somewhere that in the late twentieth century, the United Kingdom, as it was then, had the greatest concentration of close circuit television surveillance in the world. It seems that in the interests of crime stopping, people quickly took this for granted in shopping precincts and thought nothing of being spied on by multiple cameras wherever they went. And this climate softened up the public to accept the idea of ever greater surveillance of criminals, probationers and eventually potential terrorists.'

'Exactly – so surveillance is another area with small beginnings in commerce but with a growing role in public and state security. The question people had and still have to ask themselves is this: is the government to be trusted any more than big business when it comes to intruding in their lives – whether through direct physical surveillance via CCTV or digitally every time they go near a computer?'

Emily had something to say on this point:

'It's probably six of one and half a dozen of the other. Governments potentially want to know every last detail about their subjects – and that's practically official given all the questions asked in the annual national census. And then there are the endless surveys conducted by the Office for National Statistics that people feel obliged to take part in if approached. But the motivation has to be better than with big business which only wants to know facts about people it can exploit commercially...'

Hendricks smiled approvingly. Then Roger entered the discussion for the first time since he introduced the minister.

'It's been a fascinating discussion so far, but I hope you don't mind me bringing us back to VETS and what this agency is about! So far, we've talked about the various powers that be and people or the public in the abstract. I'd like to mention here how serious the government is these days about trying to fully appreciate what makes people tick from a psychological point of view.

'We know that human evolution and the struggle to survive has made people like any other species essentially egocentric and selfish. This is the reason why governments have traditionally been at loggerheads with the mass of the population who want to take as much as possible that the State has to offer and give back as little as possible in return. Society is just the macrocosm and the individual is the microcosm.

'However, unlike the first economists who presumed the selfish gene to be predominant, modern research has shown that the altruistic gene is a natural and potentially equal force in the human psyche, especially in societies which function on broadly egalitarian lines and with greater wealth equality. Indeed, the selfless or altruistic side of human nature can be cultivated or nurtured to a large extent and the VETS programme has a huge role to play here. True, the selfish, acquisitive and competitive aspect can only be tamed so far, but individual citizens demonstrate a huge capacity for self-control and self-censorship when educated in the right way.'

Mathew came in, again in a supporting role:

'I've heard that idea before – that even largely selfish people can persuade themselves that in the long run itIs in their own interests to be outwardly altruistic and cooperative rather than competitive if they have a deeper understanding of the dynamics of human interactions. I've heard too that people who practise altruism for pragmatic reasons actually become less selfish in the process.'

'Yes, and going back to the macrocosm of society, a good example is getting better off citizens to see the wisdom of paying higher taxes to reduce poverty, as the removal of a social underclass will virtually eliminate crime, so that everyone will be safer as a result. For generations, the real obstacle to achieving this was that politicians talked incessantly about being tough on crime and tough on the causes of crime, but did precious little to tackle the primary causes of crime – poverty and inequality. Moreover, being tough on crime tended just to mean longer sentences which produced only hardened criminals in overcrowded prisons. Giving a criminal a longer prison sentence just protected society at large from that one individual for a little longer, while dehumanising offenders and making things worse for society in the long run.

'The ideological barrier to eliminating crime was the capitalist establishment mentality. This was perpetuation of the myth of social mobility as a means of rising out of poverty and the fallacy that economic growth which would enable surplus wealth to drip down to the poorest members of society.'

Roger, apparently buoyed up by his well-received contribution earlier, came in again:

'Of course, there are many ways of keeping people in poverty. I'm just old enough to remember my parents talking about a huge revolution in government legislation to ban all types of gambling which always hit the poor hardest. It started with removing advertising from TV and other media which used the most cynical psychology to entrap vulnerable people by convincing them that betting gave them a real chance of rising out of poverty and changing their lives for ever.

'In fact, it was designed to get them hopelessly into debt. Agencies employed graduates with psychology degrees to present an innocuous image of the socially responsible gambling companies offering legitimate forms of entertainment. In reality, those behind it were often running illicit loan shark companies with links to debt-collecting agencies. Some right-wing politicians invested heavily in the betting companies which sponsored popular sports and charities to acquire a veneer of respectability.'

Hendricks wasn't to be outdone:

'Yes, it's not for no reason that several religious sects emerging in the 19th century prohibited their members from any form of gambling and extended the ban a century later even to the National Lottery. This started out as a transparent institution based on European models run by the State. These should have been simplicity itself, usually with half the money raised going to charities and voluntary organisations. A commission was meant to consider all applications for funding fairly and impartially.

'But even this institution became tarnished with scandal as soon as an element of privatisation was introduced. Companies given contracts to run the lottery found devious ways of squeezing out a profit and enriching their directors and investors, hence short changing both the punters and charities. And besides the legitimate capitalist profit-making there were a few notable cases of corruption whereby commission panel members were bribed to favour some charities over others...'

'Most of the older generation still remember how the rot spread to charities themselves from overpaid chief executives at the milder end of the spectrum to immoral practices employed to con people into making donations at the most extreme end. A prime example of one of these techniques was moral blackmail where campaigners invented sob stories about fictitious victims of natural disasters. It was hardly surprising that public support for government taking over grew even if it meant the end to the charity as such. But the original railways started out as private enterprise before being taken over by the state. And on a grander scale and a lot longer ago, the East India Company became the

Jewel in the Crown of the British Empire.

'To come back to the point of these excursions into history, this all goes to illustrate that government, while being far from perfect, is a far better candidate for public trust than are the agents of free market enterprise, especially where extracting money from good honest citizens is concerned.'

Mathew saw the opportunity to insert another contribution into the mix by citing one of his recent readings:

'The other day, I was intrigued by a fascinating MyTube documentary on banks and what was termed 'mission drift'. Hundreds of years ago, the banks were mainly set up to keep wealthy people's money safe, to lend to governments and to finance various more or less worthy public and private projects. Up to the early twenty-first century, they had broadened out to loan money to small and medium-sized businesses and even to individuals to help them buy houses through mortgages. The system broke down over time, as unscrupulous individuals hijacked the banks and lost huge amounts of public money in rash speculative investments. With each financial crisis, the banks were bailed out by governments which had no choice, as by then the whole economy was underpinned by banking as an institution.

'It wasn't just banks either – there was the famous case of a mutual society founded by a religious sect of hardworking idealistic industrialists two hundred years ago. Their idea was to invest their surplus wealth in social improvements for the masses. Fast forward to the late twentieth century and we have just one extremely elderly member of this original group left on the board of directors. The society then converts to a bank only to be swallowed up by a transnational bank with branches everywhere, but a base nowhere and certainly paying taxes virtually nowhere. Also, a financial institution which had started life as a socialist cooperative movement ends up running a failed bank and exploitative funeral service!'

Mathew was aware that practically everything he had been contributing so far was supportive of the main thrust of Hendricks' and Roger's argument, that in the final analysis, government was eminently more trustworthy than the private sector when it came to looking after the interests of ordinary citizens. But although a proper discussion was now evolving, it could have taken place pretty well anywhere, any time and have involved anyone bright and informed enough to follow the arguments. He now needed to force Hendricks to spend whatever time was left for the interview answering his and Emily's concerns about the agency.

Given Hendrick's presence and gravitas as a senior member of a government department, Mathew still suspected that Roger had drafted him in to browbeat them into walking away from the meeting without really having taken the agency to task. He could not let this happen. Apart from anything else, he feared falling in Emily's estimation.

'So, let's take it as read that you've convinced us the agency is an expression of the government's benevolent intent. Are all its practices entirely ethical? I mean from its recruitment methods using state-of-the-art algorithms, to its staff training systems and right down to the techniques it employs to tease money out of the public?'

Mathew paused for a moment and made eye contact with Hendricks and Roger in turn. As neither volunteered a response, he continued:

'I must say I've been impressed by the egalitarian ethos of the agency with workers seeing themselves as essentially coequals capable of doing each other's jobs. But in the light of this, if I'm honest, it strikes me as odd that there seems little transparency about much of what goes on behind the scenes and no real encouragement to ask questions or challenge the agency.'

Hendricks was ready with a response this time:

'The great dilemma for government is that the more it takes control, the more the people who have granted it that control tend to expect not just higher but flawless ethics! Why do those in power in so many countries tend towards autocracy and dictatorship? Because of the paradox of accountability in democracy. The more open and accountable a government is, the worse this tends to be for efficiency and 'getting the job done', to use a favourite phrase of a particularly charismatic past prime minister.'

'We could have designed our recruitment, induction and training to contain much more background information about the agency's raison d'être, but in the grand scheme of things, it would have only unduly complicated and slowed down the process. It's more pragmatic and productive to operate a 'come and get me' policy, in other words, responding to those of our trainees and employees who want to dig deeper such as yourselves. I think that point was made by Mr Hudson. And, to prove the point, here we all are now!

'The people who want to know the inner workings of a system and get at the ultimate truth are always in a minority, it seems. Typically, only one out of ten even in most campaigning groups and organisations assume an activist role – and it's about that proportion of our workers who probe a little deeper into what we are about, though not usually quite so deeply as your good selves, I must confess.

'But to return to the 'come and get me' or 'ask and thou shalt receive' policy, it reminds me of the days of so-called 'fake news' which led many to give up on trying to follow events in the news, as they had lost faith in what they were being told even by mainstream media. However, the more discerning and braver minority always found a way of arriving close to the truth through research, hard work and critical thinking.'

'That implies that you only reluctantly yield up more information if people come banging at your door for it...'

Mathew was feeling emboldened now, but sensed the danger of sounding too provocative.

'Well perhaps that wasn't the best illustration. But, to be fair, you didn't exactly have to come banging at our door to arrange these extra discussions about our mission!' Roger countered.

Hendricks took over with no sense of having usurped Roger's pitch.

'Of course, you won't need reminding that whereas in society at large, we still have plenty of pure mischief makers to deal with such as journalists posing as champions of the oppressed and whistle-blowers who are merely after self-aggrandizement or scoops for their media companies. With our agency, however, the algorithmic sifting and selection process would be unlikely to let anyone of that ilk slip through. It would soon become apparent once they started work in any case....'

Same old ground, thought Mathew, *Let's move it on a bit*:

'Well clearly that's one type of trouble maker. But just suppose for a moment you did let in someone with a mission to subvert our work here. Say one of these people hacks into your algorithms and gets to know them inside out. They are then able to sneak into the agency and stay long enough to convince you they're fully on board with the programme. They may initially conduct multiple successful interviews with clients, but always remain intent on doing as much damage as possible once they're established....'

Hendricks squeezed in:

'Their motives?'

'They might be political extremists or hate paying taxes or just love hacking into systems and undermining them for the sheer hell of it and for the damage they can do once inside. Now how would you deal with that sort of infiltration?'

'Well, since you ask so pointedly, I can say we've had two

such cases so far and I'll tell you exactly how they were dealt with. The first case was of an angry young lady who probably did, as you suggested in your hypothetical scenario: break into our algorithms. At any rate, she was highly intelligent and eminently capable of doing so. By 'break into' I mean 'saw through', though I know that's not the best phrase either, connoting, as it does, deception on our part!'

Has he at last begun to lower his guard?

'Within days of this lady conducting semi-autonomous interviews, it became clear she opposed our programme. She manifestly held an emotive rather than ideological resentment against the government. She may well have intended to stick around much longer and undermine our VETS, but her whole demeanour and speech style alerted our trainers that something was amiss. It wasn't such a hard task to persuade her to leave our service, but a skilfully conducted debriefing session enabled us to avoid an acrimonious parting.'

'Would that have included promise of a financial settlement by any chance?'

'She was paid up to the end of the month, but this would be standard procedure with a member of staff leaving after such short service in almost any circumstances. No, in fact one of our excellent staff diffused her anger and brought her round to seeing things in a more reasonable light.'

'Fair enough. So, it wasn't exactly a major crisis for the agency such as might have been the case with a whistle-blower...'

'We've never particularly worried about the whistle-blower scenario. Indeed, why should we when all we do here is above board. As we've discussed more than once, any of our practices which might seem questionable if glimpsed at first sight are perfectly defendable when examined more closely.'

Mathew puzzled for a moment over Hendricks' – a government minister's - detailed knowledge of such a mundane case.

How much had he and Roger colluded in preparing for this interview which the devil within him still willed to turn into a 'showdown'? Mathew also wondered whether Emily had taken over the questioning at this point in order to take the pressure of him. She came in again.

'You mentioned there were two cases. What was the other one?'

'I was about to come to that. It was, in fact, a so-called whistle-blower. The individual concerned didn't reveal any major differences with us at any stage of the recruitment process including training, so it *was* a bit of a mystery, frankly....

Admission of weakness, at last! Mathew noted with interest.

'So, what form did the whistle-blowing take?' Emily pressed on.

Hendricks continued as if uninterrupted:

'... but in hindsight we suspected he may have suffered from an attention-seeking or narcissistic complex. This may be what unconsciously led him to find fault with our practices within a few weeks of working autonomously and go public criticising us. This particular gentleman accused us of taking advantage of naïve and gullible old folk to raid their nest eggs. That was how he expressed it, if I remember rightly.'

'You'd think he would have come round to that idea earlier on when observing experienced colleagues at work, wouldn't you? He'd be the one making the judgement calls once working more autonomously... unless it was just the nature of the cases that came his way', Emily mused.

Roger intervened:

'I honestly don't think it was to do with timing. I reckon it was a character flaw the algorithms hadn't picked up but which would have come out sooner or later...'

How limited is this man's script? He mentioned algorithms again! thought Mathew. He had noticed that as the meeting progressed, Roger had been casting more sideways glances at Hendricks but repeatedly failed to catch his eye. Was this out of resentment at being eclipsed or challenged by his departmental boss? Or could there be another reason?

Hendricks regained control:

'But here's the essential point: it goes back to what we were saying about only a minority wanting to dig deeper. Very few people have heard of the agency and VETS as yet and only one national newspaper was interested enough to publish an article which attracted very little attention anyway. We were available for comment, which is always a good sign in the public's eyes, and in a concise rebuttal were able to nip any potential public outrage in the bud.'

The discussion, which had lasted nearly an hour up to this point, finally ground to a halt. Mathew had picked up mixed vibes from the meeting and felt a little perplexed. On what note had the conversation ended? Had everything been said? Were all the participants now assumed to be in broad agreement or had their time simply run out?

It was Hendricks who, true to form and to his position of authority, pronounced the last remarks.

'When all said and done, history has proved that societies break down and civilisations fall for a limited number of reasons. War and conquest used to be the ancient favourite, but this is a rare event in the modern world of international cooperation and supranational organisations. In recent decades we've still witnessed a number of civil wars caused by nationalist tensions within states and revolutions born of extreme social injustice and fragile economies.

'The strongest guarantee of stability and harmony in a modern society is economic security and greater equality. This situation itself is best guaranteed by a strong state governing in the public interest by consent and consensus. To a large extent, the agency can be seen as a microcosm of society as a whole. The people it recruits require no or little persuasion to fall in with the common goals once they are understood, as they are transparent and ethical. This is positive acquiescent conformity. It's only when people recognise that their best interests are not being served that acquiescence or conformity has to be imposed, for example, in a dictatorship.'

Mathew turned his head again towards Emily who met his gaze halfway. This body language clearly signalled the end of the discussion to Roger who at once rose and lent towards them over the table in the centre of the room.

'Well, thanks to both of you for giving us the opportunity to get to know you better and have this longish chat. Even in a conformist society (he laughed, nodding towards Hendricks), it's important to get everything out into the open once in a while and remind ourselves what we're all here for!'

'Well said, Roger, and as you'll have observed today like never before, we bureaucratic Whitehall types do enjoy the odd philosophical discussion now and then and the chance to wax lyrical about what we believe makes society tick…'

As he and Emily moved back from the table back towards the exit, Mathew felt it was incumbent on him to produce a suitable parting comment.

'Too true! From what I've heard read about the recent past, we're living in an age when people don't naturally talk politics any more. Philosophy still less. No doubt it's down to that truce between the old political parties.'

Emily too was not to be denied a concluding remark:

'The paradox for me is it seems good people are always striving for consensus and harmony in society, but once it's achieved and the noise has died down, we find ourselves at a loose end and kind of miss the squabbling.'

As Mathew and Emily finally left Roger's office, they

instinctively joined hands. This was the grand dénouement they'd been planning for what seemed an eternity and yet Mathew's emotion was more akin to deflation and a sense of anticlimax than exhilaration.

They were not to know that less than two minutes after their exit, the chairs they had vacated at the table in Roger's office had already been occupied by the two mystery men who had caused them so much mirth just days before.

As soon as they had skipped through reception and got outside the agency building, Emily looked down at her watch:

'Heavens! We went in there at three thirty on the dot almost exactly an hour ago...'

Mathew, who had successfully supressed the urge to periodically look down at his own watch at various points during the discussion, had nevertheless measured the passage of time quite accurately using his internal clock.

'Yes, but just think: we've still clocked off only half an hour later than most of our co-workers. Do you reckon we'll be paid overtime?'

Emily looked puzzled, as the term was not familiar to her.

'Apparently, overtime's what my grandad's generation lost early in their working life – a higher rate of pay for working extra hours.'

Mathew had allowed himself a measure of levity for his first unself-censored remark all afternoon. It would serve as a buffer before he and Emily launched into a more profound analysis of the past hour's discussion.

Emily, however, made it clear that she preferred to sustain the light-hearted tone of their conversation for a little longer and so Mathew let himself be persuaded to call in at a nearby café where they knew they could talk in private for a few minutes before the teatime crowd began to appear.

Seated at an empty table, Emily teased Mathew saying she'd seen him blush when Hendricks alluded to violent video games which used to be popular in the past.

'I did feel a bit awkward and feared my body language might give something away, but I didn't actually blush, surely? I know you're only kidding as I'd have felt the blood go to my cheeks and it wasn't like I'd been called out and publicly disgraced or anything!'

'Yes, I'm just pulling your leg, but don't you think it's about time you asked me about my eccentric pastime or aren't you really interested?'

'Well, I do recall your saying I'd have to wait until the right moment for you to reveal it to me...' Mathew repressed a yawn which belied how eager he actually was to learn Emily's secret.

'Clever response. I hope you're not always so ready with the rejoinders when we're sharing our lives together. We ladies have to put down our men folk somehow, you know.'

'It's a proven fact that women do that best through smarter use of language and I do admire your choice of the word *rejoinder*, though myself, I'd have gone for *repartee* from the French.'

Noticing that the café proprietor had begun to cast frequent glances in their direction, Emily at last got up to order their drinks.

Mr Hudson broke the news to Jonathan and Peter that Mathew and Emily had made a snap decision to leave the agency for personal reasons.

Peter remarked that the couple had visibly become more devoted to each other than to their work, as evidenced by their constantly being seen together and the way they had challenged almost every aspect of the agency's operations. His tone suggested 'good riddance'.

Jonathan said nothing, but his look of anguish on hearing the news betrayed a realisation that he had lost a significant prop for moral support during his more fainthearted moments.

Mathew's mother called Paula to ask if he'd been in touch. Paula unable to get a response either, took a bus to Mathew's house and let herself in with her spare key. There were no signs that her brother had planned a trip away: various articles of clothing were draped over backs of chairs and the fridge was stocked with fresh food.

Before long, Frank who in any case was gaining confidence at his new job and beginning to make new friends, assumed that Mathew had lost interest in their relationship.

Having shared his wisdom with Mathew just days previously, Rory was a little hurt that his university friend hadn't troubled to update him on the latest developments at his new job. However, like Frank, he would eventually assume that he and Mathew had at last outgrown each other.

Andrew, now back with Paula, shared her concerns about her brother's disappearance and wished he had quizzed Mathew about his new job. He might have learned the whereabouts of the agency offices and made enquiries.

Then, suddenly all the people in Mathew's life seemed to come before him at once, producing a clamour of voices, some of them pointing accusingly….

Had there been an accident? The two dark figures? Where was Emily? Was she safe?

Mathew awoke with such a start that he nudged the table, almost upsetting the cup of coffee which Emily had placed there just moments before.

Seeing his bewildered expression as he came to his senses, she gave a shriek of involuntary laughter.

'As good a time as any to snatch a nap, I suppose. Imagine if you'd fallen asleep during Hendricks' concluding speech!'

But Mathew's bewilderment, far from passing turned into something darker.

'That was no ordinary dream. It was as though I was hovering in space, totally paralysed, looking down on everyone I knew – family, friends, work colleagues. People were talking about me or just thinking about me as though I'd disappeared. I wasn't aware it was me they were concerned about until our two mysterious friends from the agency appeared, grinning maliciously at me. Then it became like a typical nightmarish dream which is just about to break. I was betwixt and between, wondering if or when I was going to snap out of it or….'

'Or those two bastards murdered you and there you were – or rather your soul – floating off to wherever souls go after death!' Emily instinctively made light of Mathew's pseudo-psychic ordeal. 'I wonder if you'd have made it out of the dream at all had I been a moment longer ordering the coffee…'

It wasn't long before the two had completed their analysis. An anxiety dream was perfectly natural under the circumstances. Mathew revised his initial assertion that this was a dream like no other: as its effect wore off, it seemed not unlike his other recent anxiety dreams. Except, of course, it had occurred not in his bed during nighttime, but in a café during the late afternoon. Even the lingering sense of dread on waking was common enough following his anxiety dreams. Probably just having Emily there to relate the experience to had magnified the psychological effect.

The dream episode dealt with, the couple turned to why they'd actually come to the café – to discuss their future within or without the agency. It was too big a decision to make that evening, barely an hour after the Hendricks showdown, so they agreed to 'sleep on it' and, subject to any further nightmares, reconvene the next day.

CHAPTER 16. SHOWDOWN WITH HENDRICKS

But there was one other outstanding – almost burning - issue which to Mathew's mind needed to be tackled before they parted. Surely by now he'd earned the right to insist that Emily reveal to him her enigmatic hobby or pastime.

'Alright, you win. I must confess, I've quite enjoyed keeping you guessing all this time, but it's not fair to torture you any longer. Sorry to be a bore, but my secret passion is for...' she paused, starring at Mathew fixedly to heighten the suspense, '... making up cryptic crosswords.'

Mathew tried to looked surprised rather than deflated with anti-climax.

'Ah, so that just confirms we're ideally suited to each other as complementary opposites – me the amateur sleuth and you as the one who creates the enigmas for me to solve. Looks like there's a great future for us together...'

'Yeah, it's a cop-out really, as it's actually easier to set crosswords than to solve most of the clues.'

She got Mathew to suggest a word to fit into her next puzzle. He came up with what he felt was a topical word: *mysterious*. Emily now challenged herself to invent a cryptic clue.

'Give me two minutes. I'm thinking how it sounds.... It starts with *mister*...., so how about something like: 'Mrs Strange's partner sent the credit notes, we hear.'

'What? How on earth do you get that?!'

'Mrs Strange's partner would be Mister. Strange is a near synonym of mysterious and credit notes are IOUS. Mister-ious! *We hear* is a well-known indicator to focus on the sound rather than the exact spelling.

'You'll give me nightmares about cryptic clues next.' Mathew recalled the bizarre dream involving his fleeting infatuation with his trainer Theresa, but now wasn't the time to bring this up with Emily.

'Talking of IOUs, it must be my round to buy the next coffees…..'

'But you take my point – it took me about ninety seconds to create the seemingly clever clue and explain it to you, whereas even an experienced crossword solver might be poring over it for several minutes.'

Emily anticipated Mathew's next question, explaining that a splendid bespoke computer programme was all she required to insert her words into a conventional crossword grid.

EPILOGUE

Mathew and Emily's suspicions around the two mystery men hadn't been entirely wide of the mark.

Rufus Wilde worked for CID before moving to the agency at its inception. His primary role was to investigate potential clients suspected of illegal activity. In such cases, he would then advise the agency in determining whether to pursue a criminal prosecution or whether resources would be better spent persuading subjects to stump up meaningful VETS contributions.

His colleague, Marcus Foyle, had a rather murkier background. An IT whizz kid in his teens, he had specialised in hacking into anti-virus programmes, analysing their weaknesses, then marketing his own enhanced versions. He'd made quite a good living, sometimes passing off his tweaked products as entirely his own, but often daring to pose as an official market leader. In his early twenties, he was recruited by GCHQ as an IT security manager, which allowed him to further hone his hacking skills. A few professional interludes later saw him at last working for the agency.

His government recruitment officer stressed that in return for a handsome salary and exceptionally vague job description, he could expect to be assigned to a range of covert and even potentially dangerous operations, some of which would be unknown even to senior agency staff.

Discreetly breaking into Mathew's home two weeks earlier and installing an audio-visual surveillance system in every room was one of his least demanding assignments. Analysis of the recorded material provided him with two main highlights. Emily's visit had piqued Foyle's voyeuristic interest, but disappointment followed as it became clear there would be no bedroom scene. However, the second highlight came just a little while later during that same visit.

Initially, Foyle had taken little notice of Mathew's wargaming interest as he watched him pottering around the hobby room. However, listening to his mark's impassioned exposé to Emily again excited his curiosity. He reviewed the earlier wargaming sessions and finally zoomed in on the episode where Mathew had marked the M on the soldier's base representing his own role in the battle.

When called in by his bosses immediately after the long interview, Foyle had been instructed to remove the surveillance equipment from Mathew's house. Knowing that his mark travelled by public transport and was heading for a post-work social interlude with Emily, he saw this as his opportunity to drive to the house, arriving a good hour before Mathew returned.

Foyle effected his second discreet ingress into Mathew's home and made straight for the hobby room. On the wargaming table, he quickly discerned the remaining figure standing with Mathew's pose. He lifted it to reveal the M marked clearly under its base.

Probably in less than an hour, Mathew was due to inspect this very same piece, and learn that, as the final figure standing, he had scored some sort of victory over the agency....

Foyle gleefully swapped this figure with one of the fallen figures, quietly mimicking to himself what Mathew had muttered just audibly enough for him to make out from the recordings: 'M marks the spot for Me – Mathew!'

Foyle inwardly smiled: *That'll teach the smug bastard to take on the agency when he gets home and finds he's not got away with it unscathed.*

During his drive home, Foyle entertained himself by repeatedly chanting the alliterative words:

M marks the spot for Me – Mathew

Then, creatively inspired, he continued with his own variations.

M marks the spot for Mathew the mug

M marks the spot for my mark Mathew the mug and meddler...

Until several *m* words later, he was struck by an uncomfortable realisation. His darkest desire was that one day, if not for the agency, then for a future employer, he would commit MURDER.

ABOUT THE AUTHOR

Christopher Cooke

is a retired modern foreign languages teacher who has been a Green Party councillor in Wirral since 2019. His writing is informed by his background in education and political activism.

Over the past several years, he has written in a wide range of genres and for various purposes. His second novel, Green Necropolis, follows the fortunes of a family struggling to survive in a dystopian near-future society faced with climate breakdown and an increasingly intrusive authoritarian government.

Printed in Great Britain
by Amazon